THE RED CARNELIAN

I turned and it seemed that the acre of owls had moved in behind me. They sat on the floor, hundreds of them, watching me with empty, staring eyes, and it was as if they were saying, "Go on, go on! You cannot go back!"

It was then that I saw a square patch of moonlight on the floor at my feet moving like smoke, like the rippling of water. I glanced up at the big window. A silver edge of cloud was creeping over the moon. It moved quickly and already the light was dimming.

With the fading light the figures about me seemed to come into a shadowy life of their own. They wavered in the gloom, whispered among themselves.

But their whispers were unreal, imagined. The sound I heard close at hand had frightening reality. It was no more than a creak, as if something moved stealthily and sought to tiptoe away.

I wanted to scream, to cry out to Bill, but my throat muscles were tight and choked and no sound came.

In that instant I heard clearly the sound of running feet. Feet no longer stealthy but bent on escape.

The Red Carnelian

Phyllis A. Whitney

CORONET BOOKS
Hodder and Stoughton

To MAX SIEGEL, fine bookman and friend, and with grateful acknowledgment to REED SCHLADEMAN who answered all my questions about window display.

Copyright © 1943 by Ziff-Davis Publishing Co.
Copyright renewed © 1971 by Phyllis A. Whitney

First published in 1955 by Warner Paperbacks Library

Coronet edition 1976
Fourth impression 1984

The characters and situations in this book are entirely imaginary and bear no relation to any real person or actual happening

Printed and bound in Great Britain for Hodder and Stoughton Paperbacks, a division of Hodder and Stoughton Ltd., Mill Road, Dunton Green, Sevenoaks, Kent (Editorial Office: 47 Bedford Square, London, WC1 3DP) by Hunt Barnard Printing Ltd., Aylesbury, Bucks.

ISBN 0 340 19928 8

CHAPTER 1

Cunningham's department store is quiet again now. Sylvester Hering still puts his head in the door of my office whenever he goes by, to call out, "Hi, Linell!" and perhaps to linger and study the pictures on my walls, to speak briefly of the past. But his days are given over to the humdrum of catching shoplifters and petty thieves, instead of trailing a murderer.

He never mentions that one picture we hunted down together, or the tragic denouement to which it led. But now and then we cock an eyebrow at each other because we are conspirators and know it.

Not that the law was in any way defeated. Payment in full was made for all those terrible things that happened. But still, Hering and I know what we know and the case as it broke in the papers told only half the story.

There are still things about Cunningham's that make me shiver. I can never cross that narrow passageway that leads past the freight elevators into the display department without a feeling of uneasiness. I cannot bear the mannequin room at all, and I will go to any length to avoid setting foot in it. But most of all I am haunted by the symbols that came into being during the case.

The color red, for instance. I never wear it any more, because it was the theme of those dreadful days. It ran beneath the surface of our lives like a bright network of veins, spilling out into the open now and then to accent with horror. And there are the owls. Sometimes in my dreams that eerie moment returns when I stood there in the gloom with all those plaster creatures crowding about me, cutting off my escape.

Nor will I ever again breathe the scent of pine without remembering the way the light went out and those groping hands came toward me. Strange to have your life saved by the odor of Christmas trees.

But the worst thing of all is when I imagine I hear the strains of Sondo's phonograph. For me, those rooms will never be free of ghostly music and I break into cold chills in broad daylight whenever a radio plays *Begin the Beguine*.

Yet, before that Tuesday afternoon in late March, I'd never thought of myself as a particularly jittery young woman. That was the day it began—the day Michael Montgomery came back to Cunningham's.

I sat at the desk in my little eighth floor office and stared helplessly at the sign copy before me. I'd been under a strain since early morning and it was beginning to tell.

I didn't want to watch the door. I'd been assuring myself all day that it wouldn't matter in the least when the inevitable moment came and Monty walked into my office. Why should it matter? I wasn't in love with him. All my feeling for him had died and left only a faint bitterness. Even though this was his first day back from a honeymoon with another girl, still it didn't matter to me.

But my eyes strayed to the door and my nerves were keyed to a tense pitch of waiting.

I wasn't alone in the office. Across the room—no more than three paces—Keith Irwin sat at his smaller

6

desk shuffling papers and watching me with moody dark eyes whenever he thought I wasn't noticing. Keith was my office force, often embarrassingly loyal to my interests, but at that particular moment he was getting on my nerves.

Helena Farnham stood at the single small window, staring down through drizzling rain at the strip of alley that ran back of the store. She wore black, as always, but with that big-boned frame of hers she wore it with distinction.

Helena and I had shared an apartment for several months and I was fond of her. But I could tell by the set of her dark, gray-streaked head that she was in a disapproving mood, and the fact left me a little defiant.

I forced myself to scribble industriously for a moment and then tossed down my pencil.

"Listen to this, you two," I said. *"Bold* is the word for new spring colors. Taunt windy March in a green hat. Laugh at April showers in a suit of yellow or rust."

Keith's eyes flicked my way and then off toward the window where a sickly yellow sun was trying to break through the drizzle. Helena didn't even turn around.

I tore the sheet of paper across with a sharp nervous gesture and dropped the pieces in the wastebasket beside my desk.

"Thanks," I said. "I agree with you. Corn, pure unadulterated corn."

I pushed back dark hair that had a tendency to tumble into my eyes and leaned my head on my hands. The small office was intensely quiet for a few moments and then Keith coughed and rustled his papers, and Helena turned away from the window where that curious sulphur glow hung over Chicago's Loop.

"You shouldn't have come down today, Linell," she said. "I told you this morning it would be a hard day to get through."

That was the trouble with sharing an apartment with

7

an older woman, I thought rebelliously. Sooner or later she tried to mother you. Helena should have had a comfortable husband, a suburban bungalowful of children. But somewhere in the past there had been a divorce, and unhappiness had left its stamp on a face that was still handsome in a faded way, but must once have been lovely.

"I have to go through with it sooner or later," I protested. "Michael Montgomery means to go on being window display manager of this store, and I mean to go on writing sign copy. Since we'll have to meet, talk to each other, work together, I don't see why we can't do it impersonally and ignore the fact that we were engaged until—until—"

"Until Monty ran out on you and married Chris Gardner," Helena said. "But you're well out of it. It's Chris I'm sorry for. She'll break her heart over him before she's his wife a year. Your heart's still in one piece."

What she said was true, I hoped. Maybe my heart was a little frayed around the edges, but that was all. Since Monty had come from an eastern store some eight months before, life had been a gradual disillusionment for me. A slow falling out of what I knew had been a foolish infatuation. So the worst hurt was over and done with.

Why, then, had the gray drip of rain on the window sill set my teeth on edge the moment I'd entered the office that morning? Why did the queer yellow glow against the window pane seem so depressing?

But I knew why. I sat at my desk, aware of the defiantly bright splash of color I made in my red and white striped blouse—no sackcloth and ashes for me—pretending I could work. And all the while I waited for the sound of Monty's step, for the moment when I'd meet him face to face.

I hadn't told Helena or anyone else, but I'd already

seen him earlier in the day. I'd come upon him by accident, and the shock of that brief glimpse had left me disturbed and a little sick.

It had happened when I'd gone on an errand to the sign-lettering department that morning. The corridor takes a turn and forms an alcove that is shielded from view unless one is right upon it. The man and woman who stood there were so engrossed in each other that they didn't hear my approach. He had his back to me and his hands were on the shoulders of the woman, but I recognized them both at a glance.

The man was Michael Montgomery and the woman who stood so intimately close to him was Carla Drake, our most exotic dress model from the fourth floor.

They were talking in low, tense voices, but I didn't stop to listen. I turned and hurried back to my office, more disturbed than I cared to admit. Even if what Monty did no longer concerned me, there was still Chris to consider. I hated to think he might already be carrying on a flirtation with someone new.

All this contributed to the tenseness of my nerves, so that by now I was keyed to a dangerous pitch, where only some explosive action would relieve the tension. And I knew there mustn't be an explosion. There must not be.

I liked my job. I wanted to keep it.

The letters on the door of my office read: LINELL WYNN, SIGN PROMOTION—which meant that I wrote copy for advertising posters used throughout Cunningham's and for what I modestly considered the most cleverly sophisticated window signs on the street.

When I came to Cunningham's two years before, my office had been a cubbyhole of a place, and about as inspiring to the eye as a cell. But Keith and I had worked evenings for a week hiding those blank walls beneath pages torn from Vogue and Harper's Bazaar.

9

We picked all the striking color photographs and the most interesting black-and-whites and the change worked wonders with the room, brought it to life, turned it gay with color.

Now, ordinarily, when my mind had a tendency to go blank and ideas wouldn't come, I had only to search those colorful walls for inspiration and a new start.

But today was different. Today was deadly.

"It's being on a spot I hate," I explained to Helena. "I was downstairs talking to the handkerchief buyer this morning and every clerk at the counter was watching to see how I was going to take it with Monty back from his honeymoon today. And I don't want to take it, or not take it. I just want to go about my work and not be stared at and pitied."

Keith's somber eyes seemed to darken. "I'd like to fix that Montgomery the way you'd wipe out a rat."

I glanced at him, startled by his intensity.

"Never mind fixing anybody," I told him. "I'll do my own suffering, thank you, and fight my own battles. Here, these signs are ready for lingerie. Take them down and don't hurry back."

I watched him go and Helena shook her head.

"Be careful with that boy," she warned. "He's crazy about you and he knows it's hopeless. At nineteen that's dangerous."

I tried to dismiss her words with a laugh, but the look I'd glimpsed in Keith's eyes was disturbing. I changed the subject hastily.

"I wish Monty would walk in and get it over with. It will be much worse if he feels guilty and tries to avoid me."

"I don't imagine a guilty conscience has any part in our display manager's make-up," Helena said drily and glanced at her watch. "I suppose I'd better get back on the floor. That plastic jewelry ad Chris made the drawings for has been pulling crowds all day. I just wanted

10

to stop in for a minute and see how things were going with you."

"Thanks," I said. "If I could get some decent work done I'd be better off."

But I was glad she was going and it made me feel jumpy when she turned back at the door as if she wanted to say something more. I didn't want to be like Helena when I grew older—a lonely woman working in a small, department store job. That was why Monty's action had frightened me a little.

It had been an open secret for months that young Chris Gardner, over in advertising, had a crush on Michael Montgomery, but as far as I knew, he'd never paid much attention to her until that day two weeks before when he'd run off and married her without any warning at all. I kept wondering if it was something in me that had made him do that. Even though we'd been moving toward a break-up, he needn't have humiliated me so. He needn't have—

"Don't!" Helena said. "He isn't worth it."

I'm afraid the smile I gave her wasn't a very happy one. I hadn't known my face was giving me away and I didn't want her to think I really cared. Perhaps I'd have tried to explain, if there hadn't been an interruption just then. Quick footsteps came down the corridor and a girl slipped past Helena into the office.

She stood for a moment with her back to the door and her chin up defiantly. Her gray yellow print frock was jaunty, but her eyes were swollen from crying.

"Hello, Chris," I said. "Won't you sit down?"

Chris Gardner—she was Chris Montgomery now—went to the chair opposite me. But she didn't sit down, she crumpled into it, her mouth trembling childishly.

"You've always been so good to me, Linell!" she wailed. "You've helped me more than anyone else in this store. And now I—I've treated you like this. I've ruined your life and—"

"Stop it!" I said, to check her rising hysteria. "You haven't ruined anything. The fault was Monty's. I think I know."

Helena gave us both a dark look of pity and slipped away from the door. Chris pulled off her hat and her head went down on my desk in the curve of her arm. I suppose, considering everything, I should have been angry and resentful, but I couldn't be angry with Chris.

She was a big, sturdily built blond girl, with wide shoulders that should have borne trouble more capably, but she always crumpled at the first sign of storm. That was her father's fault, the way he had spoiled her.

"You oughtn't to talk to me!" Chris's voice came muffled from the crook of her arm. "You ought to just throw me out for playing you such a rotten trick."

"If you don't stop crying," I said, "I will throw you out. Sit up and blow your nose and remember that you're a happy bride."

She sat up, mopping futilely at her eyes with a scrap of handkerchief. "That's just it! I'm not a happy b-b-bride at all. I've got to talk to you, Linell. I've got to tell you."

"It ought to be a pretty story," said a voice from the corridor. "Mind if I listen, *Mrs.* Montgomery?"

I looked around at the girl in the doorway.

"Hello, Sondo," I said, not very cordially. "Come in and join the party. We're having open house this afternoon."

Sondo Norgaard was Monty's right hand over in window display and the very sight of her gave me an uneasy feeling. The girl was odd, with her olive skin, tangled black hair, and thin, clever fingers. But put a paint brush or a pair of scissors in her hands and a lovely, whimsical fairyland would result.

She painted backgrounds for the Cunningham windows. She added designs to signs. She created fantastic paper creatures with shaving curl manes and flirtatious

12

eyes. In her way she was a genius, sharp of temper and bitter of tongue. Her presence in my office at that moment probably meant just one thing. That Monty had sent her.

But at least the sight of Sondo had stopped Chris's tears. The girl took out her compact and made a feeble effort to cover the streakings left by her outburst.

Sondo regarded her efforts scornfully, addressing herself to me. "Monty wants to see you. Now. Do you think you could manage to be alone if he comes over?"

I didn't care for her tone or manner. "Since he's waited this long, perhaps he might as well wait till tomorrow."

Sondo became a shade less bitter. She stood there in the doorway, looking like a sexless gnome in her straight, paint-smeared green smock, her feet set well apart in sturdy brogues. The big dark eyes that were her one good feature held no particular enmity as she looked at me, but they held no open liking either.

"Better see him," she urged. "He didn't want to just barge over without warning. That's why he sent me. But you'd better get rid of his—" her dark eyes moved to Chris, turned vindictive again "—his charming little wife."

Chris pulled on her hat without regard for appearance, her hands trembling.

"I'm going now, Linell," she said. "I—I'll talk to you some other time."

She moved past Sondo as if she were a little afraid of her, and then gathered momentary courage. "I know you've never liked me, Sondo. But be kind this once. Don't tell Monty I was here. Please don't tell him."

I looked at Sondo and saw the gleam in her eyes. That was no way to deal with her, I knew. She had too strong a sadistic streak, and Chris was too soft and helpless and open to hurt. Sondo was the kind who could indulge in a particularly refined type of torture

13

and I knew I'd have to warn Chris never to ask for quarter from her.

But I said, "I'll see you later, Chris. Run along. There's no need for Sondo to tell Monty you were here."

Chris gave me a grateful, beaten glance and scurried down the hall toward the elevators. Sondo stared after her for a moment, her wide, scarlet mouth twisted derisively.

"I hate mice," she said. "Nasty, furry, frightened little beasts. God knows why he wanted her. In fact, I don't think he did. But there she is married to him and dissolving in misery."

There was something odd about her manner. Something I couldn't quite put my finger on which left me uneasy. I'd always been puzzled by the relationship between Monty and Sondo. He treated her more like a man than a woman, yet he seemed to trust and rely upon her more than on anyone else.

Before I could speak, she went on.

"You're the one who ought to be miserable and you've been flying banners of courage ever since it happened. I know. I've watched you."

"Wouldn't it be nice," I said, "if we'd all stop watching one another and just tend to our own affairs? Suppose you go back and tell Monty I'll give him five minutes if he comes right away."

Sondo grinned.

"Okay," she said, "I'm put in my place. Trouble is, I never remember to stay there." She waved one small hand and scampered off down the hall.

I shivered. The girl was sometimes more animal than human. I wondered how Monty could stand to have her around. Tony Salvador, Monty's assistant, hated her like poison and since Monty had been away the two had been snapping at each other and indulging in temperamental clashes that echoed clear across the floor.

I sighed and rubbed my fingers wearily against my

14

temples. A department store is too full of temperament. Especially at the merchandising end. Down in the selling sections only buyers can afford the luxury, but upstairs there's always enough talent and creativeness to drive any innocent bystander crazy.

Not that I was an innocent bystander, by any means. I had a job I liked to do. Ordinarily. And I tried to do it with a minimum expenditure of temperament on my own part. The trouble was everybody knew I was a good peace-maker and I was always having to play buffer when matters became too charged with dynamite.

I didn't know what was wrong with Chris, or what she'd wanted to tell me. I didn't know what the whole miserable tangle was about. And I felt charged with enough dynamite at the moment to set off a few explosions in my own right.

It was then I heard Monty's step in the corridor. I raised my head, steeling myself for resistance. I knew Monty. I knew those charming ways of his and how his soft-spoken words could sometimes disarm and betray, and this afternoon I wasn't having any.

This was the meeting I'd been dreading since early morning. This was the moment.

CHAPTER 2

Michael Montgomery came into my office with his usual assured stride. He came straight to my desk and stood there, tall and blond, looking down at me with a face that revealed both the strength of tenacity and the weakness of sensuality. In spite of his forty-three years, he had kept the vitality of youth.

"You wanted to see me?" I asked quietly.

His brown eyes held a warm appeal. When he looked at a woman like that she was apt to forget that his chin had a softness of line and his mouth was a little cruel.

"I don't know how to begin," he said. "I've spent hours during the last two weeks planning what I'd say to you, and now that you're here before me, I can't say any of it."

"Do you have to say anything?" I asked. "Why not just let the whole thing go? We both have our jobs to do and there's no need for personalities to enter in."

But he had too much vanity to let me go as easily as that. He didn't want me. He'd married another woman. But he wanted to convince himself that I was still properly subjugated.

"There will always be personalities where you and I are concerned," he told me, dropping his voice to what

16

I'm sure he considered a fascinating huskiness. The sad part was there'd been a time when I'd considered it fascinating too. Which didn't flatter my intelligence. "You can't escape me, any more than I can escape you, Linell. I've hurt you cruelly, but——"

I was a little surprised at the sharpness of my own voice. "No! No, Monty. You haven't it in your power to hurt me. My pride, perhaps. But not me. You're very charming, when you want to be, and for a little while I was foolish enough to believe in the surface. But I'm quite free of you now. I don't understand what you did, but I don't care any more that you did it."

He went right on, as if my words had no meaning. "Linell, sweet, I think this is the first time in my life I've loved a woman as I love you."

Gracious, I thought, was he going to stand there and weave his spells until I was compelled to believe him? He was really very good at it, but I suppose he'd had a lot of practice.

"One thinks that each time, I imagine," I said. "About never having loved as one loves now. But just how do you reconcile such a depth of emotion with the fact that you dropped me without warning and went suddenly off to marry Chris?"

"That's what I want to tell you about, Linell. That's why I'm here. To ask you to have dinner with me tonight."

I felt so strong an aversion that I pushed back my chair and gathered up some papers from my desk.

"If you'll excuse me," I said, "there are some things I must attend to."

I walked by him to the door, but he came after me and put a hand on my arm.

"Linell! You've got to give me a chance to tell you, a chance to——"

I withdrew my arm with a shrug of distaste. "If you won't think of Chris—of your wife—I will. I'm very

17

fond of her, very sorry for her. The last thing I'd do would be to have dinner with her husband."

He started to protest, and to stop him I said something I hadn't meant to say.

"While we're on the subject," I told him, "knowing that you have a wife, I think it might be wise to avoid being seen in intimate conversation with women like Carla Drake."

To my surprise, he didn't display his usual swagger.

"There's nothing between Miss Drake and me," he assured me. "I barely know the woman."

But it seemed to me that he protested a little too earnestly and I couldn't forget his hands upon her shoulders. I didn't stay for further discussion.

I went out the door and down the narrow corridor to where the floor widened to meet the elevators. I was shaking inside and I was angry with myself for letting him infuriate me. But what he was going to do to Chris, what he had undoubtedly done to other women, was wicked and cruel. And Chris was so young, so dreadfully, agonizingly in love.

It was then I realized something. The encounter I'd been dreading all day had come and gone. There had been no real explosion, only a cold severing of last ties, yet my nervous tension had not relaxed. If anything I was more taut than before, as if thin strong wires drew me step by irrevocable step toward something which lay in the future.

I shrugged impatiently and glanced at the papers in my hands, copy I was planning for signs which would be used throughout the store to advertise the style show starting Saturday. I might as well go down to fourth and talk to Owen Gardner about the affair. Perhaps I'd find Chris there with her father, and could discover what was troubling her.

Fourth was my favorite floor. A floor of luxury and fashion. Huge glass showcases displayed rare furs and exquisite gowns. Deep pile carpets sank beneath the lightest step, lights were soft, cunningly arranged to reveal the perfection of the merchandise, and to flatter the beauty of women who came to buy.

This floor was Owen Gardner's pride and he gave to it all the creative genius of an artist. Which was odd, considering that he looked like a dull little man who would be more interested in Sunday golf and week-day market reports, than in the trappings of the fashion world. But I could remember one day when I'd come upon him lovingly stroking pudgy hands over a length of Chinese brocade. In that moment he had ceased to be merely a hot-tempered little man with a mind bent on bringing dollars into his department, and I knew he had made a success of the fourth floor because he loved luxury and beauty as passionately as any woman.

Miss Babcock, the buyer for better dresses, nodded toward the merchandise manager's office. "His highness is in conference, but you go right on in. It's only one of the models."

Things were evidently not going well with Miss Babcock today. But then, things were seldom going well with Miss Babcock. She liked it that way.

I could hear a low, indistinguishable buzz of voices as I approached the door of Owen Gardner's office, but the buzz stopped at my knock, as if the speakers did not want to be overheard.

I put my head in the door. "Miss Babcock said you weren't too busy to be interrupted. May—"

"Come in, come in," Owen Gardner said a little too hospitably. "Of course I'm not too busy to see you, Linell. Uh—you know Carla Drake, don't you?"

I did indeed. Since her name had been so recently on my tongue, I looked at her now with more than ordinary interest.

She turned toward me slowly, with fluid grace that

seemed to have little to do with prosaic matters like joints and bone-structure.

"Hello, Miss Wynn," she murmured in a low, whispery voice.

She was exotic, breathlessly lovely. Not young, certainly. Ageless. Her face was as unlined as a girl's, but her shining, shoulder-length bob was silver-white and her body had a full-blown maturity.

Gardner went on, explaining where there was no need. "I was just talking to Miss Drake about the gowns she's to model for the style show. That will be all now, Carla. I'll speak to you again later."

I found myself raising a mental eyebrow. What went on here? Had I imagined it, or was there a certain hurried uneasiness in the way Gardner had dismissed the model? Carla merely bent that startling, shimmering head submissively and glided toward the door. "Flowed" was the word, really, I thought, looking after her.

It surprised me a little when the model turned back for an instant at the door, one delicate hand pale against the mahogany panel, her blue eyes dark and sad as they rested briefly on me. Then she was gone and the door had closed softly behind her.

There it was again, even from this woman I scarcely knew—that look of pity beneath which I was beginning to cringe.

I went over and spread my papers on Owen's desk. "I wish you'd glance through these suggestions when you have time. Has Chris been here? I thought I might find her."

He looked up at me sharply and to my dismay I saw cold fury in his eyes.

"She was here," he said. "Crying."

I could understand how he felt. The way Gardner adored and spoiled his only daughter was obvious to everyone. Sometimes I'd even been a little sorry for Susan Gardner, his plump, self-effacing little wife, because of the way all this affection seemed to pour out on Chris. Owen's dislike of Michael Montgomery, and the feud between fourth floor and window display was already a legend in the store, so it must have been a stunning blow to Chris's father when the girl ran off with Monty. And now, if Monty was making her unhappy, Gardner must be wild with anger.

"That's why I came down," I told him. "I thought I might find her here. She wanted to talk to me, but there were so many interruptions upstairs. Do you know where she's gone?"

"Down to the waiting room to meet Susan." He closed his eyes and with the anger hidden, looked a little gray and broken. But there was suppressed violence in his words as he went on.

"Montgomery's no good. He's rotten clear through where women are concerned. And now he's going to break up Chris's life the way he's broken the lives of other women. If somebody doesn't break him first."

There was such hatred in his tone that I was alarmed.

"Please be careful," I said. "You mustn't do anything that would hurt Chris even more. Perhaps it will work out. Nobody's bad all the way through. He wouldn't have married her unless he cared something about her—"

"That's it!" Gardner pounded his fist hard against the desk. "That's just it—he didn't give a damn about her. It's my fault, but I didn't dream—"

He broke off and I turned hastily toward the door. Everything I said seemed to excite and upset him more.

"You mustn't worry." I tried to sound encouraging. "I'll see her as soon as I can. I'll talk to her."

He didn't hear me. He said, "I could break him. I could end this once and for all. Perhaps I will."

His eyes were fixed blindly on the wall and I'm sure he didn't notice when I left the office.

I went upstairs, more worried and concerned than ever. What a day! One thing piling on top of another, building up emotion and conflict until it seemed that the lid must surely fly off. Something had to explode under all this pressure. I was beginning to feel that all I wanted was to be out of the way when it happened.

When I got back to my office I found a tall young man with blue, humorous eyes sitting on the corner of my desk. He grinned at me engagingly and nodded toward Keith, who was answering the phone.

Keith grimaced and held out the phone to me. "It's Tony Salvador and he's whopping mad."

This was life in a department store. I suppressed a sigh and took the phone. Tony was Monty's first assistant in window display.

"Shut up, Tony," I said. "This is Linell."

I didn't expect him to shut up and I wasn't disappointed. But at least he brought his voice down a couple of octaves and slowed his words to a more intelligible pace.

"Look, Linell, I'm through. I quit. I'm not taking any more from Montgomery. Not any more at all. See?"

"Yes, of course, Tony," I agreed. "But you'd better go home and sleep on it before you do anything drastic."

"I don't need to sleep on this," Tony went on furiously. "I'm through. For good."

There was no use trying to talk to him over the phone. Obviously he'd had a drink or two, and he never made sense on a telephone anyway.

"Where are you now?" I asked. "Window display? All right, you stay there. I've some work to finish and then I'm coming over. I want to talk to you."

I hung up before he could protest and shoved the phone away from me.

"Oh, for a nice quiet madhouse," I murmured. Then I looked up at the young man who'd perched himself

22

on my desk, "Hello, Bill Thorne. Tony's scrapping with Monty again and I suppose I'll have to go over and calm everybody down."

Bill transferred himself to a chair. "Cunningham's little angel of mercy! I'll bet it's that phonograph attachment I rigged up while Monty was away that's causing the trouble. Tony tell you about it?"

I shook my head. "Not a word."

"Well, Tony had a brainstorm. He wanted a mechanical bird to sit on a tree branch in the golf window. It moves around and ruffles its wings, while a hidden phonograph whistles *Welcome, Sweet Springtime*. A loud speaker will broadcast it on State Street. And don't look at me. I only take orders."

I wrinkled my nose. "For once I don't blame Monty. Tony can pull some awful stuff sometimes."

"The trouble with window decorators," Bill said, "is that they're such snobs. Now if Dana O'Clare* did it at Lord and Taylor's, stores out in Podunk would be copying next week. Anyway, Tony has the courage of his convictions."

"But we're not Lord and Taylor," I pointed out, "and Tony isn't Dana O'Clare. Not that I don't appreciate the spot he's been in ever since Monty took over. Tony expected to be put in as display manager when Gregory left. He had a right to expect it. But here he is still assistant, though he produces most of the ideas while Monty takes the glory. And Tony really is good most of the time."

"Have you seen Chris?" Bill asked without warning.

I glanced at him quickly. He was looking at one of the color photographs above my head and I had a chance to study him for a moment.

I liked Bill Thorne. He had an easy-going good

---

*Dana O'Clare is now a Corporal with the Army Air Forces First Fighter Command.

nature, a friendly grin and swell sense of humor. I liked the little kindnesses he was always performing unobtrusively. He was tall, compact, and well-knit. His blue eyes could twinkle. And I liked the fineness of his long slender hands.

He was a little of everything, Bill Thorne. Artist, sculptor, inventor, mechanic. He'd inherited the Universal Arts Company out on West Madison Street from his brilliant father, and he supplied the million-and-one needs of show windows all over the country. Anything from a plaster fawn to a hundred-and-fifty dollar mannequin could be produced at Universal Arts. If a window decorator wanted a Grecian column or a paper weight Bill was there with the answer. On the side he had a little electrical shop which flourished at Christmas time when animated toys for show windows were in demand.

And Bill Thorne had been especially kind to Chris Gardner.

"She was up here just a little while ago," I told him. "And feeling pretty miserable too."

"I don't doubt it." Bill's voice was dry. "She's a nice kid. Talented. She had a real career ahead of her, I think. But I suppose she won't be coming back to Cunningham's now."

I shook my head. I was remembering how Bill had helped Chris so often with her drawings when he dropped into the store, and how he'd sometimes taken her out to lunch or dinner. And I was wondering just how hard Chris's marriage had hit Bill Thorne.

"Well, I'll be running along," he said. "I've a date with Montgomery, though he doesn't know it. A date to punch his head. I'll come back and let you know how it turns out."

This was getting almost funny. I left my chair in a hurry and caught him at the door.

"Bill, don't be an idiot! There are enough people in

24

this store mad at Monty. He'll get what's coming to him sooner or later, without any help from you."

He grinned at me. "I should think you'd be all for the idea. Though I must say you don't look like any broken blossom to me."

"I'm not," I told him. "And if I were, I'd keep it to myself."

"Good girl," he said, and I liked the way he looked at me. There wasn't any pity in his eyes. Just an acceptance of the fact that I could take what I had to take.

"When I get through," he went on, "I'm coming back to take you to dinner."

But I didn't want that. Not then.

"No, Bill. This has been—well, quite a day. I'm going home tonight and go to bed. If you see Tony, tell him I'll come over as soon as I finish here."

"Okay," he said. "Another time maybe. We, the jilted, ought to get together."

He waved a hand at me and went off down the hall.

"We, the jilted"? Had he been so seriously interested in Chris, then, I wondered? Or had he, perhaps, been trying to make me feel that I wasn't quite alone in what had happened to me? He was a nice guy, Bill.

CHAPTER 3

I was tired. Achingly tired. While I'd been talking to Bill, everything had returned almost to normal, but now the tautness was back again, the queer sense of momentum carrying me along. It wasn't through yet. It wasn't ended.

That horrid sulphur light still pressed against my window, but it had started to rain again and the drizzle came straight down through the yellow glare. As I went back to my desk I was conscious once more of Keith watching me furtively, and I'm afraid I snapped at him.

"Get those letters typed and forget about me," I told him.

I pulled a sheet of paper across the desk and looked at it wearily. It was the sign copy for the series of red windows Tony had been planning for State Street. He'd worked hard on those plans, with Sondo doing the backgrounds and contributing ideas of her own. I knew it was his intention to put in something so spectacular while Monty was away that he'd completely outshine him. Now, no matter what Tony did, the plans for those windows would have to go ahead.

I stared without interest at the words I'd written on the paper.

Red is the Color of the Year
    Red for Daring
    Red for Courage
    Red for—

"Red for *what?*" I asked Keith.

He looked up from his typewriter.

"Blood, maybe," he said somberly.

"Oh, go home," I told him. "It's only a half hour or so till closing time and I'm getting awfully fed up with people."

I knew I'd hurt his feelings.

"I'll feel better tomorrow," I called after him as he left, but he went out the door without replying.

That was the trouble with department stores. You could never get away from people. From different temperaments and dispositions and sensitivities. Including your own. Usually I liked it. I liked the rush and excitement, the everlasting pressure of work. There were always deadlines in my job, just as there were on a newspaper. For a few weeks the theme song would be spring. Then overboard with spring and on with hot weather. Cotton for warm days ahead, while one was still trailing through the puddles of April.

But right now red. I had to think of a word. Just one more word before I left the office.

I looked about at the bright pages lining the walls, but for once inspiration was a laggard. There was scarlet and gold in a ballet picture of *Coq D'Or*, there was a nail polish ad—hands with blood-red nails arranging delicately hued seashells on a dark table, there was a crimson coat on a famous model. Red everywhere—but no adjective to catch fire in my tired brain.

Let the word go. I'd get it tomorrow. Now I'd run over to talk to Tony and then I'd go home.

The section of the eighth floor leading to the window display department was deserted. A long corridor ran

27

past echoing store-rooms and closed doors, ending in a strip of floor that was like a drawbridge flung between stairs and freight elevators. The rooms of window display lay beyond.

This was one of the days when the display people came down early to work in the side windows before the store opened. Nearly everyone had gone home in the afternoon, and now the place was empty and quiet.

Window display consisted of a series of rooms of various sizes, separated by steel gray partitions rising part way to the high ceiling. Monty and Tony each had an office on the right, with a little anteroom between, where Monty's secretary usually stayed. It was empty now because the girl's brother had become seriously ill and she had taken a leave of absence to go down to her home in southern Illinois.

On the left, running along the window side, stretched rooms, like a row of boxes, open above the partitions, and open on the corridor they shared. These included numerous prop rooms, Sondo's workroom, the room in which the mannequins were kept.

Tony's office was empty and for a moment I thought he must have gone. I stood there wondering what to do next, feeling again that strong sense of predestination, of something I *must* do.

I began to walk slowly down the corridor, past the room where old sets were kept, past shelves containing bolts of material and rolls of wallpaper, past Sondo's workroom without looking in. Above my head, like the intertwining branches of a forest, hung artificial pine boughs with long green needles and white-tipped cones—decorations from last Christmas.

The whole place had a touch of the fantastic. It was a through-the-looking-glass world where anything could be found, anything could happen.

And then I heard Tony's voice and paused for an instant, startled. Ringing suddenly through that quiet place it had an eerie, insane sound. As if Tony Salvador were talking loudly to himself.

But he wasn't talking to himself. I was still more amazed as I caught the words.

"Darling," he was saying, "I don't know what I'd do without you. You're the only one who ever listens. You know I'm good, honey. You know I'm the best damn' window decorator on the street. And then I have to be up against a louse like Monty. You know why he won't let me get ahead, honey? Because I'm better'n he is."

I pulled myself together and walked quickly to the door of the mannequin room. This was scarcely discretion on Tony's part and it had to be stopped, no matter who was with him. If Monty ever overheard a conversation like that, Tony would be through whether he wanted to be or not.

The mannequin room was a huge jumble, with Tony himself in the middle of it, waving a plaster arm of feminine contour as he talked. Tony was tall and very dark, with those Latin good looks which have such a romantic appeal for women. But it was the girl who sat in a chair with her back to the door that interested me.

She wore a hooded scarlet evening cape, and her black lace formal draped gracefully over crossed knees and fell to the point of one silver sandal.

"Come on in," Tony invited. "I don't keep any secrets from Dolores."

It was one of the window mannequins. The figure was so amazingly lifelike that for just a moment I'd been fooled.

"Tony!" I cried in exasperation. "Do you have to be such a fool? That voice of yours carries all over the floor. What if Monty came in and heard what I've just heard?"

"What difference does it make?" Tony's gesture with the arm was debonair, if grotesque. "I'm through any-

29

way." He chucked the mannequin under her papier maché chin. "Going to devote all my time to you now, gorgeous."

"Do you think you could sober up long enough to tell me what happened?" I asked.

He grinned at Dolores. "She thinks I'm tight. But I'm not half so tight as I'm going to be an hour from now. Oh, well—I'll tell her. It was that damn phonograph, Linell. That bird attachment Bill Thorne worked out. "It's a swell idea and I was ready to put it across tomorrow in the golf window on State Street. And what do you think happened?"

"Let me guess," I said. "Monty didn't like it."

He leaned an elbow against a wall cabinet labeled "Half Figures," and nodded wisely. "Smart girl. He said he wasn't going to have Cunningham's windows put on a drugstore level. And he told me to go back to the farm. Me!"

"So you're going, is that it?"

He glared at me. "No, I'm not going. But we'll see what he can do on his own for a while. He's got by on my ideas long enough."

I was scarcely listening to Tony. The mannequin room had always been the strangest, most fascinating spot in the whole store. I never could resist poking around in it to see what I could find.

All about the walls ranged deep cabinets, each with its own closed door, containing mannequins. In one corner was a collection of unclad figures waiting to be carried down to the windows, or put away for future use. While down the middle of the room stretched a long table with a scramble of hands and legs upon it, a wig or two, some hair ornaments, artificial flowers, and something that looked like a Flit gun. I picked it up curiously.

"Bothered by flies?" I inquired and squirted the green

spray experimentally out into the room. The odor of pine needles was pungent.

"There now!" Tony said. "That was one of my ideas. Remember last Christmas when the whole first floor smelled of pine trees? That was because I sent somebody down to spray it every morning. But I'm not going to think up anything more."

I put down the spray gun. "Well, it's your nose, if you want to cut it off. Aside from the bird in the tree, is the window finished? Nothing for me to look after?"

Monty had said I had a good eye for accessories and small details and lately I'd been working more closely with the decorating end.

Tony considered. "There's some new jewelry that's supposed to be promoted for sport wear. Lapel pins or something. Maybe you'd better pick out some stuff. I'm not going back."

"I'll take care of it," I assured him. "And, Tony—sleep it off before you quit. The rest of us appreciate you around here, if Monty doesn't."

Tony put out the plaster arm and shook hands with me gravely. "Thanks, lady. But I think I've had about enough of Sondo and Monty."

"All right," I said. "So long."

The light was on in Sondo's workroom, but I didn't stop to look in. It was getting on toward the closing hour and I didn't want to go home too late. There was a time later on when I was to find myself wondering if it would have made any difference if I had looked in.

I stopped at my office to pick up a smock for slight protection against the chill of the display windows, and then went downstairs.

The main floor was thronged with last minute shoppers. Around the costume jewelry counters the women were three deep. That ad of Chris's had drawn business all right. It was the last thing she'd written for Cunningham's.

I pushed through to the counter and caught Helena Farnham's eye.

"I need some things for the golf window," I told her. "Brown, maybe, to go with green. A couple of lapel pins. Nothing dangly."

It took more than a big sales day to destroy Helena's outward efficiency, but there were lines of fatigue about her eyes and as she brought out a tray of pins and set them before me, her hands trembled a little.

"If I never see another piece of costume jewelry it will be too soon," she murmured. "My feet are killing me."

"Bed for us both the minute we get home," I said. "I'll take that brown wooden seahorse with the scarlet head. And maybe the gold anchor."

I filled out a borrow sheet and gave it to Helena. Then, pins in hand, I crossed the aisle to the long section of middle windows. Here a stairway cut down to the basement, dropping away below the paneled walls, so that no counters ranged along the windows in this section.

There were padlocks on all the doors that led into the windows, but most of the time nobody bothered to lock them. I put my hand on a door that looked like a panel of the wall and then stood quite still, waiting.

Waiting because a curious sense of reluctance had seized me. A reluctance that had to do with the opening of that door beneath my hand.

But that was nonsense and I shrugged the notion aside. The door opened easily and I drew it shut behind me as I stepped into the window. It was cold and I shivered as I stepped between a wing of compo board and the framework that held Sondo's painted background.

Everything was as it should be. There was nothing strange or unaccountable about the scene. Heavy home-spun curtains were pulled across the plate glass, shutting off the view from the street. I went across and parted a fold to look out and see what the weather was like.

The yellow light was gone and rain was coming down in earnest. The afternoon was stormy dark. Street lights were on and people scurried by close to my window, the lucky few with umbrellas, the rest with heads bent against the rain.

I dropped the curtain and turned back to my little window-stage of a world. Above my head a spotlight flung its beam upon four mannequins grouped on an island of peat moss "earth."

The idea had been to contrast old style golf fashions with the new, and there were two swank, modern mannequins wearing the sport clothes of the moment and equipped with the latest in steel shafted golf clubs. These two regarded with evident amusement the two seated, long-skirted figures with golf bags that were anything but streamlined, and old wooden clubs.

The background represented a rolling expanse of grass with a country club in the distance, and there was a cleverly contrived tree of plywood with a slightly larger than life-size bird on one of its branches. Wires ran down behind the tree, so evidently the phonograph was backstage.

I smiled. Poor Tony and his welcome-sweet-spring-time!

But the window was chilly and I didn't want to stay. There's never any regulating the temperature of the windows. In summer it's like being in a hothouse behind the plate glass, and in winter it's practically outdoors. But nobody seems to care except the decorators.

One of the mannequins wore a brilliant scarlet sport jacket and the mere sight of that color made me feel jumpy again. I either wanted to get away from it, or else think of a word to describe it and banish it from my mind. Something sophisticated and challenging.

"Blood," Keith had said. Goodness knows that was challenging enough.

I fastened the wooden seahorse on a green lapel and stood back to view the effect. Good. And the gold anchor would look stunning against that scarlet. I moved gingerly so as not to step on the peat moss and track it about the window. Someone had already tracked it a little. Tony, probably, mad and not caring. It would have to be vacuumed in the morning before the curtains were opened. There was a chipped fragment of something that might have been part of a costume jewelry piece showing up dark against the carpet. I put the scrap in my smock pocket, meaning to drop it in a wastebasket later. A window must be spotless before it is uncovered.

It was then I noticed the stick lying at one of the mannequin's feet. Tony was getting careless. The thing had simply been tossed down there on the peat moss and nobody had bothered to remove it. I bent and picked it up.

It was the broken upper end of a wooden golf club. Monty should see that! The boys in window display had been known to indulge in horseplay on occasion, but they seldom broke anything. Oh well, it wasn't my problem. I thrust the stick into a golf bag leaning against a mannequin's knee and turned quickly.

Turned with a queer chill running through me. A chill that was more than the chill of the window. For suddenly, eerily, I'd had the feeling that I was being watched. It was as if someone, something, had stood for an instant behind one of the fluted wings peering out at me.

Had there been a movement over there on the left? Or was it only a trick of reflected light?

"Who's there?" I called in a low voice.

But the words fell flat, without echo or answer; the mannequins watched impassive, empty-eyed. Nerves, I

34

thought in annoyance. This day had been too much for me and the sooner it ended the better.

I forced myself to stand quietly for a moment with my back to the street, looking over the display for any further flaws, considering the lighting. That baby spot wasn't just right. I could go around to the switch box at the back and adjust it. Then I'd be finished.

I slipped carefully between wings and background, accustomed to the difficult task of moving in such cramped quarters without knocking anything askew. "Backstage" there was a narrow strip of passageway leading to an intersection where the switch box was located.

The window decorators were forever leaving props about behind the scenes and I stepped past the unclad half figure of a mannequin, ducked to miss a pair of silk stockings which dangled from a hanger hooked carelessly on a strip of framework. I reached the alcove which contained the switch box and came to a dead stop.

This, I knew, was the moment toward which I had been moving with dreadful certainty all day long. All the wires which pulled me had been stretched so taut that I had only to scream to snap them.

But I couldn't scream. I could only stand there staring at the man who lay at my feet beneath the switch box. He was sprawled face down, and beside him was the steel-clubbed head of a broken golf stick.

There, too, was that ruddy hue I could not escape. Dulling the shine of steel, staining the floor, crimsoning the blond hair of that limp and grotesque figure.

It was Michael Montgomery and I knew, instinctively, that he was dead.

I could only stand there sharply aware of small things that were of no consequence. The chill of the window, the shine of Monty's shoes, the way his right hand was tightened into a fist. How many times later

I was to recall all those small details, recall them frighteningly in my dreams, and unwillingly when I was awake.

All that was Monty, his cruelty, his charm, his vitality, had been resolved at last. Someone had taken upon himself the meting out of justice. Someone—*someone*. It was the significance of that word that brought me back to life.

For all I knew the murderer might be hiding in that very window. I had to get away quickly. I had to get back to the bustle and safety of the store, call for help, raise the alarm.

But at the very moment when I turned toward the single passageway of escape, I heard a sound that was more frightening than any sound I'd ever heard in my life. It was faint—a clicking and fumbling.

A sound made by the latch at the entrance to the window. Someone was opening the door.

CHAPTER 4

I stood there in that narrow passageway, my blood drumming wildly in my ears and Monty's body sprawled on the floor behind me. Stood there, waiting agonizingly through seconds that seemed like years, while someone climbed into the window.

The head and shoulders of a man appeared first, then his whole body, and I experienced an instant of almost agonizing relief. But with recognition came a guarded tightening.

It was Bill Thorne. But why was Bill Thorne coming into this window? As far as I was concerned, who was Bill Thorne? What did I really know about him? And how could I forget that only a little while before he had threatened to punch Monty's head?

"What are you doing here?" I asked in a voice that sounded strained and cracked.

He looked at me queerly, but I must have been a strange sight with my face bloodless with terror.

"What's up?" he asked.

I could only repeat my question as if I knew no other words. The second time he answered me.

"I'm looking for Monty. I got tired of waiting around upstairs for him to show up. Thought I might catch him down here. Linell, what's the matter?"

He sounded natural enough and if he was looking at me a little strangely, that too was natural, considering how I was behaving. I made a feeble motion toward the alcove and the switch box.

"Back there," I gasped. "Back there on the floor! You're too late!"

He gave me one look and strode past to the alcove. When he saw, he made no sound, no outcry. His eyes turned back to meet mine for just an instant, then he knelt at Monty's side. I watched while he felt for a pulse and I knew by his face that there was none. He shook his head and stood up, looking white and shaken.

"We've got to get you out of here," he said.

Then, while I watched, he leaned down and gingerly picked up the broken golf stick. Working carefully, to avoid the area where blood had spattered, he wiped the shaft with a handkerchief, replaced the stick beside the body.

37

"Now then," he said, "come on."

He had wiped the fingerprints from that stick. His hand hurt my arm and I tried to pull away.

"We—we've got to call s-s-somebody!" I said between chattering teeth. "G-g-get a doctor!"

He shook me quite sharply. "It's too late for a doctor. Pull yourself together. You've got to get back upstairs."

His fingers were cruel and tight on my arm and I was too terrified to protest. We walked to the entrance of the window and then he bent to whisper grimly in my ear.

"We're going out into the store now and you're going to walk past the counters and over to the elevators as if nothing had happened. It's busy out there, and if we move quickly, the chances are we won't be noticed."

There was no resisting the tight band of his fingers grasping my arm. I found myself walking along the wide aisle, conscious in a confused way of the bright lights of the store, of spring decorations overhead, of the gleam of crystal at the perfume counters. Then we were in the elevator and a girl in a green uniform was saying, "Floors, please," as the car moved upward.

Just as we reached the eighth floor the closing bell jangled harshly and I jumped as if the sound had released some lever that controlled my normal will to think and act. But I didn't try to talk to Bill until he led me to my office and thrust me none too gently into the chair behind my desk.

Then I sat up and started in.

"I don't know what you've had to do with this, Bill Thorne," I said angrily, "but I don't like the way you wiped that golf stick with your handkerchief. Or the way you sneaked us out of there. Or—"

"Stop it!" he said. "It's no go."

He'd perched himself on the corner of my desk again, just the way he had earlier that afternoon, only

38

now there was no twinkle in his blue eyes. Only grim purpose.

I could only gape at him blankly, numbly, until the straight line of his mouth softened. He leaned over and put his hand beneath my chin and I had a swift, incongruous memory of Tony doing the same thing to that mannequin.

"You can trust me, Linell," he said. "I'll see you through. Begin at the beginning and tell me exactly what happened. Was there a quarrel? Where did you get the golf stick?"

I began to understand and the stunning realization that Bill thought I had killed Monty did what even the sight of that crumpled body had not managed to do. It snapped the tension.

I put my head down on my arms and began to laugh. Crazy, choked laughter that shook me clear through and must have sounded more like sobs than laughter.

Bill put his hand gently on my shoulder and the concern in his voice made me laugh all the harder.

"Linell," he said, "you mustn't. You poor kid! Monty got what was coming to him all right, but why did it have to be you?"

I couldn't stop. All the strain I'd been under that day was releasing itself in laughter. And there was horror too, because I sensed that the moment I stopped laughing I'd have to face the terrible fact of murder.

I raised my head and Bill saw that I was laughing. He looked so shocked that I knew he must think I'd gone crazy—and that made me laugh still more.

"It's so—f-f-funny!" I gasped. "You're so rid-d-diculous!"

He said, "If you don't stop, I'll slap you."

He looked as if he meant it too, but I couldn't stop. He did mean it. His hand whacked smartly across my cheek and I could feel the blood tingle under the blow.

I stopped right in the middle of a giggle, so mad I wanted to throw things.

"How dare you!" I stormed. "How dare you strike me! How dare you think I killed Monty!"

He caught me by the shoulders and turned me toward the light. "You mean—you didn't kill him?"

We looked at each other for a long moment. There was something guarded in Bill's eyes that I didn't like. It meant either that he was still suspecting me, or that he had something to hide himself. Even in my numbness, I couldn't quite accept the way he'd behaved through all this.

My lips must have trembled, for he bent over me at once. "If you switch to tears, I'll slap you again. Regardless of what's happened, you've got to get out of this store. I've never seen such a nice mess of circumstantial evidence as you handed me down in that window, and I can't turn in an alarm till you're safe."

"My prints weren't on that stick," I told him indignantly. "If you hadn't wiped it off, the police could tell I'd never touched it. But maybe you were wiping your own prints off."

He didn't deny it. "We can go into the details later," he said. "Right now I've got to get you out of this."

"Get her out of what?" asked Sondo's voice and we both swung guiltily about to see her standing in the doorway.

There was no telling how much she might have heard, with her stealthy way of sneaking up before you were aware of her. But though her big dark eyes looked brightly curious, there seemed nothing in them of suspicion.

"Hello, Sondo," Bill said. "I've just been offering a little free advice. Linell takes on more than her share of work, it seems to me. Can't your bosses look after their window job themselves?"

"It's Linell's job too." Sondo presented her usual

chip-on-the-shoulder attitude. "Monty can't do every-thing. And Tony's no good. Right now he's over in window display getting gorgeously drunk. You're the only one he ever listens to, Linell. So how about coming over and clearing him out?"

Bill didn't give me a chance to answer.

"Not tonight," he said. "Linell's in a hurry. You'll have to get rid of all incidental drunks yourself."

He picked up my hat and plunked it on my head with about as much skill as you'd expect from a man.

Sondo said, "Oh, stop playing the dominant male. I'm talking to Linell, not you. Look—I don't care if Tony gets fired tomorrow, but I've got some work to finish and he keeps cruising through the place getting in the way. And if he turns mean he may start smashing things."

Bill had a hand on my arm again and I knew the way he was squeezing meant that I wasn't to waste any more time on Sondo. Thanks to his tender protection I was going to be thoroughly black-and-blue tomorrow, and the soreness of my arm didn't make me feel any more amiable toward him. But there was something else that kept me from turning down Sondo's request.

Tony.

Tony was pretty decent really, and he'd always been nice to me. But he was reckless and impulsive and excitable. If the—the body (I winced from the picture that word brought up) was discovered and then Tony was found in the store, drunk and spilling over with indignation against Monty, it might go hard with him. Tony hadn't had anything to do with this, of course, and I didn't want to see him get into a lot of trouble. It would only take a couple of minutes to collect him and get him out of the store with us.

I took off my smock and hung it over the back of my chair.

"Come on," I said, "we'll go get Tony."

41

And I started off, with Sondo at my heels, and Bill reluctantly following. Short of picking me up by the hair and dragging me off to the elevators, there wasn't much else he could do.

Tony was in his office this time and he was still conversing loudly with his plaster and papier maché dream girl, Dolores.

"Tony," I said, "we've come to see that you get started home all right. Be a good guy and get your hat."

Tony dazzled me with his smile. "Linell, honey, this *is* my home. I like it here. Besides, I got Dolores now."

"You see what I have to put up with?" Sondo said. "Well, I'm going back to work. I leave him to you."

She went off and I tried again. "Listen, Tony, this is serious. It's important that you go home right away. Please come."

"Oh, you mean it's important," Tony said. "That's different, isn't it?"

Bill started in on me. "Stop wasting time. I'll give you one more second to persuade him, and then you're coming if I have to carry you. And I mean—"

He stopped and looked around with a listening expression on his face. "What's that?"

I knew right away, but I'll admit it had an eerie sound echoing through those deserted display rooms. It was the phonograph in Sondo's workroom. She'd brought it when she first came to the store and Monty had humored her and let her play it. She said she could always work better to music, and though the window decorators claimed it drove them batty, Sondo's phonograph could be heard in the department at almost any hour.

"It's that damn *Bolero!*" Tony said. "Some day I'm going to smash that box to tinders."

I explained to Bill, and while I was talking, trying not to listen to the monotonous beat of the music, something quite dreadful began to happen way down inside me.

I began to be terribly aware. Aware of the fact of murder. Until now shock and hysteria had held me, but that music was beating right in my blood. With my mind I knew now that Monty was dead. Violently, horribly dead. Beaten to death with a golf club. I couldn't yet cope with the question of who had done so terrible a thing. I knew only that I wanted to get away from Cunningham's as quickly as I could, get home to the safety of my own apartment, to Helena's comfortable, soothing presence.

So the first thing I did was to lose my head. I put both hands on Tony's shoulders and shook him as hard as I could.

"Something awful's happened!" I cried. "You've got to come right away."

To my relief he stood up, swaying a little.

"Okay," he said. "I'll come. But Dolores is coming too."

He reached down to gather her up in his arms and I pictured the three of us trying to walk past the doorman with one of Cunningham's prize mannequins in our company."

"Tony," I said, "Monty's dead." I felt Bill's warning hand on my arm, but I didn't care. "Somebody's killed him, Tony. I tell you he's dead!"

Tony stared at me and for a second there was no sound except the maddening drum of the *Bolero*.

Then, echoing on the bare floor of the passageway that led toward the display rooms, came another. The sharp purposeful sound of someone walking toward a chosen goal. Not the clicking heels of a woman, but the heavier tread of a man.

I put a hand to my throat. "There's somebody coming."

"It's all right," Bill said, but his eyes were alertly on

43

the door. "We belong here. We came to talk about that bird and phonograph attachment for the window. Understand, Tony? That's all we came to talk about."

I wobbled and leaned against Bill, with my back to the door.

"Sure," Tony said. "That phonograph's gonna stay too. I left it right there in the window. I don't care what Montgomery says—" a shock of realization crossed his face, a stunned look. He was beginning to get it too now. "Maybe it won't have to come out. Maybe—"

The footsteps had come very close and Bill broke in breezily. "It's a good idea, Tony. And the contraption I've rigged up sounds fine. Ought to pull the crowds just as a novelty."

Even in my confused state I sensed that Bill was doing the wrong thing. A few moments ago he could still have turned in an alarm. But he had committed us to conspiracy, to silence. It was already too late to tell.

The steps had reached the door, but I was too terrified to look. I tried to read Bill's face, or even Tony's. But Bill just looked blank and Tony had his head down and was running a finger around his collar."

" 'Evening, Miss Wynn," said a drawling voice. "Hi, Tony."

I turned around as slowly as I could. The man in the doorway had been put together on a large scale. He had massive shoulders and arms, the profile of a poet, and dark dreamy eyes. His name, ridiculously, was Sylvester Hering, but he was not a ridiculous person. Merely a sad one. He regarded the three of us in mournful speculation. Ominously mournful speculation.

"Thought maybe I'd find somebody up here," he said as if he did not in the least relish his discovery. "You ought to go home right away after work, Miss Wynn. You been looking sort of tired lately."

He broke off, listening to the music that came from Sondo's workroom.

"That's nice, isn't it?" he said dreamily. "Swell tune. *Dum*-da-de-um. The Norgaard jane, I suppose?"

I managed somehow to nod, but my nerves were screaming. I wanted to bombard him with questions. I wanted to cry, "Have they found—do they know— who was it—?" But I just nodded dumbly.

Hering looked at Tony. "Too bad to interrupt the concert, but you better go bring her here."

Tony walked a little unsteadily to the door and Hering turned back to me.

"Sorry to break the news," he said, his brown eyes concerned, "but Mr. Montgomery's been murdered. Downstairs in window five. You—you won't faint, Miss Wynn?"

I've often wished I could faint. I always admire heroines in stories who slip into convenient blackness every time the going gets tough. But I always stay wide awake and watch the whole operation. However, I thought it might be just as well if I clung with touching weakness to the hand he held out to me. Sylvester Hering was a good friend of mine. We'd always got on fine together. He often stopped in my office to chat, and he never seemed to tire of studying the pictures on my walls. But of course I'd never had any professional dealings with him before.

Sylvester Hering was one of the store detectives.

CHAPTER 5

Somebody turned off the music and Sondo came back with Tony.

"Look," she said, "I'd like to get home sometime tonight. Couldn't you all go have your social hour somewhere else?" Then she saw Hering and a certain wariness came into her manner. "Well! And to what do we owe the pleasure?"

"It ain't my fault," Hering told her. "Your boss has got himself bumped off down in one of the windows."

Sondo turned a yellowish color and fumbled for a pack of cigarettes and matches in the pocket of her smock.

"You ain't supposed to smoke up here." Hering was reproachful.

Sondo lighted her cigarette and blew smoke insolently in his direction, but her hands were shaking. "What—what happened?"

Hering's gloom deepened. "This kind of matador don't sign his autograph. But there's a couple of people in this store who never gave Montgomery no popularity vote."

"You mean it was—murder?" Her control was admirable, but I sensed that it was hard won. And beneath her shock there was already speculation. I could see it in the swift look she gave Tony.

"I might have a candidate to suggest myself," she said with venomous sweetness.

"Then you better come downstairs and talk," Hering said. "That's what I'm up here for—to round up anybody in the department. Come on now, folks, all of you." Then he dropped back beside me. "Gosh, Miss Wynn, I'm awful sorry."

I thought I might as well make good use of any stand-in I had with the police, so I clung to the arm he offered me and walked along beside him toward the elevators. Goodness knows I didn't have to act. I was upset and frightened and confused.

The sight of the main floor after closing hours was no novelty to me, but when I stepped out of the elevator the whole place seemed strange and unfamiliar. The lights had been turned down, of course, dust covers shrouded the stock, and the store had been put to bed. But it wasn't that which disturbed me.

And then it came at me again with a sort of rush— that awareness I'd experienced upstairs. This wasn't Cunningham's as I knew it. This was a place where murder had been committed. Perhaps the murderer was still in the store. He might be hiding anywhere. In the shadowy aisle beyond the next counter. Crouching to—

"You all right, Miss Wynn?" Hering inquired anxiously in my ear.

I tried to nod brightly and he gave me a look of doubt as we walked toward the one part of the main floor that had not been put to bed. There the lights burned brightly and several benches had been drawn about the doorway to window five. The Homicide Squad had taken over and the place was overrun with photographers, fingerprint men, detectives. A man named McPhail was in charge and he threw our little group a look markedly lacking in enthusiasm as we came up.

I recognized several girls from the jewelry and perfume counters gathered on one of the benches, all looking frightened and shocked. It couldn't have been very quieting to know that a murder had been committed a few yards away while they went on with their usual work.

Helena Farnham was among them and she turned my way with a question in her eyes. Helena knew I'd been in that window. I gave her a stiff smile that was meant to be reassuring and went over to sit down beside Chris Montgomery.

Chris was hunched over, sobbing, and a woman I recognized as Susan Gardner, Owen's wife, was trying without much success to calm and comfort her. Susan was one of those vague, colorless people who make good backgrounds. Nobody ever paid much attention to her and I'd always wondered why Owen, with his passion for beauty, had married her.

She looked up and nodded at me, her pale blue eyes wide with distress.

"Perhaps you can do something with her, Miss Wynn," she said. "She'll be ill if she doesn't stop crying."

I put an arm about the girl's shoulders. "You mustn't. It doesn't help. They'll be wanting to question you pretty soon, and you've got to be ready to answer sensibly."

Chris jerked her head up and there was very evident terror mingled with the grief in her face. "But I don't know anything! I haven't anything to tell. Oh, Linell, make them let me go home. Don't they understand that I've just lost my husband? Don't they—"

"Hush!" I tightened my grip on her shoulder, glad to have this task of quieting her. It helped me get myself in hand and keep a rein on my own emotions. "This isn't an ordinary death. That's a terrible thing to face,

48

but we all have to face it and do what we can to help the police."

This only brought on a fresh attack of sobbing, so I gave up and sat patting her shoulder.

Another bench had been pulled up and Sondo, still smoking, had plumped down on it between Bill and Tony, her scrawny legs crossed and the green smock hitched carelessly above her knees. It was impossible for Sondo to fall into a position remotely resembling feminine grace.

Tony looked dazed and he was still not entirely sober. He had slumped down on the end of his spine, his long legs thrust inconveniently into the aisle, where everyone who passed had to step over them.

Bill was the only one who looked unconcerned and natural, and I didn't like that a lot. This wasn't any time to look unconcerned and natural. He must have felt my eyes upon him for he held my gaze for just a moment. Not by so much as a flicker did his expression change, but somehow there was meaning in his look.

It said, "Don't worry. You'll get through all right." But it said something else too, as plainly as words. It said, *"Be careful."*

I gave him a faint nod that meant I understood and then glanced at Mrs. Gardner over Chris's bowed head.

"Who found him?" I whispered.

She didn't have to ask whom I meant, but her lips trembled and she tried twice before she managed to form the words.

"Owen," she said. "Owen found him."

That was a bit dismaying. It would have been better if it had been someone wholly unconcerned. Now the detectives would trace the enmity between Gardner and Monty, and the tie-up with Chris. In which case I couldn't throw Owen to the wolves—I'd have to tell the truth, explain that he couldn't have had anything to do with it because Monty had been dead before Owen

Gardner had ever gone to the window. I had reason to know. It would look pretty bad for me, considering that I'd rushed off upstairs without giving the alarm. Bill's well-intended efforts would land us in hot water yet.

Just then Gardner stepped down out of the window, followed by a detective, and McPhail beckoned to him. The whispering of the sales girls on the other bench hushed as all attention focused on McPhail and our fourth floor merchandise manager.

I gathered that McPhail felt this was an inside job. Even though the store had been filled with customers, it was unlikely that one of them had stepped into the window and murdered Monty. Nothing had been stolen from his wallet. While the customer angle wasn't being overlooked, probability pointed toward some more revengeful and personal motive than theft.

Gardner told briefly about coming down to the window, looking for Montgomery, and described finding the body.

"Why did you want to see him?" McPhail asked.

Gardner was holding himself in check, but a muscle in his cheek twitched. "Why shouldn't I? There's a decided tie-up between my department and window display."

For the first time I noticed that Sylvester Hering had taken up a stand across the aisle at the perfume counter. His huge arms leaned alarmingly on the fragile glass of a showcase, and his attention seemed concentrated lovingly on the glittering display of bottles and vials. But his ears were missing nothing of what went on, for without shifting his rapt gaze, he spoke to McPhail.

"There ain't no tie-up with that golf window and Mr. Gardner's department. He don't handle sport stuff."

"Nevertheless," said Gardner, "I had business to discuss with Mr. Montgomery. I was not at all satisfied

50

with the evening gown display he gave me in the corner window. That was a botched-up job, if ever I saw one."

"So you didn't like Montgomery?" McPhail caught him up.

"Certainly I didn't like him. But I'd scarcely murder a man because I disapproved of the way he displayed my goods. If that's what you mean to imply."

"I'm not implying anything," McPhail snapped. "I'm just trying to get the set-up here."

There was a movement beside me and I realized that Chris was sitting up now, her attention wholly concentrated on her father. Gardner looked her way and his face softened.

"My daughter was married to Michael Montgomery two weeks ago," he said. "I was ready on that account to let our difference be bygones."

McPhail called to a detective who was taking everything down. "Got it all?"

The man nodded and McPhail went to stand before the line of nervous sales girls. My thoughts were busy elsewhere and I didn't listen. Owen hadn't been entirely honest with McPhail. When I'd talked to him in the afternoon he hadn't been so strong for this burying of differences. I could recall much too clearly how angry he'd looked, I could remember the threatening violence in his manner and tone.

When I began to follow McPhail's progress again I saw that he was questioning the group of girls from the perfume and costume jewelry counters. They worked nearest to window five. Had they observed who went in and out of the window?

He wasn't getting anywhere. The perfume girls had been busy on the far side of the counter and had noticed nothing out of the ordinary. The sale in costume jewelry had taken the energy and attention of the jewelry girls, so that they'd had time for nothing else.

51

Besides, as one girl explained, the comings and goings of the window decorators were routine and easily went unnoticed.

I held my breath when Helena was questioned, but she said nothing of those lapel pins or the fact that I'd gone into the window, and she carefully avoided any glance in my direction. I was only slightly relieved. Sooner or later I was going to be dragged into this and the fact that I'd been in the window would come out. There was that borrow sheet with my name signed to it, for one thing. It might be better for Helena if she told the truth.

Tony Salvador came up for questioning next and my uneasiness and suspense increased. For once Tony was moving cautiously. Some realization of his own peril must have made its way through the fog, because he carefully avoided all mention of his quarrel with Monty.

Sure he'd worked in the window that afternoon. That was his job. But he'd left before Monty did and had gone back upstairs. He'd been up in window display ever since. I glanced at Sondo and saw that she was intently watching the whole procedure. She knew about that quarrel and she had no love for Tony Salvador, but evidently she meant to bide her time.

During Tony's recital one of the fingerprint men came out of the window and spoke to McPhail.

"We've covered the ground pretty thoroughly. Not much to go on. There's dozens of assorted prints all over everything except the one thing that counts. Somebody wiped off the shaft of that broken golf club."

Tony forgot his caution. "What golf club?" he asked suddenly.

Immediately suspicious, McPhail said, "I suppose you don't know how it was done?"

"You mean—" Tony was sober enough now and plainly shocked. "You mean they—whoever it was—used a broken golf stick?"

"That's right," snapped McPhail. "What do you know about it? What do you know about that club?"

Tony's finger tugged at his collar. "Me? I don't know anything about it. Just that there were golf clubs in the window. I put 'em there myself. Linell—Miss Wynn knows about that. I phoned her right after I left the window and told her to finish up with the accessories. She's been doing that a lot lately." He turned and looked at me. "You did take care of that job, didn't you? Say—!"

He stopped short and I could almost read his thoughts. Not until that moment had he recalled that I had told him Monty was murdered, or wondered how I'd known. But he'd made that dangerous connection now and if he betrayed the fact to McPhail, I was in for it.

"That's all I know about it," he said. "Montgomery was alive when I left the window."

Sondo snorted, but when McPhail glanced her way, she pretended to be blowing her nose.

The detective wasn't satisfied with Tony, but after all this was merely a preliminary investigation.

He said, "I'll come back to you later. Which one is Miss Wynn?"

I took my arm from about Chris's shoulders and braced myself for what was ahead.

"I'm Miss Wynn," I said.

McPhail's eyes were cold and hard. The letter of the law might read that a man was innocent until proved guilty, but this man saw guilt wherever he looked. It was difficult not to feel guilty with his suspicion probing into my soul. I blinked in spite of myself and shifted my gaze, and I could sense McPhail's satisfaction in beating me down in even this small way.

There was a moment of silence in which I was sharply aware of the minute details of my surroundings. Aware of a jumble of sounds and voices from the window, aware of the bright lights, the scent of perfume from across the aisle, of McPhail waiting, playing cat and mouse.

Then it began.

As simply and quickly as I could I told of coming down to the window. Yes, it was my job to look over accessories, to make selections and last minute touches. I told about choosing the lapel pins—without mentioning Helena—of going through my routine work in the window. I even remembered that queer sense of being watched and told him about that.

He pounced on it right away, but when I couldn't produce anything substantial concerning the experience, he dismissed it impatiently.

I said I'd gone right back upstairs when I was through and that I hadn't seen Monty at all. I left Bill out entirely.

McPhail looked as if he hadn't believed a single word I'd told him, but that seemed to be his attitude toward all witnesses anyway. He did check on whether it was possible to enter and leave the window without discovering Monty's body, found that it could have happened, and was about to let me go.

But right then Hering chose to lift his unhappy gaze from the array of perfume bottles and turn it my way.

"You got to know it sometime," he said despondently. "Up to a couple of weeks or so ago, Miss Wynn was engaged to Montgomery."

He looked so unhappy that I felt sorry for him. He hadn't wanted to give me away. Not that it mattered. I was relieved, really, to have the whole thing out. Hering went back to regarding the perfume bottles with an air of tragedy.

This time I was in for it. McPhail's questions were like machine-gun fire. Why had the engagement been broken? Had we quarreled? Had I known Monty was interested in the Gardner girl? Then back over the win-

54

dow routine again in an effort to trip me, followed by a new barrage of questions.

It was pretty unpleasant and after a while it got so monotonous it was almost numbing. I was terribly afraid my mind would just go off to sleep and I'd begin to give all the wrong answers. I didn't dare so much as glance at Bill. I had to stand on my own feet and get through as best I could.

McPhail left me, finally, unsatisfied, but unable to wring any incriminating evidence from me.

There was a break now in the questioning. The photographers were through in the window, the Coroner had made his examination and stated that Montgomery had been dead no more than an hour.

Two men carried a stretcher past us and Chris screamed hysterically and clutched at me. I tightened my arm about her and hid my face against her hair. That was a bad moment for me too. No matter what Monty had done or been, he had paid for everything now, more than even he deserved.

I didn't look up again until one of the detectives came out of the window and held something out to McPhail.

"What do you make of this?" he asked. "Montgomery had it clutched tight in his right fist."

McPhail took the small circlet of gold and examined it curiously. Then he came over and held it out on his palm before Chris and me.

"Ever see this before, either of you? Did it belong to Montgomery?"

I looked closely at the ring. It was of yellow gold, with worn, antique carving on the wide band. The prongs of the setting were bent, the stone was missing, and there was no way to tell whether it had been lost long before, or broken off recently. It must have been an unusually large stone. The ring might have been a woman's, or a man's little finger ring.

"If it was Monty's I never saw it before," I told McPhail, and Chris, between whimpers, disclaimed all knowledge of it too.

McPhail passed it about the entire circle, but no one admitted to recognizing it. All of which annoyed him extremely. He gave orders that the window be carefully searched to see if the stone could be found. And then he turned his attention to Chris.

The girl promptly went to pieces again and for a few minutes nothing could be got out of her at all. It was Bill Thorne who brought order out of the emotional chaos. Probably he had learned by practicing on me.

He went over, put his hands on her shoulders, and shook her. There is something decidedly startling about being suddenly shaken or slapped by a nice young man you've always considered quite mild-tempered. Chris reacted just as I had. Her mouth dropped open in shocked surprise. But Bill's eyes were kind.

"We all know how you feel, Chris," he said. "But you're a big girl now. You've got to sit up here and answer all Mr. McPhail's questions. He doesn't want to hurt you. He only wants to get at the truth."

The soothing voice stopped her hiccoughing sobs. She actually sat up and faced McPhail with an effort at self-control.

He repeated the questions he had asked and she answered them in a voice so low that sometimes it was difficult to catch her words. But the picture she was giving wasn't exactly true to the character of Michael Montgomery as I had known him.

I felt a little sick. It was dismaying to realize that one human being could so trick and fool another. But Chris held firmly to her idealizing and it wasn't until McPhail brought her to an accounting of her actions that day, that she began to falter. It was a stubborn faltering, however, as if she were trying to evade something which terrified her.

"My reason for going to Miss Wynn's office hasn't anything to do with what has happened," she said. "I won't talk about it. You can't make me."

He saw the signs of returning hysteria and left the subject hastily. "All right, go on. We just want to know what you did next."

"I went down to the fourth floor to see father," Chris continued. "I talked to him for a few moments and then I went down the escalator to the waiting room on third to meet mother. We were all going to have dinner together."

"And then?" McPhail prompted.

Chris waved her hands vaguely. "Why—why that's all. We went downstairs. We—were just looking around at things, and all of a sudden somebody came running up to tell us about Monty and—" she broke off and her head went down on my shoulder.

Hering interrupted again, gently, sorrowfully.

"I was up in the waiting room," he explained. "I had to get some stamps for a letter and I had to stick around a while before the girl at the desk could wait on me. I guess I've got a kind of photographic memory. I mean, I see a thing and it sticks."

"Okay, okay," McPhail broke in impatiently. "What did you see that stuck?"

"Mrs. Gardner was up there all right," Hering said. "But she was alone. She was alone all the time I was there. She kept looking at her watch, and then after a while she got up and went off. Miss Gard—Mrs. Montgomery never came to meet her at all."

There was a faint sound from one of the opposite benches and I looked across to see Sondo leaning forward, her eyes upon Chris. There was a burning intensity in them that startled me. Then she became aware of my regard and relaxed, with her usual wry smile.

McPhail appeared anything but pleased with Hering's contribution. Nobody would let this thing go through to a smooth, logical finish. Somebody always had to gum up the works. But there was no help for it. He had to follow the new tack.

"Well?" he demanded of Chris. "What have you got to say to that?"

But Chris was having hysterics again—on my shoulder.

CHAPTER 6

McPhail was ready to give up. "You'd better take her home and put her to bed. I'll talk to her tomorrow when she's feeling better. Then maybe she can explain why her story doesn't match our friend Hering's. Or maybe you can explain it, Mrs. Gardner?"

There was heavy sarcasm in his voice and Susan started. But she showed more presence of mind than one would have expected.

"I—I think I can," she faltered. "The reason Mr. Hering didn't see Chris come up to me in the waiting room, was because we didn't meet till I reached the escalator and found her coming down. That would have been out of even Mr. Hering's photographic range, I'm afraid."

I looked at her in surprise. Susan Gardner had returned the detective's sarcasm with a gentle variety of her own. McPhail wasn't noticing, however. The look he gave Hering was anything but complimentary and the store detective's gloom deepened by another degree.

Bill, next in the questioning, was disposed of quickly enough. He explained that he'd come to see Montgomery about some special figures he'd wanted for a window. The display manager was out of the department and he'd waited in his office. No, he couldn't say much about who had come and gone in the department while he'd been there. He'd talked to Sondo Norgaard briefly. Once the phone in the connecting office had rung and he'd heard Sondo answer it. But for the most part he couldn't say who'd been on the premises. Later he'd given up waiting for Monty and had come over to my office just for something to do.

He got through smoothly and easily, skirting all quicksands. For once McPhail actually seemed to believe what was being said, and there went our last chance to make a clean breast of things. Bill hadn't been telling the whole truth any more than I had. And how many others?

Sondo was last on the list and I sat up to listen with interest. Here came trouble, if I knew a storm signal when I saw one. Sondo knew all about Tony's quarrel with Monty, and I'd caught a look in her eyes once or twice that made me suspect she might know a few other things too.

But Sondo was in anything but a manageable mood. She showed no proper respect for the law and McPhail disliked her on the spot.

"Just what was your relationship with Montgomery?" he barked.

Sondo recrossed her legs, managing to convey an

insult to majesty by the length of time it took. "What do you mean, relationship? He was my boss."

"Oh, sure," McPhail said. "You know what I mean. What did you think of him? How did you like him?"

"Very much." Sondo's tone was bland. "He was a very brilliant and capable man."

I expected her to go on and drop a few disparagements about Tony, but she let the opportunity pass. McPhail led her through the usual maze of questions and she answered impertinently whenever impertinence was possible, but not a word did she say about the feud in window display. She said she'd been in her workroom all afternoon, and admitted cheerfully that she couldn't prove it.

I thought of that moment when I'd gone to Tony's workroom and had passed Sondo's door without looking in. The light had been on, but her phonograph was silent. Had she really been there or not?

McPhail questioned her about answering the window display phone while Bill was waiting for Monty. She dismissed the call as routine business, but it seemed to me that an odd flicker came into her eyes.

Whatever she knew, she wasn't telling. I think McPhail would have enjoyed getting something on her, but her answers were glib and gave nothing away.

Hering sauntered back from an excursion into the window.

"She said upstairs she might have a candidate for murderer," he told McPhail.

"Well," said McPhail. "If you know anything, Miss Norgaard, this is the time to spill it."

But Sondo smiled venomously and disclaimed knowledge of anything. She'd just been talking. She didn't know a thing.

McPhail was disgusted with the whole affair, and particularly tired of Sondo.

"Did they find the stone from that ring yet?" he asked Hering.

The store detective shook his head gloomily.

McPhail glanced around at the rest of us. "Now look, all of you. What's happened here this afternoon is bad business and you're not any of you clear of suspicion. So no skipping out of town, see, or you'll land in jail. You can all go home now and report back to your jobs in the morning. I'll let you know when I want you to answer more questions. Some of you will be called for the inquest."

A sudden commotion started at the other end of the store. Several large, important-looking gentlemen were advancing down the middle aisle with the air of a parade. Sondo caught my eye and winked.

"The heavenly hosts themselves? Do you suppose we'd better get down and salaam?"

The procession was headed by Mr. Cunningham, president of the store, flanked on each side by the first and second vice-presidents respectively and it was apparent that he had been thoroughly affronted.

A murder had been committed in his beautiful store. Murders were not good for business. Murders were definitely low, messy, and uncharacteristic of the high Cunningham level of quality. The man who had been murdered was a valued employee of the store; a man who had been imported some months before at considerable expense. Mr. Cunningham was in a very critical mood. He looked around at us lesser mortals as if he'd have preferred to part with the whole lot, rather than to lose Montgomery.

McPhail had evidently met executives before. He sighed and signaled to Owen Gardner. "You had better stay a while. The rest of you can go."

We went willingly enough.

Near the door Tony put a hand on my elbow to draw me quietly aside.

"Thanks for trying to get me out of the store," he whispered. "I won't be asking you any questions, see? And I won't be answering any either. Whatever you do is okay by me."

It was a promise of secrecy and I hated to be in a position to have to accept it. Sondo's eyes were upon us suspiciously, so I gave Tony a nod of thanks and went over to join Bill.

As I came up, Bill said, "I've got my car outside. Suppose I drive you and Miss Farnham home?"

In spite of the suspicions about Bill that had flashed through my mind, I was relieved. We were certainly in no state to take a bus. And probably Bill's connection with the whole thing was innocent. Strain and shock had made me suspicious in a direction where I'd never have entertained a doubt in a more normal frame of mind. At least those were the arguments I used on the ride home.

He came up to the apartment with us and suggested that he be fed a sandwich or two. That was the first time Helena and I thought about the fact that we hadn't had supper. But even when we thought about it, we weren't hungry, and it took Bill's bullying to get us out to the kitchen.

It was queer how matter-of-factly we were behaving by that time. I suppose the human mind cannot live intensely through a period of horror without becoming somewhat numbed. In spite of all I'd endured since the discovery of Monty's body, I think I accepted the fact of murder only in brief flashes of realization. The rest of the time I was too confused to face the enormity of what had happened.

Just the same, it was I who voiced the question that was in all our minds.

"Bill," I said, buttering rye bread automatically. "Who do you think—"

He shook his head at me. "Better let it go for a

while. You've had a nasty shock. Can't we talk about something else?"

There was a heavy silence in which we all tried to think of something else—anything at all. And couldn't. Then Helena looked up from arranging slices of cold meat on a plate and asked a point-blank question.

"Did you find him when you went into the window, Linell?"

I had a bad moment as remembrance swept back, but my mind was weary of horror. There was no use trying to keep the truth from Helena.

"Yes," I said. "I found him and Bill found me. Then Bill rushed me off upstairs and we've each been suspecting the other ever since."

Bill helped himself to the makings of a sandwich and took a bite. "You can see what a nice tidbit that would make for McPhail. And it wouldn't help the case any for him to know."

Helena's silence seemed a little ominous and I dropped my butter knife in anxiety.

"You don't think we—we ought to—" I began, but she cut in on me.

"I don't very well see how you can now. Bill's right that it wouldn't help. But I was just thinking how much worse it may be for you if it comes out later on."

She'd finished with the plate and was standing there examining the palm of one hand absently. Helena's hands were lovely. They hadn't aged as her face had, and as I went shakily past her to get the coffee from the stove, I saw a long red scratch which ran down one finger and clear across the palm.

"Heavens!" I said. "How did you do that?"

She started, as if she hadn't been aware that she was looking at the scratch. Then she shrugged.

"One of the girls from upstairs came back to exchange a pin she didn't like. One of us was clumsy and that's what happened."

"You'd better put something on it," I told her, but I doubt if she heard me.

She went on looking at her hand as if she were really seeing that scratch for the first time. And an odd look came into her face, as if she were remembering something. But whatever it was, she evidently didn't mean to talk about it. She picked up the plate and carried it into the living room where we'd set up a card table for our impromptu supper.

"I'd hate to be in McPhail's shoes tonight," Bill said as we sat down. "This is going to be smeared all over the front pages tomorrow, and he has a good portion of the city of Chicago to choose from in selecting the murderer."

"I thought he was going to discard the outsider theory," I put in.

Bill shook his head. "He can't discard anything, though the chances are that whoever did this is someone who hated Monty. Somebody he'd hurt. Somebody reasonably close to him."

"That would tie in the store," I said. "His personal life was pretty much connected with it, I think."

We couldn't keep from speculating to save our souls. In a moment we were deep in discussion. I began checking over the people who had strongly disliked Monty.

"There's Tony," I said. "And of course Owen Gardner. Monty wasn't exactly popular, but most of the boys in window display got along with him all right, I think. Besides, everybody up there went home early today except Tony and Sondo."

"Hm," Bill said. "Well, McPhail will check their alibis fast enough. What about his secretary?"

I shook my head. "Not Monty's type. Plain and efficient. And anyway, she's gone home to be with her mother. She left last week. But there must be more than one woman in Monty's past who had reason to detest him."

"That's a green field," Bill said. "Now we've got half the country to choose from. He's worked in stores all over the east and middle west."

Helena made her contribution. "Linell didn't list that office boy of hers. He didn't sound very fond of Monty this afternoon."

That was funny. I hadn't thought of Keith since he'd walked out the door of my office. Yet he had his small place in the pattern too and McPhail would probably get around to talking to him in the morning. But to think of Keith as a possible murderer was absurd and I said an emphatic no to that.

"Just the same," Bill said, "we'll put his name on the list. He's a queer egg, to say the least. And there's another name. Yours, Linell."

I choked over my coffee and put my cup down with a hand that shook.

Helena said, "Don't tease her like that," and Bill reached over and gave my hand a friendly pat.

"Don't take it too hard," he told me. "Just to show you I'm open-minded, I'll put my name down too." And he actually took a notebook from his pocket and wrote down the names. "Now then—where does Sondo fit in? She was sticking up for Monty with McPhail. That mean anything?"

I tried to focus my mind on Sondo, but my thoughts had a tendency to gallop off in four directions at once.

"I don't know," I said. "She always seemed to get along all right with him. It was Tony she disliked. If Sondo was going to murder anybody, I'd expect it to be Tony."

He put down Sondo's name with a question mark after it.

"Anyway," he said, "there's something she's not telling. Did you see how suspiciously she watched everybody? She was a clam with McPhail, but I have a feeling that she has a finger on some point that wasn't brought out."

I bit into a sandwich that seemed to have no taste, and swallowed only because I felt I ought to.

"Where does Chris fit in?" I demanded.

Helena passed Bill his fifth sandwich. There was nothing wrong with his appetite.

"Does Chris belong on your list at all?" she asked. "She seems a sweet girl and she was certainly broken up over this. I felt sorry for her when McPhail was hammering away."

"Oh, I didn't mean as the murderer," I explained hastily. "She was in love with Monty all right. But it was queer about that waiting room business. And there's certainly something troubling her."

I was watching Bill as I spoke. That interest of his in Chris—what did it amount to?

"Non-suspect," he said. "We can't use her at all. I was sorry for her today too. She looked so different from the happy kid who won that dress design contest a year ago. Remember, Linell?"

"Of course I remember. National recognition, with her picture in papers all over the country."

But I was feeling hurt, and even a little frightened that Bill should put my name on the list and so readily eliminate Chris Montgomery's.

All our nerves were in a jittery state by that time, so when the doorbell shrilled suddenly, the three of us jumped up in alarm.

I got to the door first and opened it to Chris. Her yellow frock was rumpled and her eyes red. She flung herself past me into the room as if pursuing hordes were on her heels.

"I had to come!" she cried. "Oh, Linell, I couldn't

66

go home tonight till I'd said what I came to your office to say this afternoon."

It was Helena who took charge in her usual capable manner. She settled Chris beside Bill on the couch and took away her purse and gloves.

"I'll get you a cup of coffee," she said and went to the kitchen.

"Take it easy, kid," Bill told her. "Where did you leave the others?"

"Susan stayed to wait for father," Chris said. "But I couldn't stand it there in the store any longer, so I slipped out on my own and took a bus over here."

Helena came back with the coffee and Chris sipped it, becoming slightly less wilted.

"Linell," she went on earnestly, "I wanted you to know that it was really you Monty loved. I—I think he hated me. If I hadn't been so blind and selfish and—"

I patted her hand. "We've been over this before. You mustn't go on reproaching yourself. I know how charming and compelling Monty could be when he chose, but I'm afraid I haven't much belief in his ability to have loved anyone but himself."

Chris shook her head. "Oh, but he did love you. He even told me he did. That's what I wanted you to know. I thought it might make all this a little easier for you to bear."

I knew it cost her something to tell me and I was touched. I was shocked, too. What a talent for sadism Monty had had to marry the child deliberately and then tell her that he loved me. And why had he done such a thing?

"Chris dear," I said, "you must try to understand that I haven't been in love with Monty for a long time. We were moving toward a break-up and he knew it as well as I. So stop worrying about how you may have hurt me."

I was aware of quickening interest on Bill's part, but

67

Chris's expression was blank. It was evident that the idea of anyone falling out of love with Monty had never occurred to her.

"Sometimes in the last couple of weeks I've hated him as much as I loved him," she said in a puzzled tone. "But it was love and hate all mixed up together in some queer way and it wouldn't let me go," she paused. "I mean after—I found out."

"Found out what?" Bill asked.

She started to answer, then stopped. "I can't talk about that. I mean I really can't explain. But I don't want you to think I'm completely a fool. All those things I was telling McPhail—I didn't believe them really. I just had to say them for him."

"You mean about believing Monty was such a wonderful person?" I asked.

"Yes." She looked very young and very sad. "I couldn't believe in him the way I did before. Not after the last two weeks. But, Linell, it didn't matter. I don't care how bad he was, or how cruel—I loved him anyway. I always will. I guess I've got a lot of my mother in me after all."

She sat up very straight on the edge of the couch. Her face, with its youthful prettiness, looked suddenly older, more adult, and there was the shadow of deep unhappiness in her eyes.

I was puzzled. Somehow this older aspect of Chris didn't fit in with what I knew of the rather vapid Susan Gardner. She saw my bewilderment.

"Didn't you know, Linell? Susan isn't my real mother. She's been wonderful to me and I love her dearly, but she's not my mother."

I think we were all a little surprised and there was a silence before Chris went on, groping uncertainly for words to explain.

"My own mother ran off before I was two years old. With some man. Father hasn't ever talked about it much, but he's told me a little. He says the man was no good at all. But mother must have loved him to do a thing like that. She must have loved him the way I loved Monty, who wasn't any good either. That's what I mean about being like her. I guess I even resemble her a little, though I'm fair like father and she was dark. I found an old picture of her a while ago and it looked almost like a picture of me, the way I look now."

Chris's inclination toward hysteria had passed, but it wasn't good for her to go on this way, brooding over past tragedy, magnifying the present. Helena and I exchanged glances and then she spoke to Bill.

"Why don't you drive Chris home? She ought to get to bed as soon as possible."

"Of course," Bill said. "Come on, kid. You're staying at your father's aren't you?"

Chris nodded. "Oh, yes. I couldn't bear to go back to that awful, empty apartment of Monty's."

Helena brought her things, but Chris stopped, as if there were something more she wanted to say. Even though her emotions were under control, strain was visible in every line of her face. Strain that had its roots in fear.

"You see," she said to me, "father's had such a bad time that I—I don't ever want anything to hurt him again. She made him unhappy. My mother, I mean. And I've made him unhappy by marrying Monty. So now all I want is to try to make it up to him. For everything."

"I understand," I assured her, though I didn't quite. There was something I couldn't put my finger on. Something that left me faintly uneasy. But I patted her arm soothingly. "Get a good sleep. And drop in to see me next time you're downtown."

Bill said, "Call me out at Universal tomorrow, Linell, if anything new comes up at the store."

There was a moment in which Bill and I looked at

each other and I knew that we were friends. Allies. He didn't want to suspect me, any more than I wanted to suspect him. The realization was comforting.

I don't know why my mind chose that particular instant to fly off at a tangent and recover a memory that had slipped from me entirely. But without any warning at all, the picture was there, sharp and clear. The picture of myself in the window, going through certain motions.

"The golf stick!" I gasped. "Oh, Bill, the golf stick!"

"What about it?" he asked.

"The other half—the part they didn't find. I had it in my hands. My fingerprints are on it!"

And I told them about trying to clean up the window; about picking up the upper half of that stick and thrusting it into the golf bag just to get it out of sight. A hiding place that would be discovered sooner or later. And if they checked my fingerprints—!

Bill shook his head at me despairingly. "That makes it all a bit worse. Maybe instead of trying to put what's happened out of our minds—which isn't possible anyway—we'd all better turn our wits to the business of discovering the real murderer, before someone innocent is blamed."

Helena had put an arm about me because I'd started to shake again and I leaned against her.

"There's something else too!" I cried. "Something I'd forgotten all about. You know that ring McPhail was so puzzled over? I think I must have found the stone to that. Or a piece of it anyway. I picked a fragment of something from the carpet in the window, but I thought it was a broken bit of costume jewelry. If it was the stone from that ring, perhaps it's important."

"What did you do with it?" Bill asked.

I could remember the very feel of the thing in my fingers. It had been smooth, but jagged on one side from the break. I could remember the careless movement of my hand as I put it away.

"It's in my smock pocket," I said. "I left the smock hanging over the chair in my office."

"Good," Bill said. "Get it the first thing in the morning and take it to McPhail. It's likely it does mean something. And try to get some rest tonight."

Then Helena closed the door and we had the apartment to ourselves. I walked around restlessly, desperately, for all my weariness.

"Helena," I said, "who could possibly have—"

She cut me off at once. "No more supposing tonight. Let the police do the worrying. You've had a terrible day and I'm a bit limp myself. To bed we go."

Later, in the bedroom I shared with Helena, all the awful pictures began to return, and the pounding of all those unanswered questions. I lay there for a long while, with my eyes closed against the soft darkness, listening to the rain against the windows.

Monty's death must have been the climax of some secret story the rest of us had yet to read. But it wasn't an ending in itself. It was the beginning of a new story in which all of us who had been close to him in any way must now play our unwilling parts. A story filled with terror and uncertainty and despair. These things followed murder as surely as night followed day. Tomorrow the new chapter would begin. What would be my place in it? When would the part I'd already played come to light?

I tossed for a long while on my pillow before I dropped off into a dream-haunted sleep.

CHAPTER 7

The next morning I overslept and Helena was considerate enough not to wake me. She was gone when I got out of bed, but she'd left a newspaper on the dresser for me to see. The murder of Michael Montgomery had hit Chicago's front pages.

It had hit Cunningham's, too. Hit it hard. The minute I walked in the store that Wednesday morning, I sensed the nervous excitement. I was aware of it as the chatter hushed when I stepped into the elevator. The few good mornings which greeted me were packed with unspoken questions. I responded when necessary and tried to ignore the eyes I was sure were boring into my back.

How many of these people, I wondered, were connecting me with Monty's murder? How many were saying to each other, "Well, he threw her over, didn't he? A woman scorned, you know!" And if they were wondering about me now, how would it be if they ever learned what I was hiding?

But the thing uppermost in my mind at the moment was that bit of something I'd picked up in the window and which might be part of the stone missing from the ring Monty had held clutched in his hand. I meant to get it from the pocket of my smock at once and I walked quickly as I left the elevator.

The door of my office stood open, as always. There was nothing of value there and I never bothered to lock it at night. Keith hadn't come in yet and I walked straight to my chair.

The smock was gone.

My first thought was that I must have hung it somewhere else. The hook behind the door perhaps. Another instant and I would have turned, but in that instant some faint sound reached me and I knew I was not alone in the room. Knew, with horror running like ice water through my veins, that something waited for me behind the door.

And then, before I could recover the power of movement, there came a rush from behind me. Something caught me a heavy awkward blow behind the ear and I pitched forward across my desk, stunned and groggy.

I wasn't out cold. The blow, though struck with desperate intent, had glanced off the thick padding of my hair. I could hear the thud of footsteps down the corridor, yet I couldn't summon the will to move or scream. I seemed to be swimming through space without being able to make the effort to return to a more solid world.

Then heavy hands were pulling me up from the desk, shaking me. I started frantically to struggle, thinking that my assailant had come back. But the hands held me firmly and squeezed me back to consciousness. As the red mist cleared from before my eyes, I realized that the hands belonged to Sylvester Hering and that he was muttering over me in concern.

I stood on my feet for an instant and then collapsed in a chair.

Hering bent over me anxiously. "You all right now, Miss Wynn? What happened? You faint?"

"No," I told him "No!" The throbbing lump behind my ear didn't help to clarify my thoughts.

"Somebody hit me," I said. "Somebody hit me and ran away!"

Hering took one look at the lump and then rushed off down the corridor in the direction I'd indicated. I felt that search would be useless. Whoever it was would have had time to make the stairway by now and lose himself in the store. I looked about my small office, trying to force my mind to function.

It was the sight of my flowered smock on the floor behind the door that whipped me back to full consciousness. I leaned over dizzily and picked it up, searched the pockets with trembling fingers.

The stone from the ring was gone.

Hering came back, shaking his head. "Couldn't find nobody. Don't you know who it was?"

"No," I said. "But I think I know what he wanted."

I told him about the stone I'd dropped into the pocket of my smock, and he picked up the phone on my desk to try to get in touch with McPhail. But the detective was off on some hunt of his own. Hering reported what had happened and left word for McPhail to call the store.

When he hung up, I pointed to the floor. "Look. That must have been what hit me."

There was a shelf halfway up the wall and on it had stood a pair of small onyx book ends from Mexico. One of them lay on its side on the floor. Hering picked it up carefully, using a handkerchief.

"Looks like it all right. Let's see that bump." He examined my bruises. "That'll hurt for a while. But you got off easy. Skin's not even broken. Your hair's thick and a book end ain't the handiest slugger in the world. How you feel now?"

"My head hurts," I said. "But I'll be all right."

"Then maybe it's a good thing it happened," he told me solemnly.

"What do you mean?"

He shrugged heavy shoulders. "Look, Miss Wynn, I'm your friend."

"Of course," I said. "Thank you."

"That's why I want to tip you off. You watch your step. There's a lot of people in this store who've been plenty mad at Montgomery at one time or another. But *you* got the motive. A better one than anybody else. McPhail could make things pretty hot if he got anything on you. Maybe this attack kind of lets you out. So maybe it's a good thing."

I pressed my fingers against throbbing temples.

"Look, Miss Wynn," Hering went on, "if you think you can stay on the job today, it might be better to keep still about this. Not go blabbing it around right away. Watch how people act. See if anybody looks surprised to see you okay, or gives himself away."

I nodded. I was willing to keep still about the affair. The news would bring half the floor around me in sympathy and I felt I wanted most of all to be let alone.

"Well," Hering said, folding his handkerchief tenderly about the book end, "guess I'll take this over to the fingerprint boys. Oh—that's what I was coming to tell you. That you're supposed to go get fingerprinted."

"Fingerprinted?" Sickness flashed through me as I remembered that golf club.

"Yeah. Over in window display. Mr. Cunningham's got a few pals among the higherups and he put up an awful yowl about pulling a flock of people off their jobs and taking 'em over to headquarters to get fingerprinted. What with the publicity and all. So to keep him quiet they're doing it over here."

"When's the inquest to be?" I asked.

"They were going to hold it today," Hering explained, "but McPhail asked for a continuance, so the Coroner's set it for Monday. This is a screwy case. Too many witnesses. McPhail wants to get 'em all rounded up before the inquest. Well, I gotta run along. You think you'll be okay now?"

I gave him a stiff smile. "I think so. Whoever it was got what he wanted. I don't think he'll come back."

"Mm," said Hering. "Unless he thinks you might have seen him. Then he might want to finish off the job."

And with that cheerful thought, he left.

Nothing seemed real or solid any more. I wasn't even very frightened as yet. Too many things that simply couldn't happen had happened, and my mind hadn't gotten used to accepting them.

Someone had killed Monty. Someone had hidden in my office and struck me down. And a fragment of stone was gone from my smock. There—there lay the clue. Who had known where I'd put the stone?

There were just three people. Helena, Bill, Chris.

Helena had left before I had this morning. She would have had plenty of time to slip upstairs to my office before I arrived to get the stone from my smock. But Helena was my friend.

As for Bill and Chris—I'd come down after the store opened. Anyone at all could have walked in among the customers and come upstairs unchecked ahead of me. But it couldn't be Bill. It couldn't be! I wasn't going to think again those ridiculous thoughts that had tormented me the night before.

Yet it couldn't have been Chris either. She was big enough and strong enough. But she had seemed to worry about what she had done, so anxious to make her peace with me.

Bill and Chris were my friends, too. Still—even a friend who was desperate, trapped, might strike out against discovery. Against any person who meant discovery.

Or had one of these three told others? In that, there was a thread of hope. I'd check on it later when I could see each one alone.

The whole thing was so baffling. What had that ring

76

meant in Monty's hand? And if it had been part of the stone from the ring I had found, why should such a fragment be of importance to the murderer?

The questions were endless, impossible to answer. And on every hand there were threats to me, dangers I might be unaware of even now. I wished Keith would arrive so I needn't be alone. In a few moments I'd have to go over to be fingerprinted, but first I wanted to collect myself a bit. Perhaps work might help.

I searched my desk and found the copy I'd been working on the day before, with its bold words: "Red is the Color of the Year." But that was no way to settle my mind. "Red for blood," Keith had said. But now I could go him one better. In my mind red would forever stand for "murder." I thrust the paper out of sight just as Keith came in.

The boy looked ghastly. His naturally muddy complexion had yellowed and his hands were shaking so that he could hardly hang up his hat.

"What's the matter with you?" I demanded.

"I—I didn't know till this morning," he stammered. "About Mr. Montgomery, I mean. It's awful."

"You'd better straighten up," I said. "We're both supposed to go over to the display department and get fingerprinted."

"Fingerprinted!" The word came out shrilly. "But I didn't have anything to do with this. Oh, Miss Wynn, I've got to stay out of it!"

He looked so green that I turned mercifully away. It wouldn't do to take the boy over to the police in such a state of jitters.

"I'm going ahead," I said over my shoulder. "As soon as you can, follow me."

I went out without looking at him again. I was still a little wobbly, I discovered, but I felt lucky to be alive at all.

Bill had been doubly right last night when he'd said

77

we'd better all put our wits to work and try to clear this thing up. Not only to save some innocent from arrest. To save our own lives. I thought of that last remark of Hering's about the murderer coming back to finish the job, and shivered as I stepped into the empty corridor.

The fingerprint expert had grumblingly set up his materials in Monty's office. He didn't care for the irregularity of the procedure and was letting everyone know just how he felt. I could hear him the moment I stepped into the department. Another detective plodded systematically through Monty's papers and files, pausing now and then to ask questions of Tony Salvador.

I tried to notice if anyone watched me warily, or seemed surprised to find me walking about in good health. But I saw nothing suspicious.

Sondo came out of the office, wearing her usual green smock and a yellow kerchief tied about her tangle of black hair. She waved inky fingers at me and motioned with her thumb.

"A lot of work we can get done with that crowd of flatfeet trampling all over the scenery! I tried to explain that a department store is like the theater. Come hell, high water, or murder, the show goes on. But it didn't register."

Her words were flippant and callous, but there were smudges beneath her big dark eyes and the hollows under her cheek bones were more marked than ever. Sondo hadn't been sleeping well either.

But as I stepped to the door of Monty's office, I forgot her.

This room was Monty's own and very familiar to me. In the months he had worked here, he had stamped it with the imprint of his vital personality. Last night in Tony's office it had not been like this. Then death had been too horrifyingly new to be accepted. I could make

78

no real connection in my mind with that crumpled body down in the window and the Monty I knew.

But now it was real. There were reminders of him everywhere. Things he had touched and left his mark upon. Rough drawings he had sketched for window plans. Pictures he had chosen for the walls. It seemed as though at any moment his vibrant voice might echo through the department, his footstep sound upon its floor. A voice that would never echo again, a step that would never fall.

That knowledge made him really dead. And the thought that the same murderous hand which had struck him down had been raised against me, made reality all the more keen.

I became aware that Sondo was still at my elbow, her dark penetrating gaze upon me.

"Stop in to see me when you're through here," she whispered. "I think we could do a little note comparing." And with that enigmatic remark she went off toward her workroom.

Two of the girls from the perfume counters came past me out of the office, whispering together, and as I stepped through the door, I saw that Helena Farnham was just pressing her fingers to a card. Behind her, Owen Gardner awaited his turn, looking completely outraged at the thought of this indignity.

Helena quirked a sympathetic eyebrow at me as she went out and whispered, "I'll wait for you."

Tony nodded as I approached and then switched his gaze speculatively to Owen.

"Say!" He spoke abruptly. "How about getting Carla Drake up here to be printed?"

Gardner looked up from wiping his fingers. "What for? She hasn't any possible connection with the case."

"Who's Carla Drake?" a detective demanded.

"She models dresses down on my floor," Gardner said. "I doubt if she's spoken to Montgomery more than twice in the three months she's been in the store."

Tony shrugged. "Maybe so. But she's always sneaking in and out of the display department and she's been pretty darned thick with Sondo Norgaard."

The detective nodded. "Call the fourth floor and get her up here."

Gardner glared at Tony and strode out of the office.

The fingerprinting didn't take long, but I was barely conscious of what was going on. Tony's words had recalled to my mind that moment so long ago—yesterday morning!—when I'd come upon Monty and Carla in the corridor. If what Owen said was true and Monty scarcely knew Carla, then that was a strangely intimate scene I'd happened to witness.

Helena was waiting for me when I left the office and we walked over to Sondo's workroom together. The phonograph was playing as usual, but this time it was Cole Porter, instead of Ravel. *Begin the Beguine*. The effect, however, was just as melancholy.

I shivered as we went in. "Gracious, Sondo, don't you have any cheerful records?"

"I'm not in a cheerful mood," Sondo said. "I'm remembering that Monty's dead, if no one else is."

I glanced at her in surprise. It wasn't like Sondo to display sentiment of any variety.

The girl was up on a stepladder, a paintbrush in her hand, and tacked on the wall before her was a huge sheet of heavy, seamless paper. Sondo was at work on a background for one of the red windows Tony had been planning.

"Red is the color of the year!" Sondo announced derisively, and smeared a streak of scarlet casein paint across the paper.

The workroom was as wildly untidy as Sondo herself. Rolls of paper and bolts of cloth spilled over a table. There were tacks scattered on the floor and a hammer balanced precariously on the edge of a shelf. A half-finished sketch smeared by a penful of India ink was tacked to a drawing board.

This room was wholly Sondo's. Monty might have left his more orderly imprint on the rest of the department, but here Sondo had gone her own untidy way. The work she produced was first-rate, her salary small, so it had been wise to let her alone.

Not that many people ever dared give orders to Sondo. She was a domineering little person with a will like a hurricane. What she chose to do she did, and left destruction in her wake if she was opposed. Even Owen Gardner was a little afraid of her, and I could remember more than once when Sondo had flown furiously to Monty's defense and vanquished the merchandise manager himself.

"You said you wanted to see me," I reminded Sondo. "Has anything new come up?"

"Nothing new," she said. "Our friend Hering was over here this morning telling me all about his photographic memory. I'll bet he was right about Chris never coming up to the waiting room at all. He was taking one of his mental pictures of that perfume counter during the questioning last night and he could rattle off the names of every perfume bottle on display. In order, too. So I think there's something fishy about Chris."

"Why?" I asked.

"Look," Sondo said, "I'm no fool. I was around Monty enough to know something about him. He wasn't in love with Chris. What possible appeal could she have had for him? A big, husky kid with that empty kind of prettiness that means no brains."

"You're a little hard on her," I protested.

Sondo sat down on the top of the ladder and waved her paintbrush at me. "How can you be so generous when she sneaked in behind your back and took him away from you? How can you stand the sight of her when—"

81

"If that's all you wanted to talk about, I'll be getting back to work," I told her quietly.

Helena was glancing at the sketch on Sondo's drawing board, and she laid it down and turned around. But she didn't say anything.

Sondo went right on. "It's not all I wanted to talk about. I think it's up to somebody to find out the truth about that marriage. Those dumb coppers never will. There was something worrying Monty before he got married and if we could find out what it was we might have a key to the whole thing. And once we get that key in our hands—"

I looked up at her, startled. There was something so utterly vindictive about the expression on her ugly little face that I was dismayed. A surprising thought began to form in my mind, but before I could get used to it and accept it, Helena took the play away from me.

"So you're another one who was in love with Montgomery," she said calmly to Sondo. It was no question, but a quiet statement of fact.

Sondo didn't take it quietly. "Don't be idiotic!" she snapped, and went furiously back to her painting.

I felt a little upset. It had been no secret to me that Monty exerted a tremendous attraction for women, and that he was not above the dubious enjoyment of exerting it consciously, even where he had no interest in the woman. And Sondo, for all her lack of feminine appeal, was a woman. But if Monty had done this— and he must have known he was doing it—

I turned toward the door and saw Carla Drake standing there. There was no telling how long she had been there, or whether she had heard anything of our conversation. She wore a beautifully-cut suit of powder blue that emphasized the rather lush curves of her figure and set off her fair skin and silver hair to advantage. But she didn't look quite real, quite flesh-and-blood.

She came into the room like a sleep-walker, apparently seeing none of us, and went straight to the phonograph. There was a packing box beside the machine and she sat down, clasping graceful hands about her blue-skirted knees. Her head tilted back so that her silver hair hung below her shoulders and her eyes were rapt and dreamy.

Sondo looked down at her and said sharply, "Cut it out, Carla!"

But if the model heard, she gave no sign, listening with all her being to the baritone's voice.

"To live it again is past all endeavor,
    Except when the tune clutches my heart. . . ."

Sondo dropped her paintbrush and came down from the ladder. In three catlike steps she crossed the room, lifted the needle from the record. Carla started, blinked, came out of her trance.

Her eyes looked old, somehow, in her youthful face. That was something I'd never noticed before. If ever a woman had a tragic past, it was Carla. The evidence was there in her eyes.

But now they flooded with tears and she spoke sadly to Sondo. "You don't understand. It's that piece. It has wonderful memories for me. You said I might come up here and listen to it any time."

"The trouble is you get drunk on it," Sondo said curtly. "You've got to be able to take music or leave it, the way I can. But you get tight on it the way Tony gets tight on liquor."

"Who gets tight?" It was Tony himself. He came in carrying a portable phonograph of the same make as Sondo's and set it on a table. "Let me have one of your records, Sondo. Not that damn *Bolero!* This is the contraption Bill Thorne made for the window, but there's something wrong with it."

Carla got up from the packing case and Tony glanced her way.

"What are you doing here?" he asked. "You're supposed to be over in Monty's office getting fingerprinted."

The model glided smoothly toward the door. "I know. I just happened to hear the music and—" she broke off, turned back to Tony. "Do—do they know anything more? About *him*, I mean?"

"I wouldn't know," Tony said. "The police aren't exactly showering information around. If they have any to shower."

"I just wondered," Carla said gently. "There's nothing anyone can do anyway. It's all written there ahead and what must come will come."

Across the room Helena was studying her palm again and Carla looked at her.

"How is your hand today, Miss Farnham?" she asked.

Helena opened and closed it a couple of times. "A little sore. But it will be all right."

"I was so sorry about scratching you," Carla said. "It was very clumsy of me."

"The fault was just as much mine," Helena told her.

I think I was the only person in the room who paid much attention to the little byplay. But I was curious because I'd caught again in Helena's eyes that odd look I'd seen the night before, as if she were remembering something. And it seemed to me that the two women were regarding each other with a certain wariness of expression.

Then Carla slipped noiselessly out the door and Tony glanced after her.

"I'll take Dolores any day," he said. "That jane gives me the creeps. All that stuff about what-must-come-will-come. She's nuts. What do you let her come up here for?"

"I like people who are slightly nuts," Sondo told

him. "And she can come up here any time she likes. Nobody's promoted you to the position of display manager yet."

Tony picked out a record haphazardly and slipped it into place in the machine he'd brought. "Maybe not. But they will after those windows I'm putting in the end of the week. They'll make State Street sit up and take notice."

Helena glanced at her watch and murmured that it was time she got to work. Sondo and Tony were paying no attention, so I put a hand on her arm as she went by me.

"Helena," I said softly, "did you tell anyone about that piece from the ring that I put in my smock pocket?"

She looked a little startled. "No—I don't believe I did. Why?"

"Never mind," I whispered. "Tell you later."

When she'd gone, I turned back to Tony and Sondo. Tony's interest was entirely on the machine and Sondo was watching him with open curiosity. The record whirled and the music started, but it came out with an odd, tinny vibration. Tony listened for a moment and then lifted the needle.

"See what I mean? It was all right when I played it yesterday. So what's got into it now? I suppose some of Bill's gadgets have come loose."

"You'd better let Bill tinker with it then," Sondo said. I've seen what's happened before this when you go taking things apart."

Tony ignored her. "Linell, that office boy of yours lives west, doesn't he? How about letting him off early tonight so he can drop this at Universal Arts? I'm still going to put that golf window across."

"I don't mind," I told him. "Keith's just sitting around waiting for me to get to work anyway. Which reminds me that that's what I'd better do."

But I didn't hurry back. I ran into one of the girls

from advertising and she wanted to hear the latest, so I stopped to talk a few moments. By the time I reached the office it was empty. Evidently Keith had gathered up courage to face the fingerprinting.

Until this moment I hadn't been really frightened, but a reluctance to step through the door swept over me. Suddenly, I was afraid.

I looked around quickly to make sure no crouching figure hid behind the door. The room was quite empty, but I was uneasy, disturbed. It was as if some mark had been left upon it, as if it had in some way been changed. I'd been too dazed before to notice details, but now I was sure that something was wrong.

I sat down at my desk, with sweat breaking out on my forehead and on the palms of my hands. Something was different, out of line.

I couldn't find it at once and I began to check carefully in my mind. On the wide window ledge, conveniently ready to my hands, were stacks of current and back issues of all those magazines that are bibles of the fashion trade. My desk was heaped with clippings of ads from Cunningham's and rival stores—all the usual litter. But an ordered litter, because it made sense to me.

What, then, was different?

The glue pot on my desk was uncovered. Leaving sticky things around like that wasn't a vice of mine, and Keith was essentially neat. Whoever had used the glue brush had been hurried and untidy about it, for there were smears on the desk and down the side of the pot.

I sat back in my chair and began a systematic study of the walls. It was there the trouble lay, I felt sure. There was something different, something changed. And then I saw it.

On the wall just behind my desk, fitted neatly in among the other pictures, was a portrait that had not been there before. It was a black-and-white, a coyly posed beauty winner in a lastex bathing suit. A very Hollywoodish sort of picture and not one I would ever have chosen to grace my collection.

I got up and walked over to the wall, slid my hand over the paper. The glue wasn't dry. This page had been pasted on my wall that very hour.

CHAPTER 8

I stood for a moment with my fingers touching the picture. Then I went over to the magazines stacked on the window ledge and paged hurriedly through the top one. It didn't take long to find what I was looking for—a ragged edge where a page had been torn out.

Sure enough, that bathing suit pose had been ripped from a current issue. Selected at random, to hide a blank space left where another picture had been peeled from the wall?

Whoever had struck me down earlier that morning had been in my office not only to get that bit of stone, but also for the much stranger purpose of removing a picture from my wall.

Carefully I lifted an edge of the newly glued page. It had been fastened roughly, the glue smeared on the back in splotches so that it wasn't fixed tightly. It tore a little as I pulled it off. The picture underneath had been torn too as it was removed, but there the glue was old and easily pulled loose. Only one corner of the former picture remained—not enough to give a hint as to the identity of the picture.

Of course I knew I'd remember it. I'd arranged those walls myself, with Keith's help. And I'd looked at them six days a week for months on end. I could almost recite by heart the order of my little art gallery. In just a moment now the image of that missing picture would flash before my mind's eye. I could almost grasp it—almost—

But each time it eluded me provokingly and I was sitting there with my palms pressed over my eyes, struggling vainly to remember, when Keith came in.

"What's the matter, Miss Wynn?" he asked in a startled voice.

"It's nothing," I said. "But I want you to do something for me. Do you see that space on the wall there? I want you to remember what the picture was that was pasted there."

Keith looked at the space for a moment and shook his head in bewilderment.

"Never mind." I was weary. "I can't remember either. But keep it in mind. It will come back to us sooner or later. Someone came into this office, tore down one picture and pasted up another. Your guess as to why is as good as mine."

He looked about the office with quickly shifting eyes. It made me nervous just to watch him.

"Forget it," I said. "You'd better get to work and go through the store to check any torn or soiled signs that need replacing."

Anything, I felt, to get him out of sight. He left with an air of being more than willing to go. The phone rang and I picked up the receiver.

"Hello," said a very faint voice, "this is Chris."

I tried to sound cheerful. "Oh, good morning, Chris. How is everything?"

There was a moment's silence, as if that were not a matter she cared to go into. Then she went on hurriedly.

"Listen, Linell. I'm in the store using a house phone. But I don't want to go roaming around and have people ask me questions, so I can't come up to see you. But I've *got* to see you. Alone. I need your help, Linell. I need your help, Linell. I need it terribly. Will you meet me for lunch?"

"Of course," I assured her. "Wherever you say."

"At a quarter to twelve then. Do you know that little Polka Dot place over on Washington? Father's taken me there to lunch several times and it's fairly quiet. If we get there before noon perhaps we can get a booth and be able to talk in privacy."

"I'll be there," I agreed. "Take care of yourself, Chris."

She rang off and I thought about this new complication. So Chris was in the store. And Sondo was behaving very queerly about Chris. Which meant—what, if anything?

But I wasn't going to sit there any longer struggling with problems that were too much for me. I took out a fresh sheet of paper and this time I went straight to work and got the thing done.

> Red is the Color of the Year
> Red for Daring
> Red for Courage
> Be Dramatic in Red!

That settled that. Now it could go over to the sign department to be lettered. But if it was going to take me two days to write four very ordinary lines, where would my job be in a week's time?

Someone said, "May I come in?" Susan Gardner was

standing in the doorway. I laid down my pencil in surrender. There was no use even trying to work.

"Hello," I said. "Of course you may come in."

Owen Gardner's wife sat down hesitatingly in the chair opposite my desk. She was wearing a frock that was a masterpiece of style and quality but, as usual, on her it was a little dowdy. She had the sort of figure which encouraged a dress to ride up in the wrong places, and fostered a relief map of wrinkles. She made habitual little gestures of smoothing out and pulling down, but the result was negligible. Then she gathered her forces for a plunge into frankness.

"This has all been so awful," she began in a hurried, breathless voice. "Monty murdered and Chris a widow in two weeks. There were reporters out to our place this morning, and more detectives. But I want to talk to you about Chris."

"I'm very fond of Chris," I assured her. "I'd like to help if I can."

Susan nodded. "I know. You've been so kind to her all along. Though sometimes I think she's had too much kindness. I've tried so hard to make it up to both Owen and Chris by being all the things Owen's first wife was not. But sometimes I feel that I've failed completely."

Her voice fluttered off into silence and she looked around at the bright pictures on my walls.

Owen admires beautiful things. He admires beautiful women like those models up there in your pictures. *She* was like that, you know. Glamorous. His first wife, I mean. He's never talked about her much, but I can guess. And sometimes I wonder—when a man has a taste for women like that, does he ever really get over it?"

It was disturbing to realize that back of Susan's manner, back of her self-effacement, existed so wistful an envy of all that she was not.

"Oh, I don't know," I said, in an effort to be reassuring. "It seems to me that once a man has been fooled badly, he'd be more apt to turn to a woman who was entirely different from the first one."

"Do you really believe that?" Susan said, with touching eagerness. Then she went on apologetically. "But I didn't come here to talk about myself. I believe Chris is worried about something more than Monty's death. She's in a state of fright that borders on hysteria. And she won't talk about it to me at all. But I know she's having lunch with you and I thought she might tell you what she won't tell those who are close to her. If we could just find out what's wrong, perhaps we could help her."

"Well, I'll try," I said, feeling more inadequate by the moment.

Her kind, plump little face took on a surprisingly grim expression. "Michael Montgomery was a very wicked man. I'm glad he's dead. I hope they never catch the person who did it." Then she added, "So there!" like a reckless child.

But her indignation died out almost at once and she stood up, her own amiable self again. At the door she paused.

"There's one thing, Miss Wynn. I know I can trust you. Mr. Hering was right. Chris never came to the waiting room to meet me. I made it up about meeting her on the stairs. I found her wandering around down on the main floor in a dazed sort of state, but what she was doing there I don't know."

That was rather startling information. But before I could comment, she went still further.

"Did you find the stone from that ring in your smock?" she asked. "And did it mean anything?"

I couldn't suppress a start. "How did you know about that?"

"Why—why Chris mentioned it to Owen and me

when she came home last night. Wasn't she supposed to tell?"

"It doesn't matter," I said. "Not now. The stone was gone when I got to the office."

I watched her for any reaction, but she so often looked disturbed that it was difficult to gauge her state of mind. She fluttered out of the office shortly after.

So Chris had talked. Which brought both Owen and Susan into the thing, and left me no closer to a solution, or even an opinion. Knowing Owen and Susan, I couldn't imagine either of them in the murderous role that had been played in this very office. But as far as that went, I couldn't imagine anyone I knew killing Monty.

Later on I'd get Bill Thorne and we'd go over the whole thing together. When he heard what a close call I'd had that morning, perhaps he'd change his tune. And when he knew that Chris had never really gone to the waiting room to meet Susan, he might not be so gallant about listing her as a non-suspect. As for the suspects, there were a couple of others we hadn't included on our list last night.

Susan Gardner, for one, with her unexpected bitterness against Monty and her strongly protective mother love for a girl who wasn't her own daughter. And Helena, who had something on her mind about that scratch. And the model, Carla Drake, though her connection was obscure.

The next three-quarters of an hour ran along on a more normal schedule. I had no further time for making wild deductions for the phone rang repeatedly, people rushed in and out of the office, buyers issued orders no one had any intention of obeying and had to be quieted and placated. It was a relief to throw myself into the whirlpool of my ordinary life.

On top of everything else, the newspaper reporters suddenly discovered the eighth floor and were in our hair, until Mr. Cunningham furiously pulled strings and got them called off.

Once, when the telephone rang, it was Hering, to tell me he'd talked to McPhail and that the detective wanted to come over that afternoon to question me and to get an idea of the set-up of my office.

The hour for my appointment with Chris seemed to arrive in no time at all. I left the store with a sense of release from unbearable surroundings and hurried to the Polka Dot.

Chris was already there, holding a place for me in one of the small booths. There were dark circles under her eyes and her lips had a tendency to quiver.

"Oh, Linell!" she cried. "I was so afraid you wouldn't come!"

I slipped into the seat opposite her. "Of course I'd come. Have you ordered yet?"

She shook her head. "I don't want any food. I just came here to have a chance to talk. Everywhere else there are always people around you."

I couldn't urge food upon her. I felt so little like eating myself. We ordered soup and I settled back against the wall of the booth.

"Now then—what's troubling you?"

"It's Sondo. Linell, she frightens me. She's an awful person. I've always known she had no use for me, but now she hates me. She hates me because I married Monty and she wants to hurt me."

"But there's no way in which she can hurt you," I said, "other than using her sharp tongue when she gets a chance. And you have to accept that with Sondo."

"But why should she want to hurt me?"

I reached out and patted Chris's hand. She had large hands, long-fingered and broad across the back, but somehow useless, helpless. Not tough, sinewy little paws like Sondo's.

"It's not hard to see," I told her. "You're young and

93

very pretty, and you married Monty. Probably if I'd married him, she'd have wanted to hurt me too. I've never realized it before, but I think Monty has been something of an idol to her and his death has hit her pretty hard."

Quick tears came in Chris's eyes and she was silent, remembering. The waitress brought our orders and I waited till she'd gone before I spoke.

"Was that all you had to tell me?" I asked at length.

"No, there's something else," she said, blinking back the tears. "The thing I've really been wanting to say. Monty had some reason for marrying me, Linell. Something that hadn't anything to do with me personally. He even threw it up to me while we were away. He said the only thing I meant to him was protection, that I was a weapon in his hands. A weapon to keep him safe."

"What did he mean by that?"

"I don't know. I don't know at all. Perhaps I couldn't keep him safe after all from whatever it was he feared. So if we could just find out what it was, then we'd know why he died and who killed him."

"Have you any ideas as to how to go about it?" I asked.

She nodded. "Yes. That's where you come in. I want you to help me. I want to go up to his apartment and go through his things."

"The police have already done that," I said.

"I know a place to look they might have missed. A place he told me about. He said if anything ever— happened, to look there."

"Then why don't you tell McPhail and have him help you?"

Chris's lips began to quiver and I thought she might break into tears again. But she made an effort and quickly recovered.

"No, Linell! I just want you to go with me. What I

find might be something I wouldn't want the police to see."

"Well," I said, "I don't know why you shouldn't go in and out of the apartment as you please, even though there's probably a guard stationed outside for the time being."

Chris looked dismayed. "A guard? Oh, dear! I never thought of that. I don't want them to know. Anyway I've lost the key to the apartment."

I glanced at her sharply. "Lost the key?"

"Well, I can't find it. And Monty gave me one, you know, when we came back to town—though I spent just one night there and haven't been back since."

Somehow I didn't like the idea of that lost key. Particularly if there was evidence hidden in the apartment which might incriminate someone. That made another puzzler.

Suddenly, as I watched her, Chris's face seemed to crumple into confusion, doubt, fear.

"What is it?" I demanded. "What's the matter?"

In frozen silence, she was looking toward the front of the restaurant.

I reached out, clasped her shoulder and shook it. Chris jerked away, shrank far back in the booth.

"We've got to get out," she whispered. "Quickly."

"But why?" I asked. "Stop acting like a baby, Chris."

The jibe had no effect. She was up, pulling at my arm. We paid our checks and went hurriedly out of the restaurant. But not so hurriedly that I missed the two in the front booth.

Owen Gardner was leaning forward, his interest wholly absorbed in the woman who sat opposite him. In passing the booth, I had a glimpse of powder blue, of the fall of silvery hair beneath a smart little hat. The woman was Carla Drake.

CHAPTER 9

Chicago's Loop was aroar with the noon hour rush, and elevated trains rumbled above our heads as we turned down Wabash Avenue. The lights changed at the shrill of a policeman's whistle. I slipped my arm through Chris's and marched her along briskly.

"Do you think they saw us?" she asked, without turning to look at me.

"I doubt it," I assured her. "But why didn't you want to be seen? What's up?"

Her voice was so low that I had difficulty catching the words above the din of traffic.

"I've been afraid he was meeting her, Linell. But I haven't been sure till now. Oh, how can he? How can he hurt poor Susan like that?"

I tightened my grip on her arms. "Don't leap to conclusions. The world hasn't come to an end just because your father is taking one of the store models to lunch. It's been done before without any dynasties collapsing. Don't be an infant!"

Somehow I couldn't pack a great deal of reassurance into my words. I remembered only too clearly that moment, yesterday, when I'd gone to Gardner's office and there'd been something almost guilty about the way he'd ushered me in and dismissed Carla. However, Gardner's peccadillos, unpleasant as they might be for his wife and daughter, had nothing to do with the more immediate matter of Monty's death. Chris had enough concern without this added distress.

"You mustn't worry," I told her, managing to put some conviction into my voice. "I'm sure it can all be explained quite harmlessly and that you'll feel foolish and ashamed of your suspicions. After all, Carla's no young girl. She must be close to forty, if not more."

But I doubt if Chris listened to a word I was saying. We said good-bye at the foot of the elevated steps and I stood looking after her for a moment, before cutting over to State Street to get back to Cunningham's.

I knew what I was going to do before I turned my attention to anything else.

Keith looked up as I walked into the office. "Tony wants to see you right away. He says never mind the crime wave—his windows have to go in and you're to hurry over."

I picked up the phone, called a number.

"I'll go see him in a minute," I told Keith and then spoke into the phone. "Hello, Mr. Thorne? . . . Oh, Bill, I'm glad to talk to you! Bill, when can I see you?"

His voice was cheerful. "How about tonight? I have to finish up some work here, but it won't take too long. Suppose you come out to the shop when you're through work and we'll have dinner together."

"Wonderful!" I cried, feeling that several tons of worry had slipped from my shoulders. "I'll be out around six."

"Anything wrong?" Bill asked.

My fingers felt the lump behind my ear. His voice had such a sympathetic ring, I had to make a real effort to keep from blurting out what had happened to me.

"No—well, I suppose there is in a way," I told him. "A lot of ways. But I can't tell you now. See you later."

I felt considerably better when I hung up. Bill was that kind of person. He had a level head on his shoulders and he'd help me to see everything clearly. Until then, I'd simply stop puzzling and worrying.

That's what I thought.

Keith was watching me. He spoke as soon as I hung up the receiver.

"Tony said I was to take that phonograph out to Universal Arts this afternoon. But if you're going out there—"

He looked unhappy and I knew how badly he must want to get away from Cunningham's.

"You can take it out," I told him. "It will be heavy, I expect, and I don't want to juggle it on a crowded street car."

He cheered up right away and I went off to the display department.

I could hear Sondo and Tony wrangling long before I reached Sondo's workroom. The girl was up on her ladder, working on a background for Tony's red windows.

She had painted two or three figures coming down a corridor of big red and white checks. The checked floor of the painted corridor would continue into the window itself and mannequins would be set upon it.

The two of them were behaving as if nothing had happened to disturb their show-window world, and their manner jarred me. I couldn't immediately look beneath the casual surface of their flippancy for the tension that must have existed.

"How do you like it?" Tony asked, "We'll be putting the red series in Friday, so you'd better count on working late that night."

"Maybe they'll go in," Sondo snapped. "I've still got the navy blue background to do and the decorations for the window signs. And now you're howling for screens."

Tony ignored her. "You get the set-up, Linell? The golf window, then the red series in the middle. And next week we're putting gray in the corner window. Babcock says they'll be showing a lot of gray this spring and she wants all gray dresses in the display. That's why I want to put in some folding screens for background. Something to liven up the color scheme."

I suppressed a desire to call them back to the reality of horror. Too much that was dreadful hung over our heads. If we snatched at a familiar routine, perhaps we could for a little while avoid the quicksands. I made an effort to join the discussion.

"I saw a hat down in millinery a couple of days ago that was a honey," I told Tony. "Flame color. If it hasn't been sold it would give you your color keynote."

That was the way the decorators worked. One striking note of color gave them their key and they built around it, repeating it in background and accessories.

Sondo came down from the ladder. Fresh smears of red brightened the already stained smock, and her black hair escaped in careless tendrils from beneath the yellow kerchief. She pulled a wallpaper book from a shelf and began to ruffle through its pages.

"Here you are, Tony!" she cried, shoving the book toward him. "There's flame for you in those flower clusters. If they match the hat, we can use wallpaper to cover the screens. And I can copy the flower motif on the window signs in flame, too."

"Good girl!" Tony said, and they beamed at each other amiably.

Then Sondo climbed back up the ladder and returned to work, and Tony sent one of his helpers to millinery to pick up the hat.

"That's a start," he said. "Now if you'll get going on the window signs, Linell."

I closed my eyes and attempted half-heartedly to play the game the others were playing. It wasn't as

99

easy for me as for them. There was nothing hanging over Sondo's head, or Tony's. No one had made an attack on their lives. Even though I didn't want what had happened to me publicized, still I felt a twinge of resentment that these two could be so casual and matter-of-fact in their ignorance of how close I'd come to death.

"Shimmering gray for spring," I chanted. "The gray gleam of April rain, accented by all the hues in your garden."

Sondo Bronx cheered lustily. "Talk about tripe! I'm glad I only have to paint signs, not write 'em."

"Don't pay any attention to her," Tony assured me. "She's a frustrated sign writer herself. Anyway, these new windows are going to be something. Better than anything Michael Montgomery ever put in." The name carried a spell with it that hushed our forced cheerfulness.

"You're glad Monty's gone, aren't you?" Sondo said bitterly.

Tony glared up at her. "What do you expect me to say? I never wasted any love on him while he was alive, why should I pretend to now that he's dead? I'm running this department and I can't be sorry because Monty's not around to interfere."

"What if they put in another display manager over your head?" Sondo asked. "Will you get rid of him too?"

"Oh, stop it!" I broke in. "We're all in this together and it doesn't do any of us much good to go flinging ridiculous accusations around."

"How can you be so sure it's a ridiculous accusation?" Sondo demanded. "There's just one thing I'd like to know, Tony. Why did you get that peculiar look on your face and shut up so fast when McPhail told you Monty was killed with a golf club?"

"You know what you can do," Tony said. "And if

I get the job of running this department permanently, don't think you're going to stay in it."

Sondo tossed her kerchiefed head. "I'll be here longer than you, *Mister* Salvador. Lay you odds on that."

I stopped listening to their squabble because I was thinking of that golf club and my own fingerprints upon it, prints the police now held in duplicate in their records. I had to tell McPhail about finding the club. I had to tell him before he discovered those prints.

I started out of the room and Tony stopped quarreling with Sondo to call after me.

"Hey, Linell! Will you go down and talk to Babcock? You know how to handle her. She's just had another brain child. A perfectly stinko idea about having mannequins lined up in the window holding block letters in their hands spelling out GRAY FOR SPRING. Discourage it, will you?"

"I'll try," I said wearily and went off toward the elevators.

I didn't care much about Babcock's ideas, or the continual war that raged between some of the buyers and window display. I felt as if I walked a narrow ledge with an abyss on either side. On one hand waited the police. It was true that I, more than anyone else, had the motive for Monty's murder. And too much circumstantial evidence, still unknown to McPhail, had piled up against me. I might have some nasty times ahead unless I moved carefully.

But on the other hand lay a more terrifying danger. The very real attack on my life, and the unpleasant possibility Hering had suggested—that the murderer might watch for an opportunity to "finish off the job."

It was no wonder that I went down to see Miss Babcock in a most indifferent frame of mind.

When I reached fourth I found that the buyer for better dresses was taking life the hard way, as usual.

It wasn't easy to turn an idea which she considered divinely inspired into something slightly less antique, but I'd had plenty of practice and set about it almost automatically.

I began by planting the flame colored hat and the screens in her consciousness, and then gradually circling until she came out dramatically with them as her own idea. That would annoy Tony considerably, but would give us our way and at least keep peace.

As I was about to leave, Miss Babcock put a sympathetic hand on my arm.

"I want you to know, my dear, how sorry we all are about what happened. So unfortunate. So bad for the store. Have they, have they found out yet who—"

"No," I said curtly. "Nobody knows."

Miss Babcock looked disappointed and reluctant to allow me to escape.

"How would you like to see one of the numbers we're going to present in the style show?" she asked. "The model who is to wear it is back there trying it on. Miss Drake is so stunning, don't you think? So unusual?"

I'd been anything but vitally interested until I heard Carla's name. The woman had crossed my path so often lately that I was beginning to have a fatalistic feeling about her.

Miss Babcock led me to one of the dressing rooms. A fitter knelt on the floor, while Carla turned slowly before the triple mirrors.

Beautiful gowns and beautiful models were nothing particularly new in my life, but I caught my breath in tribute.

The dinner gown Carla wore was as modern as tomorrow, but it's ancestry went back to the classicism of old Greece. It was white and straight in line, flowing, full, yet clinging to the lovely curves of her body with revealing simplicity. It was banded at the neck and wrists in gold and a golden girdle circled her waist.

If you discounted the silvery hair, falling in beauty to her shoulders, if you missed the tragic wisdom of her eyes, she might have been as young as Juliet.

"It's beautiful," I said. "You're beautiful, Carla."

Her eyes flooded unexpectedly with tears. "Thank you, Miss Wynn. But it is the dress." She lifted the white folds in her slender hands and turned before the mirror.

I had never seen a motion so graceful, so lovely. Then something like dismay came into her eyes and she stilled the swirling of the skirt. I had a queer feeling that she felt she had made some disclosure. The fitter picked up the hem again and I followed Miss Babcock back to the department.

"Where did you find her?" I asked.

The buyer shrugged. "She came from New York. I understand she lost her husband some time ago. She's a good model, but the other girls don't seem to care for her much. There's something peculiar about her."

I left the department thoughtfully. So Carla Drake had "lost" her husband, whatever that meant. And on the day Michael Montgomery died, he had stood talking to her in an eighth floor corridor, so intent that his hands had rested on her shoulders. At the time I had thought that the gesture was one of affection. But now I wondered.

When I reached the middle aisle, I saw that my signal was on in the light box between the elevators. I stepped to a house phone and learned that I was wanted at once in my office.

Though such a summons was familiar enough, I couldn't suppress the sense of alarm that swept through me. I went upstairs at once and found McPhail waiting for me. Keith, working at his desk, did not look up, but even his ears looked frightened. My uneasiness increased as I sat down opposite the detective.

His greeting was curt and he went at once to the point. He wanted to know exactly what had happened

103

that morning and I gave him the story in full, conscious all the while of Keith listening.

McPhail prodded me with sharp questions about the identity of my assailant and about that bit of stone from the ring. But I could tell him nothing that would help. I had done no more than glance at the fragment before I put it in my pocket, and I'd had no glimpse at all of whoever it was I'd surprised in my office.

I told him about the queer business of the picture which had been torn from my wall and the substitute pasted up in its place, but that made as little sense to him as it did to me, if he believed the story at all.

"Now then," he said, with a cold, unwavering look, "suppose you come clean about what happened in that window yesterday."

So it had come. Somehow he knew about my finding Monty and running away. I longed for Bill's sane presence more than I'd longed for anything in my life. But there was no Bill. I had to get through this on my own.

Before I could form an answer, McPhail shifted the papers on my desk and I saw what lay beneath them, the upper half of a broken golf stick. There were powdery traces on its varnished surface and I knew I'd waited too long.

Even so, my relief was tremendous. The fingerprints on that stick looked bad for me, but they weren't as bad as the other. My cheeks cooled and my tenseness relaxed.

"Oh, that!" I said. "I'd meant to tell you about it. I forgot it entirely until last night. It was there in the window when I went to take care of last minute details. I wondered at the time how it came to be broken, but I didn't think about it especially, any more than I thought about the stone. I just picked it up and put it in the golf bag to get it out of the way. I meant to ask somebody about it later. And then I forgot."

"Very convenient," McPhail sneered. "A man gets murdered with a golf club and you forget that you had the other half of that club in your hands. Until we find your prints on it and you have to remember."

"But I did forget!" I protested. "Everything was so shocking and horrible. It went right out of my mind at the time you were questioning us. But I'd have got around to telling you today if you'd given me time."

"You've had time enough," McPhail said. "And here's something else. The only prints on that book end that was used to knock you down are yours and your office boys."

Keith's head sank a little lower between his shoulders and I had a sudden unpleasant vision of him hiding behind the door and leaping out at me. I dismissed it at once as ridiculous.

"That's silly!" I told McPhail. "Keith and I have both handled those book ends many times. You'll find our prints on the other one too. All it means is that the person who attacked me must have worn gloves."

"Maybe," said McPhail, his mouth grim and straight, his eyes cold with suspicion.

"Oh, come now!" I cried. "Do you think I picked up that book end and knocked myself out with it? Ask Mr. Hering. He knows how groggy I was. And there's no getting away from this lump on my head."

McPhail would have loved to get away from it. I'm sure that lump and the fact that Hering had vouched for the attack on me, were the only things which kept him from taking me to headquarters as a suspect then and there.

As it was, I went through a bad twenty minutes or so, while he shot the same questions at me, over and over. But somehow I kept my story straight and suppressed that moment when I'd gone back to the switch box.

McPhail left at last and I phoned Helena to let her

105

know that I was having dinner with Bill Thorne and wouldn't be home till later. I told Keith he might as well go pick up the phonograph and take it out to Universal Arts. Certainly, neither of us was good for any work after McPhail's visit, and the despairing look Keith gave me was the last straw.

"What's the matter with you?" I demanded. "You haven't anything to worry about. McPhail's not taking your prints on that book end seriously. There's no possible tie-up you could have with this affair. So stop going around with that I-am-a-leper expression on your face!"

"It's that attack on you, Miss Wynn. That's awful. It's—"

"Well, don't go broadcasting it," I said. "I don't want the whole store in here oh-ing and ah-ing."

He shook his head mournfully. "The trouble is you can't tell where all this is going to end. There's something pretty awful loose in this store and it's out of control now. It's killed once and it'll kill again. And how can any of us stop it, or get out of its way, when we can't even see what it is?"

"The trouble with you," I said, "is that you read too many detective stories. It's not an "it," but a human being. Somebody who had something against Monty. Eventually the police will catch up with the murderer and we'll know the whole story. But it won't be anything supernatural."

Keith shook his head. "I don't just read detective stories, Miss Wynn. I've read a lot about the psychology and pathology of crime too, and we're not dealing with anything normal now. There's nothing more awful than this kind of insanity. Where the person goes right on wearing his ordinary face and ordinary actions and you can't tell the difference. But inside he's gone stark raving mad and he's not going to do things that are normal and sensible. He's going to do treacherous,

106

crazy things to fool you and blind you. So he can strike again."

I'd known the boy ever since I'd come to Cunningham's and I'd always thought him more or less inarticulate and futile. Yet behind his quiet exterior was all this teeming unpleasantness.

He saw he had startled me and tried to smile. It was a tight, thin smile that was a little frightening.

"Miss Wynn, I'm sorry. I wouldn't scare you for anything. Gosh, I like you better than anybody I know. It's just that—that—well, you better be careful. Don't you trust anybody. Not anybody at all."

With those cheering words, he left in search of the phonograph.

I went over to the single small window and threw it open. I was chilled to the bone, but I wanted fresh air. Eight stories below trucks rolled in and out of the alley, midget figures of men moved and gestured and spoke with midget voices. All about crowded the walls of stores and buildings, alive with lighted windows like unlidded eyes that watched until the light was quenched.

The wind from the lake was raw, smoke-laden, grime-laden, its first clean freshness gone the moment it struck these hills of steel and concrete.

I shut the window and turned back to the office. The blank space on the wall behind my desk challenged and tantalized me. What had a page from a magazine casually pasted up with a hundred other pages to do with the murder of Michael Montgomery?

If I could remember that picture would I perhaps have the answer?

CHAPTER 10

The Universal Arts Company was far enough out on West Madison Street to make a tiresome streetcar ride at the rush hour.

I clung to a strap and lurched with the stopping and starting of a car streamlined in everything but motion. I was thankful that I'd sent Keith on earlier with the phonograph. It wouldn't have been any fun handling it in a jam like this.

Universal Arts occupied the fourth floor of an old brick office building and I went up in an ancient, creaky elevator. Bill had talked about moving into new quarters, but as yet the change hadn't been made.

I stepped into a tiny hall opposite the receptionist's vacant desk, and Bill came out of his office to greet me.

"I've a job to finish up," he said. "Some designs I want to have ready for morning. But we can go out to dinner now. Then, if you don't mind, you can come back with me afterwards, and when I'm through I'll drive you home."

The plan was agreeable and we went downstairs again in the elevator.

"The neighborhood's nothing to brag about when it comes to eating," Bill said, "but there's a place around the corner where the meat balls and spaghetti can be recommended."

We went to the place around the corner and found ourselves a small table with a slightly spotted, red-checked cloth, and an old-fashioned vinegar-and-oil cruet set.

The minute we'd ordered, I went into my story, beginning with the attack on me. It was nice to see Bill look so concerned and sympathetic, but he lost no time getting busy on the same angle I'd taken.

"There were three of us there when you remembered about that stone," he said. "Chris and Helena and I. And I haven't told a soul. Do you suppose the others talked?"

"Helena thinks she didn't. But Chris told Owen and Susan. Susan came up to see me today and she knew all about it."

Bill sighed. "Then it's probably all over town by now."

"I should think you'd be glad," I said. "It gives you more of an out."

He grinned at me a little absently. I could see that my story had shocked him considerably, and somehow I was glad it was I—instead of Chris—who had his concerned interest for a while. I gave him the rest of the story—my tilt with McPhail over the golf stick, the picture torn from the wall, and then I told him things I hadn't mentioned to anyone else. About seeing Monty and Carla Drake engaged in secret and earnest conversation the morning of the day Monty had died. About the oddness of the moment when I'd happened upon Carla in Owen Gardner's office, and about seeing them together later in the restaurant when I'd been with Chris. Nor did I forget that Carla had "lost" a husband. And last of all, her connection with that scratch on Helena's hand.

Bill couldn't recall ever having seen Carla, but my description, and the way she seemed to thread herself

109

in and out of the affair intrigued him. "Your lady of the silver hair sounds like trouble to me. I'd like to meet her."

"I'll try to arrange it," I said. Carla wasn't the type of woman a girl goes throwing at men she likes.

Bill's grin was maddening. "I'm good at arranging things like that myself. Don't mix in. Tell me about that scratch business again."

"Oh, it wasn't much of anything," I said, regretting that I'd ever mentioned Carla. "Just that I noticed a queer look on Helena's face last night when I inquired about her scratched hand. And then today it developed that Carla had scratched her when she was exchanging a pin. It all sounds perfectly innocent and yet there was a moment this morning when Carla and Helena gave each other a look that I'd swear had some special meaning. But I don't think it has anything to do with the murder. After all, Carla wasn't anywhere near the window at the time."

Bill's blue eyes had a glint in them. "How do you know?"

"Why—why, it's never come out if she was."

"Maybe nobody's thought of it," Bill said. "Evidently she knew Monty, and she seems pretty chummy with Gardner. Another thing that's funny is her friendship with Sondo. They don't sound as though they'd appeal to each other, if you ask me. Linell, do me a favor."

"Of course, if I can."

"Find out from Helena just what time of the day Carla came down to exchange that pin."

"Oh," I said, "I'm beginning to see."

It had been there all the time, of course, quite plainly, but my mind was confused with so many details. At some time yesterday Carla Drake had gone to the jewelry counter to exchange a pin. And Helena had been there all day, except for her lunch hour and the

110

time she'd run up to see me. If that exchange had been made within an hour of closing—!

"The trouble with this whole thing," Bill went on, "is that there are too many unconnected threads lying about. Who broke the golf stick? Where did that ring come from Monty was clutching?"

"And what about the rest of the missing stone?" I put in. "It was only a fragment I found."

"Right. Was the other piece lost in the window, or somewhere else, and what has it to do with the murder? And then there's that picture torn from the wall. Somewhere, somehow, these things are tied together. When we begin to hook them up, perhaps we'll get somewhere. Not before."

We were silent for a while, struggling with all the small mysteries. Then I remembered Keith and the phonograph and asked Bill if he'd brought it out.

Bill nodded. "Yes, he came up an hour or so ago. I had him take it straight to the shop, but I haven't had time to look it over yet. He's a queer duck, that office boy of yours."

"So I've discovered," I said.

Just thinking about Keith was enough to give me the creeps again and I found myself glancing uneasily about the little dining room. I didn't like what I saw.

"Bill," I said in a low voice, "don't look now, but there's a man sitting a couple of tables away. I noticed him shortly after we came in. He pretends he's interested in the menu, or the wall over our heads, but it's us he's watching. I'm sure of it!"

"My innocent!" Bill's smile was dry. "Of course he's watching us. More particularly you, I think. You're being honored by the police department. As far as I know, I haven't had anybody tailing me as yet, but after the suspicious company I'm keeping this evening, I'll expect a like honor tomorrow."

"Oh, Bill! But that's awful. I'd never have come out if I thought—"

"Don't be a goop," he told me. "I wanted you to come out. And if I'm going to be followed, all I ask is to lead 'em as merry a chase as possible. Besides, this makes things safer for you. You're not likely to be attacked again with the police on guard."

That was a thought. But the sense of privacy, of being alone with Bill was gone.

"Let's go back to your place," I said. "They can't follow us up there."

Back at Universal I went over to a blind in Bill's office and peered down between the slats. Sure enough, our friend of the restaurant was lounging in a doorway across the street, smoking a cigarette. It gave me a queer feeling to realize that I couldn't take a step from now on without being observed and trailed.

"I've got to get to work," Bill said. "Maybe you'd like to look around the workshop till I'm through."

He pushed open a door, switched on a light or two, and I stepped past him into a huge room.

I'd never thought much about the shop where our plaster figures originated and it caught me unprepared. There was no picture in my mind to match the reality and I could only stand there in stunned dismay.

The place had the vast echoing reaches of a cathedral. Except for Bill's office, it occupied the entire floor, vanished into ghostly distance at the opposite end of the building, and went endlessly upward toward the high ceiling. Plaster dust lay over everything. It covered the floor and spread in drifts on every shelf. The dry smell of it hovered in the air and choked my lungs.

"Come on in," Bill said.

The place frightened and fascinated me. I was torn between an impulse to turn back to the bright compactness of Bill's office, and an even stronger desire to explore this strange world before me.

112

I walked around some piled packing cases and then drew close to Bill with a gasp of horror. A foot away from me hung a horrible, brown, desiccated thing like a crumbling mummy.

Bill laughed. "That's only an armature. You know— the foundation for the first clay model. Come over here and I'll show you the start of a mannequin."

I followed him to a big table on which stood a half figure in plaster. It looked ghastly in naked white, all the more horrid since lips and eyes had been touched with color and artificial eyelashes had been fastened to the lids. The thing was bald and a cheap wig, to give the sculptor an idea of how it would look when completed, lay on the table beside it.

"Our master mold will be cast from that," Bill explained, "and then a papier maché foundation will be made, with a light plaster composition over it. Over there are the booths where the figure can be sprayed with color."

It was all very interesting, but somehow I couldn't focus my attention on Bill's words. The place held me in its grip and I waited with tense expectancy for him to go away and leave me alone with it. It was as if the whole vast room was waiting too. Waiting to share some secret with me—if only I would come quickly and alone.

"You go back," I whispered. "I—I'll just roam around and get acquainted."

I stood there in silence, hearing his steps move away, hearing the click of the office door, waiting with a queer compulsion until I could do whatever it was the place demanded of me.

Two naked electric bulbs hung down from the ceiling, casting a thin light where I stood. But it was not dark beyond. Windows ranged the entire length of the walls on both sides, and through these, moonlight flowed, making patterns of light and dark.

I moved forward softly, as if stealth, too, were part of the compulsion. Behind me lay the work tables and the area of packing cases. Ahead a new and shadow-haunted world beckoned.

Everywhere stood ghostly plaster figures—forests of them, with a single narrow path of clear floor winding between. There were creatures of every form and description. Prancing plaster horses, eagles, unicorns, swans. And there, directly at my feet, was surely an acre of small plaster owls, still unpainted, waiting to be made ready for next Halloween.

I moved on into the dimmer reaches, but still it was not dark, for the plaster figures glowed luminously in the moonlight, casting a reflected radiance of their own. I'd felt the creatures behind, and now tall Grecian columns towered above me and I found myself in a maze of gods and goddesses. A pointing Mercury caught my sleeve and cold sweat came suddenly to my fore-head.

Why was I here? Under what spell had I wandered so far into the depths of this eerie place, leaving Bill and safety behind?

Safety? What nonsense! I tried to get myself in hand. This place was peopled only by things of cold plaster and there was nothing to fear. I had only to turn and walk back along the path to reach Bill again.

I turned and it seemed that the acre of owls had moved in behind me. They sat on the floor, hundreds of them, watching me with empty, staring eyes, and it was as if they were saying, "Go on, go on! You cannot go back!"

The path had disappeared. It was there, of course. But some trick of light and shadow had hidden it for the moment. I ignored the squeamish rise of panic and turned my back on the way by which I'd come. Because I'd suffered a savage attack that morning didn't mean that I must be fearful of shadows. This place was far removed from death and murder. There was nothing here to fear.

A path lay ahead and it would undoubtedly circle the floor and lead back to Bill.

It was then that I saw a square patch of moonlight on the floor at my feet moving like smoke, like the rippling of water. I glanced up at the big window. A silver edge of cloud was creeping over the moon. It moved quickly and already the light was dimming.

Panic surged up again, but I refused to give in to these tricks of the imagination.

With the fading light the figures about me seemed to come into a shadowy life of their own. Where before they had seemed stiff and white and inanimate—now they wavered in the gloom, whispered among themselves.

But their whispers were unreal, imagined. The sound I heard close at hand had frightening reality. It was no more than a creak, as if something moved stealthily and sought to tiptoe away.

But even as I tensed to listen, the sound was gone, the whole vast place hushed into deathly silence. An unnatural silence. The silence of waiting. I saw the shadow then, a few yards ahead. A shadow darker, more dense than the shadows all around; a shadow more human than those other shadows that merely mocked the human.

I couldn't be sure if the thing moved, or only *seemed* to move. A second later I was sure. The outline had changed, wavered into a new form.

I wanted to scream, to cry out to Bill, but my throat muscles were tight and choked and no sound came. But I could move; I could walk. I turned and ran blindly back along the path to the place where the owls had crowded in—and still I couldn't find the way. I turned helplessly from side to side, sick with terror, brushing at last against an Olympian figure which tottered on its pedestal, and crashed to the floor.

In that instant I heard clearly the sound of running feet. Feet no longer stealthy but bent on escape.

"Bill!" I screamed. "Oh, Bill!"

But he had already heard the crash and rushed to find me.

"Don't worry," he said. "You haven't done any great damage. I should have turned on more lights."

I clung to him, shaking. I liked the comforting feel of his arm about my shoulders. I had to tell him quickly. "Bill, someone was hiding there among those figures. Someone who ran away."

I could sense his disbelief, but he went to a wall switch and in a moment the entire place blazed with light. It was not an easy place to search. There were too many objects to afford temporary shelter, and where we were standing a wide aisle ran past benches and tables, troughs, and vats.

I went to the place where the shadow had crouched.

"Look, Bill," I said.

The thick plaster dust had been recently disturbed, trampled, though no distinct footprints showed.

Bill glanced at the telltale marks and then ran into the aisle. "The fire escape door is open! That's the only way out, except through my office."

We ran across to where a few steps led up to an open door. There were traces on the steps, marks of plaster dust. Bill believed me now.

He said, "I'm going down. You go back, Linell."

I had no intention of facing that echoing vastness alone. I climbed out into the cold of the fire escape and followed Bill down the ladder.

But the chase was futile. The long, dark alley offered a dozen doorways to shield and conceal, a dozen passageways between buildings to furnish escape.

"You're cold," Bill said at last. "We might as well go back. But first we'll go around and pay a surprise visit to your shadow."

The man in the doorway looked bored and tired until he saw us hurrying around from the rear of the building. He took the cigarette from his mouth in astonishment.

"A lot of good you are!" Bill said scornfully. "Did you see anybody come out of the alley just now? Anybody at all?"

He hadn't seen a thing. His attention had been focused on the main door of the building. Our visitor had made his escape.

The detective went into the building with us to question the elevator operator. The man said he'd taken no one upstairs that evening except Bill and me. But since Bill hadn't bothered to lock up when he went out to dinner, it would not have been difficult for someone to give the elevator man the slip and reach the upper floors by means of the building stairs. The fire escape offered an exit, since anyone coming down could lower the last flight, but it couldn't have been used as an entrance.

The whole thing was senseless. Nothing much of value could be picked up in the shop by a petty thief; in fact most of the things were too large to be carried off. What could the prowler have wanted? I thought of Keith and what he'd said about a mind ready to do crazy, treacherous things, but there couldn't be any possible connection between Universal Arts and the death of Michael Montgomery.

After Bill and the detective, a young man named Jones, had given the shop a quick search, we gave up and went out for coffee and doughnuts. Our new friend was gloomy and guarded and suspicious—not very good company. But when Bill drove me home, we were generous and offered him a ride in the back seat. I've an idea he believed as little in the hidden watcher as McPhail had believed my story of the picture torn from the wall. I suppose it's the job of detectives to be suspicious and disbelieving, but it makes them very difficult to get along with.

Helena met us at the door of the apartment, opening it the moment she heard the sound of my key.

"Thank heaven!" she said. "I was beginning to get worried. I phoned Bill's place once, but I couldn't get any answer."

"We were probably roaming the alleys about then," I told her. "But why the anxiety? Anything wrong?"

"Company for you." Helena glanced over her shoulder. "But I wouldn't know how to entertain her. If you ask me, the girl's a little unbalanced."

It was Sondo Norgaard. She had arrived only a few moments before, and came into the hallway when she heard Bill's voice.

"Hello, Linell," she called. "That you, Bill? Swell! I want to talk to you both."

Sondo, minus her green smock and dressed in a drab brown suit, looked more like a gnome than ever. But tonight there was something electric about her—wild black hair and eyes that flashed with triumphant light. She strode back into the living room as if she owned the place and seated herself on the arm of a sofa, swinging one brogued foot.

Bill explained what had happened at the shop and described our hunt through the alley, while Helena sat quietly sewing, her strong, well-cared for hands moving competently with needle and thread. Sondo perched on the sofa, swinging her foot and listening with that electric interest to every word.

"Anything damaged?" she asked when he had finished.

Bill glanced at her. "Why did you say damaged? Why didn't you ask if anything had been taken?"

Her teeth flashed in an insolent, secretive smile.

"A girl can ask a question, can't she?" she demanded. "And you might as well answer. Was anything damaged?"

118

"Not that I know of," Bill said. "Have you any reason to think that what happened out at the shop has anything to do with the affair at the store?"

Sondo hugged her thin arms about herself and laughed unpleasantly. "How should I know?"

I dropped down on the sofa beside her. This day had added up too many nerve strains and I wished Sondo would say her say and go home.

"Why did you want to see me, Sondo?" I asked.

She hopped off the sofa and took a quick turn about the room as if seething energy would not let her rest. Then she came to a halt in the middle of the floor and faced us, hands on hips.

"I'm going to have a party," she announced. "Tomorrow night. And I want you all to come."

Helena's needle paused in midair and Bill turned away from the bookcase.

"A party!" I said in a shocked echo. "At a time like this? Sondo, you're crazy!"

"It's scarcely appropriate," Bill said.

"Why do you want to give a party, Sondo?" Helena asked.

Sondo rocked triumphantly back and forth on her heels. She was obviously enjoying the sensation she had caused.

"I've a reason for wanting to give it," she said. "I may be crazy, but I'm going to do it. And this party will be very appropriate indeed. You see, my cherubs, it's going to be a murder party!"

CHAPTER 11

Sondo helped herself to one of Bill's cigarettes and bent her head to the match. The tiny flare caught the shine in her eyes and something made me shiver. Was Helena right? Was the girl a little unbalanced?

"Now for the details," Sondo went on. "I'm going to invite everybody who's had any connection with this affair. Even your office boy, Linell. He's going through a siege of calf love over you and he was death on Monty."

"Oh, Sondo!" I protested.

But she only made one of her monkey grimaces and continued. "We'll have Owen Gardner and dear dumb Susan, of course. And we'll have Tony—maybe. Though I might have other plans for him. We'll have Carla because she's the mystery woman in the case and—"

"I thought Carla was your friend," Bill put in.

"She is. But she picked me—I didn't pick her. And I'm afraid our stunning Carla doesn't love me for myself alone. She likes my collection of records. Say— Bill, have you looked at that phonograph yet?"

"I will tomorrow," Bill promised. "If the display department over at Cunningham's would take better care of things—"

"I didn't think you'd looked at it," Sondo said. "I suggest that you do so the very first thing in the morning."

Her eyes were dancing wickedly and she shook her head when Bill prodded for an explanation.

"Let me see—who else?" She began checking on her fingers. "There'll be you three, of course. And— why, I do believe I've forgotten Chris. Oh, we must have Chris. After all, she'll be guest of honor."

I lost my patience completely. "Look here, Sondo, why do you keep picking on Chris? You've got the child frightened half to death, and for no good reason at all."

"No good reason?" Sondo sniffed. "I wouldn't be too sure about that."

"Just what's the idea behind this party?" Bill asked.

"Oh, only a friendly little get-together. But with a purpose, of course. The purpose of finding out a few things about one another, of comparing a few notes."

Helena's needle moved evenly in and out of the cloth, but a line puckered between her eyes. "How do you know anybody will come?"

"They'll come," Sondo was confident. "People usually do what I want them to. I'm a very persuasive woman."

"What about the police?" Bill asked. "Are you planning to invite Hering and McPhail to your party? They'll be pretty hurt if you don't. In fact I think they're quite likely to attend anyway."

"You mean we're being watched?"

"Some of us are," Bill said. "Linell had a detective trailing her tonight."

Sondo was examining her fingernails. "I think there won't be any detective around tomorrow."

"How'll you manage that?" asked Bill.

She returned his look coolly. "If there was an

121

arrest the police would be withdrawn, wouldn't they?"

"Maybe," said Bill.

"Well then," said Sondo, "it's just possible there might be an arrest."

Bill scowled. "I don't know what you're up to, but I can't say I like the sound of it. Besides, if there's an arrest, what's the purpose of your party?"

"I didn't say the right one would be arrested," Sondo told him. "I just said there might be an arrest. But that's not for you to worry about. I'll invite everybody the first thing tomorrow morning. If I speak to Gardner he can arrange to bring Susan and Chris, and—"

"You'll have your trouble getting Owen Gardner," I broke in. "He doesn't like you, and he won't want Chris submitted to any more emotional upheavals. Which means Susan won't come either."

"They'll all come," Sondo was assured. "After I've talked to Owen he'll be afraid not to. You see—" her impudence mocked us, "Owen Gardner is going to have a very personal interest in the identity of the murderer."

"This is a screwy idea," Bill said, "but I suppose I'd better come and lend a stabilizing influence. I'll pick my own girl, however, so never mind any assignments."

I had a feeling Bill would ask me and I wasn't too pleased when he went on.

"I think I'll come down to the store tomorrow and see if I can scrape up an acquaintance with the lovely Miss Drake. The more I hear about the lady, the more I think we'd make quite a pair."

"She's old enough to be your grandmother," I said. "Don't make any more of a fool of yourself than you can help."

Bill grinned at me. "Older women fascinate me.

122

They have something you young things lack. Anyway, I doubt if she can quite rate as a grandmother."

He was looking disgustedly satisfied with himself and I yawned and stared at the ceiling to show how bored I was.

He said, "Come along, Sondo. I guess we can take a hint when people want us to go home."

Sondo wasn't given to taking hints and she wasn't in the least anxious to leave, but Bill's offer to drop her off was too convenient to be passed up.

When they had gone, Helena put away her sewing.

"That young man's very fond of you, Linell," she said. "And he's really nice."

I felt snappish. "You don't know him as well as I do. If he likes me, he certainly has peculiar ways of showing it. Carla Drake!"

It was funny how much I was beginning to dislike Carla. I changed the subject.

"What do you think of this party idea?" I asked.

Helena raised her handsome shoulders in a shrug. "I don't think Sondo Norgaard is quite sane. And I think she was passionately, hopelessly in love with Monty. Love like that is dangerous."

I was startled. "You don't mean that because she loved him she might have—might have—"

"Killed him?" Helena said. "No, I don't think that, exactly. But I think she's dangerous now. I think she's out for payment in blood. And her mind is sufficiently twisted so that she won't be guided by logic in choosing her victim."

"Then you think this party idea isn't very wise?"

"I think," said Helena quietly, "that it might easily turn into a Frankenstein monster that will get out of Sondo's control. We'll be lucky if it goes through without disaster."

She was standing at a window, looking down at the moonlit street, while a finger of one hand absently

123

traced the scratch that crossed the palm of the other.

"There's someone down there watching the building," she said.

I was too tired to care. All I wanted was to get to bed. But there was one more question I had to ask.

"Helena, what time of the day was it that Carla Drake came down to exchange that pin?"

She was so quiet for a moment I thought she wasn't going to answer. Then she turned away from the window and gave me a long, slow look that was completely inscrutable.

"I don't remember," she said, and I knew she was lying.

Cunningham's was becoming accustomed to murder. Excitement still ran high on Thursday, but the element of horror was less keen among those whose lives had touched the tragedy only from a distance.

For those of us who were close, it was not like that. I thought of a violin whose strings were being tightened to reach a certain pitch.

Keith was in the office when I arrived and I was glad to see him. I'd probably never again be able to step into that room without a twinge of painful remembrance. The swelling behind my ear was down, but I could still recall that moment all too clearly.

"You've been invited to a party," I told Keith at once.

He looked at me without comprehension and I explained.

"Sondo Norgaard wants to have a cozy little group out to her apartment this evening. Just the select few she suspects might have murdered Monty."

Keith's eyes fairly popped. "I won't go to anything like that. I won't!"

"Good," I said. "If enough people refuse there won't be any party." I was offering him an out, but for some reason he seemed uneasy about taking it.

"I don't understand, Miss Wynn. What's she want to have a party for? Do you suppose she'll be mad if I don't come?"

"It's quite likely," I said.

His gloom increased. "Anyway, there'll be another one who won't be there. Tony Salvador."

It was my turn to be startled, "What do you mean?"

"Tony's been arrested. They've got him over at headquarters now. It happened this morning right after he came to work."

"I don't believe it!" I said. "Not Tony. Tony does a lot of barking, but he wouldn't hurt a fly."

"I don't believe it, either," Keith said. "Tony didn't do it."

He sounded so sure that I asked a point-blank question. "What do you know?"

I began to consider him with a more serious interest than I'd shown before. Now that I thought about it, the state of fright he'd been in ever since the murder seemed a bit too intense to be accounted for by jittery nerves.

"Keith," I said more gently, "if you really know anything, you ought to tell me. Perhaps I could help you decide what to do. I know you've been frightened and worried the last day or so and it would be much better if you got the thing off your mind, whatever it is."

I saw his eyes turn toward that blank space on the wall.

"I wouldn't tell you, even if I knew anything," he said. "There are times when it's safer not to know. They say that after a person has killed once its easier to kill again—to kill for protection. So I don't know anything, see? I just don't think Tony's the one. I think this arrest is a trick of some kind."

That was what I thought myself. And I thought I knew who was behind the trick.

"Come along," I told him. "We're going over to see

Sondo. You'll have a chance to explain in person that you won't come to her party."

He wasn't anxious to accompany me, but he didn't dare to refuse. We went over to window display and found Sondo on her knees, busily pasting wallpaper over the panels of a folding screen. The phonograph was wailing *Dark Eyes* and the first thing I did was to lift the needle and turn off the machine.

"I want some words with you," I said grimly, "and I can't think with that thing going."

She looked around at us with her usual grimace. "Okay, but don't expect me to stop and serve tea. Even with Tony in jail, those windows have to go in. I've had executives in and out of here tearing their hair ever since I arrived. But they have to trust me—there's nothing else they can do."

"What's this about Tony being arrested?" I asked. "You're behind it, aren't you?"

She smoothed a strip of bright-patterned paper with annoying deliberation. "And what if I am? Can I help it if I've piled up such a nice stack of evidence against Tony? What could I do except take it to McPhail?"

"What evidence?" I demanded.

"Oh, just odds and ends." Her manner was airy. "About the perfectly whopping scrap he had with Monty when he went after him with that golf club."

"Tony went after Monty—?"

"Yes, of course. Didn't you notice how uneasy Tony was over that club. I finally got the truth out of him. He threatened to bash Monty's head in, but Monty just laughed at him and snatched the club out of his hands. It was one of those old wooden clubs, you know, and Monty took it and broke it over his knee. Then he threw the pieces down and went around to the switch box. Tony picked up the heavy end and followed him to finish the job."

"I don't believe it," I said. "I don't believe any of it."

Sondo was unperturbed. She sat back on her heels and surveyed the screen.

"Hand me that hat, will you, Linell?" she said. "And by the way, what do you think of my idea for Easter?"

I followed her pointing finger and saw that she'd arranged a large green paper plant in a red flower pot. The plant was jauntily wearing a flame colored hat. I handed the hat to her without a word.

"I'm going to have a line of those plants across the back of a window," she went on, "all wearing hats. Nice, don't you think?"

"What I think couldn't be printed," I said. "Are you trying to send Tony to the chair?"

Her dark eyes were mocking and wicked. "But it's almost all true. Tony's admitted it about the golf stick. He's even admitted that he threatened to kill Monty. McPhail's got his man. The case is closed."

"And there'll be no detectives trailing us tonight, is that it?"

Sondo's laugh had an ugly ring. "You're so clever, Linell dear!"

"And you're so clever," I said, "that it's a wonder somebody hasn't murdered you."

She held the bright hat up against the beige and flame background of the screen, nodding her satisfaction.

"I can take care of myself. And a night in jail won't hurt Tony. He can stand chastening. It's better that way than to go on waiting for slow police force methods. Besides, I'm looking forward to paying off this score myself."

There was a look so malevolent on her dark little face that I turned away. Helena had been right. The girl was dangerous and I didn't envy the murderer.

She changed the subject swiftly. "You're coming to my party, aren't you?" she demanded of Keith.

He cast a helpless look at me, and then nodded his head weakly. So much for Keith and his firm resolutions.

I'd have started back to my office, but Bill Thorne sauntered unexpectedly into the room. He smiled at me, but his blue eyes were grim as he looked at Sondo.

"Good morning, Madame Machiavelli," he said, "and how are all the little schemes today?"

She wrinkled her nose at him impudently. "Very well, thank you. Have you heard——?"

"About Tony, you mean? Yes, I've heard. But that's not what interests me."

He went over to stand lazily before her, his hands thrust in his pockets. Sondo was such a little thing, she had to tilt her head to look up into his face. Her eyes were wicked and unblinking.

"How did you know," Bill asked, "that the phonograph was going to be smashed?"

Sondo put her hands in her smock pockets, openly mocking Bill. "Why, Mr. Thorne! Whatever do you mean?"

Bill gave her a look full of daggers and ground glass, and turned to speak to Keith.

"That phonograph was all in one piece when you left it at the shop last night, wasn't it?"

"Sure," Keith said. "Of course."

"Bill," I broke in, "you don't mean that was what——"

He nodded. "I had a look at the electrical shop the first thing this morning. The phonograph was there all right—smashed to bits."

Sondo gave a squeal. "I knew it! I knew it!"

Bill ignored her. "How did it happen, Keith, that you took the wrong phonograph out to Universal Arts?"

Keith looked blank and Sondo stopped squealing. But she still resembled the cat who'd swallowed the canary.

Bill went on. "The phonograph you took out to my place wasn't the one I made the attachment for."

"But—but I took the one Miss Norgaard told me to take," Keith stammered.

128

Bill walked across to Sondo's phonograph. "This is the one that was intended for the window. How did you happen to send me yours, Sondo?"

Sondo's look of bewilderment was badly overdone. "Why, you're right. This is the one that belongs to the store. How could I have been so stupid?"

"I thought you said something was wrong with this one?" Bill turned on the machine, set the needle in place. The music came out clearly, the vibration entirely gone.

Sondo made a fluttery, feminine gesture of confusion that was scarcely in character. "It sounds all right now, doesn't it? I feel so foolish!"

"Yes, you do!" Bill said derisively. "You made the substitution on purpose. Because you wanted the wrong phonograph to be taken out to my place. Why?"

Sondo dropped her pose of innocence. "Wouldn't you like to know? But you won't know. Not till I get ready to tell you."

And she turned her back on us and went furiously to work.

CHAPTER 12

        I sent Keith to the office and walked slowly to the elevators with Bill.

"What's it all about?" I asked. "Why would anybody want to go clear out to Universal Arts to smash up a phonograph?"

"I can only guess," Bill said. "Did you hear the other one while it was on the blink? How did it sound?"

I tried to remember. "There was a sort of tinny vibration."

"As if something might have dropped down into the sound box?"

"Why, yes," I said. "It could easily have been that. But I still don't see—"

"Suppose the thing that dropped into it was an object of importance to the person who murdered Montgomery. Suppose the murderer had a good idea that object had fallen into the phonograph while it was in the window. Wouldn't he be willing to go to any lengths to recover it? Even to coming out to my place and smashing up the machine to find it?"

Chills went up and down my spine. If all this was true, then there was a connection between the murder and Universal Arts. The phonograph made a link. And I knew that in the frightening moment the night before, when I'd become aware of the shadow crouching among those white things of plaster, I'd again been within arm's reach of the murderer.

Bill read my face. "You're all right now. Don't start falling apart at this late date."

I made an effort to ignore my wobbling knees and attend to the confusion of my thoughts. "But why should Sondo—?"

"She probably figured the thing out herself and wanted a chance to find what was in the phonograph. So she sent off the wrong one with Keith and kept the other until she had time to investigate. Not being in a hurry, she could do it more tidily. Since the machine's all right now, the chances are she found what she was looking for. All clear?"

I shook my head. "If she had any real evidence, why is she throwing this party? Why doesn't she take the whole thing to McPhail?"

"It suits Sondo's peculiar temperament to go about it in her own way. Besides, the evidence, whatever it is, may not be conclusive."

A suddenly brilliant idea struck me. "Bill! All we have to do is figure out how many people knew the phonograph was out of order and that it was going to Universal."

"Good enough," Bill said. "Start figuring."

"First of all we can put you down," I told him. "Though I must admit you'd probably take the thing apart with something more delicate than a crowbar, or whatever was used. And you couldn't have been in two places at once. I mean in your office and hiding in the workshop too."

"Thanks for small favors," he said. "I wish I could vouch as well for you. But you certainly knew about the affair. You could even have been breaking up the phonograph while I was working. And you could easily have staged that whole episode of the prowler."

131

"I think I'll go back to the office," I said haughtily.

He caught my arm and his eyes were laughing. "Wait a minute, Miss Flighty. Let's do some serious checking."

It wasn't as easy as it looked at first glance. When Tony had brought the phonograph in to play it, there had been Sondo, Carla, Helena, Tony and myself in the room. Carla and Helena left before Tony suggested that Keith take the machine out to Universal. To all appearances, only Sondo, Tony, Keith, Bill and I knew about that. But—and here was the thing that made our checking hopeless—anyone speaking in an ordinary voice could be heard in the corridors or several rooms away.

Anyone at all could have lingered outside Sondo's workroom and heard what was going on. In that case, we'd have to include Owen Gardner, who'd been up there being fingerprinted. Even Chris and Susan had been in the store that day, and it would have been possible, though not likely, for them to have been within hearing distance.

"A lot of help you are," Bill said. "We're right where we started. But maybe Sondo will get somewhere tonight. Which reminds me that I'd better get downstairs and date up the lovely Carla."

"Without an introduction?" I asked. "Who do you think you are?"

"You underestimate my charms," he told me, with that idiotic grin on his face. "I'll let you know how I come out."

I sniffed something about not being interested and went toward the office with my chin in the air.

"Mrs. Montgomery's been trying to get you," Keith said when I walked in. "She's going to call back. She sounds excited again. Say, what was all that about the phonograph anyway?"

I had no intention of getting into a long wrangle of

speculation with Keith, so I shook my head and gave him some letters to type. The phone rang and it was Chris.

"Hello," I said. "I know—you've got to see me."

"Why, how did you guess?" she asked, and the innocent surprise in her voice pricked my conscience.

"I'll meet you," I assured her contritely, "but I can't take another minute off till lunch."

"Any time before twelve-forty is all right," she said. "That's when the train leaves."

"What train?"

"Why, the one Susan wants to take," she said, as if I should have known. "That's why I want you to meet me. So we can stop her. She simply mustn't go, Linell."

This was getting too complicated for the telephone. "I'll see you at twelve," I told her. "Wherever you say."

She mentioned the waiting room of one of the big stations and hung up. I sat for a few minutes with my hand on the phone. Now what went on?

It rang again promptly and this time it was Bill. His whistle was vulgar, but expressive.

"The lady exceeds her reputation," he announced smugly. "I'm taking her to supper tonight and then over to Sondo's."

"Do you think she'll be safe?" I asked sweetly.

"Oh, I'm the type women trust," he said. "It's my youth and innocence that appeals."

I wished him luck and hung up. Bill's kidding was something to keep the two of us sane and postpone as long as possible the inevitably approaching time when all that was frightful would crowd closely about us and laughter would die on our lips.

For the rest of that morning I managed to free my mind of questions and suspicions. The pressure of work on my desk was increasing and I had to get out from under to some extent.

133

I can't say that the copy I wrote during those days was brilliant, but I am amazed now that I could respond to necessity and accomplish anything. I did manage, however, and when I left the office to go to meet Chris, my conscience was a little clearer as far as my job was concerned.

I found Chris on one of the big benches in the station waiting room, with Susan beside her. Chris was talking animatedly, waving her hands, evidently pleading. Susan sat listening to her—plump, dowdy, silent, and very, very stubborn. Heaven preserve me from the stubbornness of a woman who is ordinarily gentle and yielding!

"Oh, Linell!" Chris wailed the moment I joined them. "You've got to talk to her. She's going off to Florida and she simply mustn't."

"I have my ticket," Susan told me, as if that settled everything.

"But just why are you leaving?" I asked.

"I don't care to discuss the matter," Susan said. "When I learned this morning that an arrest had been made, I decided I might as well leave. I'd been planning to make this trip all along, but of course Mr. McPhail wouldn't let any of us leave town before."

"The trouble is," Chris explained to me, "if she goes, she won't come back. She's leaving father."

"It's the only right thing to do," Susan said.

I felt this was a little out of my province and wished Chris hadn't called me in. After all, if Mrs. Gardner had decided to leave her husband, there wasn't anything I could do to stop her.

"You see," Susan went on, discussing it after all, "I've felt right along that I wasn't the type of woman for Owen. Oh, I've made him a good wife, and I think I've made a good mother to Chris, but a man like Owen needs much more in life than I could ever give him. Miss Drake is so lovely and I'm sure she's very charming and interesting company—"

So she knew about Carla. That was sad, but still not my affair. But it was passionately Chris's affair. She broke into what Susan was saying.

"I'll bet she's a nitwit! I'll bet father would be sick of her in two days if he actually had to live with her. Susan, you *can't* go without giving him a chance to speak for himself!"

Susan shook her head with gentle stubbornness and the hands of the station clock moved closer to train time.

Chris threw me a reproachful look for not helping and plunged into a new argument.

"Wait a while anyway, Susan. Don't leave right now while all this about Monty is still in the air. I'm so lonely and frightened. I need you, Susan."

Susan patted her hand. "You can come down and visit me in a week or so, if you like. I'd love that and it would be good for you to get away."

"No!" Chris cried. "Oh, I couldn't leave. I—I'm afraid. Susan, that's why you mustn't go. I don't think they've caught the person who killed Monty. I don't think it's over yet."

Susan and I both looked at her.

"Tony's not the one! Oh, I'm sure he's not the one. That's why we all have to move so carefully. We're not safe yet. If you leave town at this time, Susan, it might look bad for you, bad for the rest of us."

"I'm afraid I don't see—" Susan began, but Chris stopped her at once.

"Wait a few days longer, please. I think it would be better for all of us to go to Sondo's gathering tonight."

So Sondo hadn't been letting any grass grow under her feet.

"Even father's agreed to go to that party," Chris said. "He was furious about it, but he's going. And if you leave town—"

Some of Susan's hard-won resolution was crumbling. She looked anxiously at me.

"What do you think, Miss Wynn? This party sounds like a stupid, dangerous thing."

"It does to me, too," I agreed. "But Sondo's not stupid by any means. She has some purpose back of all this, I think. And if McPhail has arrested the wrong person, it might be better for all of us to see Sondo through. Something awfully queer is going on at Cunningham's."

I told them about the picture, though I left out the attack on me; about the phonograph being smashed the night before out at Universal Arts, and of my own part in that affair.

Susan listened intently and put one arm about the shivering Chris.

"All right," she said, "I'll put off my trip for a week or so. But then I'm leaving. I'm not angry or bitter. I think I've always felt I couldn't hold Owen. And now that he's found someone else, I don't want to stand in his way. You see——" she turned directly to me, "you see, I love him."

There wasn't anything to say or do in the face of that simple statement. My respect for Susan and my dislike for Carla increased.

Chris leaned over and kissed her cheek. "You go home now, Susan, and be a good little mother. Father's going to pick you up tonight. He told me he would. But I'm going with Linell, if she'll let me."

We took Susan to the elevated station and then stopped in a drugstore for a quick lunch before I went back to the store.

We were both quiet. Chris's thoughts were her own and I was lost in uneasy speculation. For one thing, it was strange that Chris should be so positive that Tony hadn't murdered Monty. And for another, I was wondering if there had been anything beneath Susan's sudden determination to leave town. I liked Chris and I was beginning to be quite fond of Susan, but just the same. . . .

When we headed for Cunningham's, Chris said she'd go along with me.

"I've something to do at the store." There was such determination in her voice that I glanced at her in surprise.

"Just what are you up to?" I asked.

Chris strode along beside me with her blond hair blowing in the wind, and her square young shoulders thrust back.

"I'm going to see Carla Drake," she announced in a voice that made people turn to look.

I had to skip to keep up with her, though there's nothing short about my legs. For the first time, I felt ineffectual around Chris. Her sudden resolve was surprising and disconcerting.

"Listen," I said, tugging at her elbows, "you can't go barging into Cunningham's to throw accusations at Carla. It isn't done. It won't get you anywhere."

"It's going to be done!"

I felt as if a mild summer breeze had turned into a cyclone right under my nose and I wished Bill was around to handle the situation. He had a way with women. I had to admit that.

"What about your father?" I asked as we flew through Cunningham's revolving doors. "He'll be wild if he finds out about this. He'll—"

Chris paid no attention. She went ahead of me down the main aisle with a stride that parted the crowd and made people get out of our way.

I decided I'd better go along to pick up pieces and nurse the wounded, so I got out of the elevator with her on fourth. Fortunately, Owen Gardner wasn't anywhere in sight. Chris might have much of her wayward mother in her, she might be young and spoiled and helpless in a lot of ways, but evidently there was a strong streak of Gardner in her, too, and I didn't like to think what might come of a clash with her father when she was in a mood like this.

"Where's the Drake woman?" she demanded of the startled Miss Babcock.

The buyer began her usual line of opposition to anything she didn't understand, but Chris brushed her off like a speck of dust and I followed in her wake.

Carla was back in one of the dressing rooms, changing her clothes. In fact, when Chris and I burst in on her she was dressed in black chiffon panties and a bra. And I must say she looked just as stunning without her clothes as she did with them, which is more than can be said for most women.

Our appearance must have been surprising, but Carla gave us one of her usual dreamy-eyed glances and took a gray frock from a hanger, preparatory to dropping it over her head.

Chris, having gone berserk, did a good job of it. She snatched the frock out of Carla's hands and threw it at me.

"I want to talk to you!" she cried. "I want to——"

Carla regarded her sadly, but without self-conciousness. "Don't wrinkle the frock," she said to me. "It just came in from the press shop."

"Never mind the frock!" Chris went on. "I want you to keep away from my father! I won't have you breaking up my home and making my mother unhappy. Women like you aren't any good. You can't get a husband of your own, so you go around picking on other women's husbands. But you're not going to take my father away. If you ever so much as look at him again, I'll take you apart."

Having shot her bolt, Chris collapsed on a stool in the corner and burst wildly into tears. It was all pretty

138

juvenile and hysterical and uncomfortable. I must say Carla took it well.

When she reached for the gray frock and slipped it over her head, it seemed immediately to mold itself to her body. She smoothed a few silver strands of hair that had been ruffled and pulled a zipper up the side of the frock, all without a word to Chris.

Then she went over to where Chris sat huddled on the stool and put the lightest of hands on her bent head.

"I'm sorry," she said. "Truly, I'm so very sorry. I know how much pain you've had. I understand pain. But in the end perhaps it will all come right."

Chris jerked up her head, her eyes stormy and rebellious. "Don't you touch me! You—you—"

"There are many words," Carla said. "But they would be ugly on lips like yours. And not so very true."

Chris had spent her fine anger. She was a little girl again, desperately hurt, and at a loss before this poised and lovely woman. Still she must try, slapping out like a child at the thing that hurt her.

"You'll be at Sondo's party tonight! And—and father will be there too, and Susan. If you so much as—"

"Hush," Carla said. "You needn't worry about tonight. Tonight I am going to Sondo's with a very charming young man named Bill Thorne, and if it will make you happier I won't speak to your father at all. Now if you'll excuse me—a customer is waiting to see this frock."

She was out of the dressing room before either of us could speak. I'd meant to ask her exactly what time of the day it had been when she had gone down to the jewelry counter to exchange that pin she'd bought. But somehow she'd eluded me, as well as Chris, and we looked at each other with expressions that admitted we were vanquished.

"I don't understand her," Chris quavered. "She just

139

doesn't act the way a woman like that ought to act. She wasn't a bit ashamed. She wasn't even angry."

"Perhaps she hasn't any reason to be ashamed," I said. "Well, now that the storm is over I'll get back to work."

We left the dressing room together and as we crossed the floor, I had a glimpse of a graceful wraith in gray, moving before a middle-aged woman who would later be disappointed because that frock declined to make her look like Carla.

The model was a downright menace, I thought unhappily. What chance would a girl with only moderately good looks have against something like that in the eyes of Bill Thorne? I hadn't thought seriously about meaning anything to Bill until that moment. Not consciously, anyway. I didn't like men much any more. After Monty, I was a badly disillusioned woman. I certainly didn't want to get my emotions tangled up over somebody new.

Chris was talking persistently and finally broke through my daze.

"So you will help me, won't you? I'm sure the janitor will let us in. And now that the police won't be watching the place—"

"What place?" I asked. "What on earth are you talking about?"

"My goodness!" Chris said. "Weren't you even listening? Monty's apartment, of course. I want to go out there tonight. Before we go to Sondo's. Linell, I just have to set my mind at rest. Maybe there's nothing. But if there is, I want to find it before the police let Tony go and start all over again."

"Oh, all right," I agreed. "I suppose it's perfectly legal for a wife to go into her husband's apartment. I certainly can't see any harm in it."

Chris gave my arm a little squeeze of gratitude. "I don't know what I'd do without you. I'd never dare

140

get into all these things alone. I'll meet you downstairs at closing time."

I left her, feeling exasperated. It seemed to me that
I'd spent half my time lately flying around after Chris
like the tail of a kite.

CHAPTER 13

Chris had the little roadster Owen had
given her the year before and it didn't take us long to
reach the apartment building where Monty had lived.
There was no police guard on duty and as the janitor
recognized Chris, we had no difficulty getting into the
apartment.

I had no heart for the expedition. The afternoon at
the store had been uneventful, but I had a heavy uneasiness hanging over me because of Sondo's party.
Shortly before closing time I ran down to let Helena
know I was going with Chris, and I'd found her
weighted down with gloom, too. And then there was
the matter of Bill and Carla having supper together,
and goodness knows what would come of that.

So when the janitor opened the door for us and Chris
switched on lights and led the way in, I was in no
cheerful, or adventuresome mood.

There is something terribly depressing about going

into rooms that have been left by someone who was alive and who expected to return to them, but will now never return.

The apartment was attractively furnished in deep tones of brown and green. Monty had had sophistication and good taste and these were the rooms of a man who had read much and had a diversity of interests.

There was much with which I was familiar. On his desk lay a book I'd given him on Egyptian art at a time when he'd been interested in using that motif in his windows. Above the mantel hung a rather violent painting in tempera that Sondo had done. A brilliant Mexican scene of cactus and blazing sky, with a little pile of bleached bones lying on desert sand in the foreground. I remembered it quite well because it had hung in one of our windows and I'd disliked it then. I hadn't known Monty had taken it for the place of honor in his own apartment.

Chris stood beside me looking up at the painting. "It's horrid, isn't it? All those greens and yellows. I hated it the minute I saw it, but Monty liked it."

She turned away and looked about the room, shivering, though it wasn't cold. I knew the strain it must be for her to come back to this place she had shared so briefly and unhappily with Michael Montgomery. There were even a few of her own things scattered about, but unrooted, not belonging.

A pipe lay on the smoking stand and Chris picked it up gently, caressed the bowl with the palm of one hand. My heart ached. She was so young and she had been so badly cheated. By Monty himself, who had not loved her. By life, which had taken Monty away from her. Sondo, too, had been painfully cheated, but how different her reaction.

In Chris there seemed to be nothing of bitterness, nothing of real hatred against the murderer. She had suffered the wild, uncontrolled grief of a child, but she had shown more bitterness against Carla that afternoon than she'd ever displayed toward the unknown murderer. With Sondo it was different. There was no softness there, no time wasted on tears. She was bitter and violent—like her painting. And I was beginning to be more and more apprehensive of the evening ahead of us.

"Perhaps you'd better do what you came to do," I said.

She seemed reluctant to move, as if she dreaded to find whatever it was she had come for. The memories she had of these rooms—not pleasant ones, certainly—were more acceptable to her than the terrible fact of Monty's death.

"Have you changed your mind?" I asked. "If you'd rather not go ahead—"

But she seemed to pull herself together. "I must," she said. "I must know."

She went directly to Monty's desk, and pulled out a middle drawer filled with letters and clippings, and dumped the whole batch out on top of the desk. Then with a heavy brass paper knife she went to work prying something loose at the bottom of the drawer.

"The police didn't find it," she said thankfully. "This is where Monty told me to look."

A thin layer of plywood fitted tightly over the real bottom of the drawer. Chris got it out with the paper knife and I leaned over to see.

There wasn't much there. Two letters and a newspaper clipping. Chris took them out with trembling hands. We sat down on the couch before the empty fireplace and looked over our find.

First the clipping. It was from a New York paper, nearly a year old, and mentioned the theft of some valuable fur coats during a style show presented by a big Fifth Avenue store.

"Does it mean anything to you?" Chris asked.

"Only that it's the store Monty came from before he worked for Cunningham's," I said.

"But why would he keep anything like that in such a secret place?"

My guess was as good as hers and Chris spread one of the letters on her knee so that we could read it together. It was typewritten and began curtly, without salutation. The signature was merely a typed initial.

Michael:

It is almost weird to find the old set-up again. Though the actors have changed their positions, and even their identities, all the potentialities for danger still exist.

I have promised to do nothing, to betray nothing—though not for your sake. But walk carefully. There is still the ring.

E.

Again Chris and I exchanged looks. Unless she was acting a part, the note had no more meaning for her than it had for me. There was just that one ominous phrase: "There is still the ring."

I sat up suddenly. "Chris, this must be it! It ties up directly with the murder."

"But what does it mean?" Chris demanded.

"Somebody's not telling what he knows," I pointed out. "This proves how important the ring is." Then I knew.

"Of course!" I cried in excitement. "It's the *stone* of the ring that counts—to someone who was in the window when Monty was murdered. I found one fragment, but the larger part was missing, so it must have been that which dropped into the phonograph and gave it a queer sound. It would have been the stone the murderer was after when he went out to Universal last night and smashed the wrong phonograph. And if that's true, then—then Sondo has the answer!"

Chris was listening to me, but without open interest.

Later, when the secret of the ring was to be placed so strangely in my hands, I was to try again and again to recall the expression of her face, the way she had reacted. At the time, though her lack of interest puzzled me, I thought she had something else on her mind and this was not the clue she sought.

She made no comment, and spread out the second letter for us to read—and I had to suppress my excitement till the time when I could confide my theories to Bill. This letter was written in black ink in a strong hand. Merely a paragraph, with a name signed to it.

You have brought about the death of the person I loved most. I know you are callous and have no regrets. I know you would do anything to save yourself. But soon you are going to have much to regret because the person you most love will have to pay this debt in full. That person being yourself.

Lotta Montez.

"Who on earth," I said, "is Lotta Montez?"

Chris shook her head. "I've never heard of her. And I don't know any 'E' either."

She got up and went back to the desk. There was nothing else in the drawer. I spread out the two letters and the clipping and read them again.

"The answer must lie here," I said. "Otherwise he wouldn't have told you to look in the drawer if anything happened to him. It certainly appears that he was up to something not too healthy and above board."

Chris put her hands over her face. "It's awful to love a person who isn't good. I wish I could stop loving him. I wish the pain would go away so I could forget."

I made no attempt to comfort her. It's no use talking about the healing of time and things like that. Each of us has to find out for himself. And there's only one way to find out—the hard way.

Chris turned back to the desk and made another search before returning to her place beside me on the couch.

"There doesn't seem to be anything else," she said. "Linell, can you connect any of these things with people we know?"

I couldn't and when I told her so she seemed oddly relieved.

"But I don't think this is for us to decide," I said. "I'd like to show these letters to Bill Thorne and then turn them over to the police."

Chris gave me a startled look. "Oh, must we?"

"Why not?" I asked.

"But—but it may just mean stirring up unpleasantness in Monty's past. And what's the good of that now?"

It might do a lot of good if it led the police to the murderer," I said.

There was a certain relief in Chris's manner, yet there was uneasiness too. As if she was glad not to have found something she'd half expected to find; and as if she couldn't be sure it still didn't lie in those enigmatic letters we'd uncovered.

I began to think of what she had told me since the murder. That Monty had married her in order to protect himself in some way. From whom? The letters from "E" and from "Lotta Montez" carried obscure threats. Who were these people and how could Monty's marriage to Chris protect him? There must be some secondary thread here we were missing.

Chris was roaming about the room and I looked after her thoughtfully. Against whom could Monty have best used Chris as a shield? Owen Gardner? Monty might have married Chris to protect himself against Owen. But what had Owen to do with the whole thing? He hadn't come to that window until long after Monty was dead. I knew that. Then what—

A sound broke into my thoughts. Chris heard it too and whirled about. Someone was at the door of the apartment fitting a key into the lock.

I suppose I realized instinctively that whoever was about to enter would be frightened away if he saw lights inside. Anyway I motioned wildly to Chris to reach the wall switch, while I turned off the reading lamp on the small table beside me.

Chris obeyed and I could hear the sharp intake of her breath from across the room. I regretted my action the moment the lights were out and the room plunged into darkness. I'd encountered the murderer twice and I'd had enough of waiting in semi-darkness for shadows to move and footsteps to fall—yet here I was going through the whole eerie experience again. This time, at least, there were two of us, Chris and I, and for safety we were separated by the width of the room.

A faint glow of light came from the tiny entrance hall just off the living room, as the door to the outer hall was opened and closed. Closed softly, stealthily. Then silence, while my heart beat in my throat. I knew someone had stepped into the apartment and was standing in the darkness, listening and waiting. Someone who was behaving in too secretive a manner to have any right to be there. Someone desperate.

Chris and I waited, too, frozen into immobility. Then there came a faint tap of steps across the bare floor before the carpet was reached and after that only whispering, muffled sound.

I turned my head stiffly and looked toward the windows, where soft moonlight glowed faintly around the edge of the venetian blinds. A hand seemed to close over my thudding heart and stop its beating.

Someone stood between me and one of the windows. The figure was tall and black and indistinct. I couldn't

147

be sure whether it was a man or a woman. It hesitated an instant and then made its way fumblingly through the darkness to Monty's desk. Hands patted over the surface, halting as if in surprise at the pile of papers Chris had dumped from the drawer, then moving on with a tiny rattle which told me they fumbled for the chain of the desk lamp.

That second or two was filled with almost unbearable suspense. An intruder had come into this room, hunting for something. Just as an intruder had hidden in my office and broken into Bill's place. Were these the same? In another moment the light would flash on and we would see—the murderer?

Fingers found the swinging chain and tugged. A soft pool of light flooded the desk, reflected upward into the face of the woman who bent above the lamp. It was Helena Farnham.

The relief that surged through me was so intense that I almost burst into hysterical laughter. It lasted no more than an instant, and was followed at once by distrust, by shock and by horror.

I lived with Helena Farnham. She was my friend. As far as I knew, she'd had no connection with Michael Montgomery. Yet she was in possession of a key to his apartment and she had come here, knowing the police guard was lifted, to look for—what?

Even though she was dazzled by the light she sensed our presence immediately and whirled to face us. She wore a long black coat and black turban and her face was dead white, her eyes set in deep hollows. I know she must have been as shocked as we were. I know the experience must have been a frightening one—to turn and see us. But her self-control was admirable.

"Hello, Linell," she said. "Hello, Chris. Evidently we're here for the same purpose." She motioned toward the papers on the desk. "Have you found it yet?"

Chris came across the room and stood beside me, her

hand on my arm. I think she was a little afraid of Helena in that moment. I turned on another lamp.

"Have we found—what?" I asked, between stiff lips.

She didn't answer at once, but looked coolly about the room. Her eyes noted the painting above the mantel, with the signature, "Sondo," drawn in yellow across one corner, and examined the furnishings, the rugs and hangings.

"Isn't it odd," she mused, "the way the most despicable men often have the most excellent taste?"

"Helena," I said, "you'd better explain why you're here."

She smiled at me remotely and her eyes came to rest on the sofa beside me where lay those two letters and the newspaper clipping.

"So you did find something?" she said, bending above the papers.

I suppose I should have prevented her from touching them, but Helena was someone I knew, or thought I did. She was someone I'd trusted. And Chris was guided by me, so we sat there in silence.

She read every word, clipping and all, and her white face and dark eyes told us nothing. Then she straightened, walked away from us to the fireplace, and stood looking down at the dead hearth.

"So they've arrested Tony Salvador," she said. "Tony didn't kill Monty. I'm sure he didn't. They'll find out and let him go."

Chris spoke for the first time, her fingers still clutching my arm. "What do you know about all this, Helena Farnham?"

Helena was studying the scratch on her palm again. She spoke without raising her eyes, and there was no irritation in her voice. Only pity for Chris.

"I know this has been a terrible thing for you," she

149

said. "But I think Michael Montgomery deserved to die. I think justice has been done and the matter should end."

I watched her in shocked silence. That was the way a murderer might talk! And then Chris surprised me still further.

"I think so, too," she agreed fervently. "I loved Monty and I still love him. But I hope they never catch the person who did it."

Helena came back to the couch, as if she had suddenly made up her mind. She selected one of the letters, picked up a box of matches and ran back to the hearth. Before I could make a move to stop her, she'd held a match to the notepaper and the flame flared upward in the draft from the chimney. By the time I reached her side, it had crumbled to black ash and Helena was breaking it up with the poker.

"Burn the others too!" Chris cried. "Burn them all!"

And if I hadn't thrust the remaining note and the clipping into my purse, Chris would have snatched them. As it was, she was all for dumping every paper on Monty's desk on the hearth and lighting a bonfire. Hysteria again. A frenzy of hysteria.

I remembered Bill's treatment and put my hands on her shoulders, shaking her as hard as I could. She was bigger than I, and I felt like a Pekinese shaking a chow. It turned the trick, however. She let the papers slide back on the desk and went over and curled up on the couch.

"I want to go home!" she wailed. "I don't want to go to Sondo's. I'm afraid to. Something awful will happen. I know it will!"

Helena and I exchanged glances.

"If we stay away," Helena said, "goodness knows what Sondo will cook up behind our backs. I think the idea is horrible, but we'd better go and defend ourselves. By the way, Chris, this is as good a time as any to return your key."

She leaned over and dropped the apartment key into Chris's hand as the girl looked up in surprise.

"It wasn't very decent of me." Helena was calm. "I mean, to go rifling your purse for the key that night you came to our place. But I had to have it, you see. So that I could do what I've done tonight."

Certainly her poise was amazing. Later on I meant to get her alone and find out a few things. Maybe what she was doing was all right, maybe not. I wasn't afraid of her and I meant to have the whole thing out.

It was time now to get on to Sondo's. I swept the batch of papers back into the drawer, so that the place wouldn't appear to have been ruthlessly searched, and trailed after Helena and Chris. I let them go into the hall, while I stopped to switch off the lights. And to do one other thing, which had struck me suddenly.

While they started down the stairs, I paused in the vestibule and glanced at the note in my purse. It was the one signed "E".

Helena had burned the letter signed by "Lotta Montez."

CHAPTER 14

Sondo lived on Superior Street in Chicago's more Bohemian quarter, and it went without saying that she had a basement apartment.

Chris parked her car conveniently near and we got out and went down a dusty, crooked flight of stairs.

Sondo opened the door and at my first glimpse of her and of the room beyond, I knew I wasn't going to like the evening.

Perhaps, under other circumstances, the set-up might have been downright funny. That night there was nothing funny about it. It made no difference that Sondo had gone dramatic in a big way, or that the whole place reeked of bad theater. The room, with all its tawdry trappings, had something odious about it, something evil.

Stubby logs burned in the fireplace. The leaping flames kept shadows dancing and scorched anyone who came too close. There were lighted candles in heavy wrought-iron candelabra on a high carved chest at the far end of the room, and in brass candlesticks on the mantel.

Sondo had gone exotic in black satin lounging pajamas and a Russian blouse embroidered in scarlet and gold. But she still looked more guttersnipe than glamor girl.

The room was thick with heat and cigarette smoke, and even a little wood smoke to sting the eyes. There was music, too—coming from Sondo's small piano, and for once it wasn't anything melancholy and sentimental. To my surprise, Bill was at the piano playing the *Carioca* in a sprightly way that cut the melodramatic atmosphere like an astringent knife, to Sondo's evident displeasure.

Carla Drake sat beside him on the piano bench, looking like a beautiful lost lady, with candlelight glinting on her hair and tears running down her cheeks. I couldn't see what there was about the *Carioca* to bring tears, but Carla was crying as if her heart would break, and Bill wasn't paying any attention.

He caught my eyes over the top of the piano and gave me a slow wink. I sniffed and followed Sondo to the alcove she used for a bedroom. We left our things on the bed, powdered our noses and went back to the heat and wavering light of the living room.

I wondered just what fruit Bill's date with Carla had borne, if any, and hoped it was the kind that pertained to the case in hand, instead of a bit of side research on his part. Maybe he'd get it after a while that I was the kind of girl to whom things happened and that he'd better stick around if he wanted to keep up with the parade. I certainly had a few things to relate that would open his eyes.

Susan and Owen Gardner arrived and I could tell by the way Owen glared about the room that the theatrical set-up offended his taste. Susan looked a little frightened, as if she longed to cling to him, but didn't quite dare. Chris went over and sat down beside her, with a defiant glance toward Carla, who was lost in her musical jag and didn't notice.

The chair nearest the fire had been chosen by Helena, who could manage to be cold even on warm summer nights, and who seemed not to mind heat that would have toasted me pink in five minutes. I picked a studio couch, well back from that scorching blaze, where I had a good view of the room and could keep an eye on Bill at the piano.

Sondo stood up and clapped her hands. "Stop it, will you, Bill? We've got to give Carla a chance to sober up."

Bill grinned at her and obligingly raised his hands from the keys. Carla gave a sigh and borrowed Bill's handkerchief to wipe her eyes. I disapprove of women who never manage to have handkerchiefs of their own. I don't think they're as helpless as they like to appear.

In a corner near the fireplace was a red lacquered Oriental screen and Sondo went over to stand before it. It made a striking background for her small, black-clad person, and I'm sure she was aware of the fact. She looked like a figure on a rather lurid magazine cover, except that she was never still.

Tense, nervous excitement ran through her like quicksilver and set her hands dancing as she talked. There was an electric gleam in her dark eyes and we could all sense the strong purpose that drove her like a whip.

"There is only one of us here tonight who has anything to hide," she said. "All the rest can talk frankly. There is no McPhail to ask questions, no record being made of our words. I've invited these few of us who are closely concerned. These few and—the murderer."

She paused and sent her brilliant glance around the circle. The silence was like a single breath held in anticipation of disaster. When the doorbell shrilled suddenly there wasn't a one of us who didn't jump.

Sondo ran to answer it and came back with Keith Irwin. We'd all forgotten him as usual. He came in like a dog who expects to be beaten, and his frightened look sought me at once.

Sondo motioned him toward an empty chair next to

Owen Gardner. He took two steps in that direction and then seemed to experience a curious reversal of purpose. There was room on the couch beside me and he turned awkwardly to choose that place. I found myself wondering in faint amusement if he were afraid of Owen.

Sondo went back to her place before the screen.

"I'm going to start," she said, "by reconstructing what happened in window five at Cunningham's day before yesterday. First of all, we know that Tony Salvador was in the window arranging the golf exhibit and setting up his idiotic bird attachment. Upstairs Monty sent me over to see if Linell would give him a few moments. Chris was in her office and left immediately."

The dark look Sondo turned upon Chris was like the flick of a lash and I saw the girl wince. Sondo continued:

"Monty stayed only a short time with Linell. From her office he must have gone directly downstairs to the window. Tony showed him the bird and phonograph arrangement and Monty laughed it down. Tony had been smouldering all the time Monty was away on his trip. I have reason to know. And when Monty told him to take the phonograph out of the window, he lost that excitable temper of his."

Sondo walked over to a small table and picked up exactly the type of cigarette holder you'd expect her to have. It was green jade and very long and exotic looking.

"So Tony snatched up one of those old wooden golf clubs," she said, fitting a cigarette into the holder, "and waved it threateningly at Monty. Monty wasn't afraid of him. He simply took the club out of Tony's hands and broke it across his knee. Then he threw the two pieces down on the floor of the window and told Tony to get out. I'm inclined to think Tony obeyed and that he left Monty alive in the window."

There wasn't a sound in the room while Sondo lighted her cigarette.

"Tony returned to window display and phoned Linell to tell her about his quarrel with Monty. I could hear every word he said. I had my phonograph turned off so I could listen. But except for a few details I'll get to later, that's where my information ends. I know Linell came over to the department to talk to Tony, and that she went down to the window after that. But what I'm interested in is what happened during the interval immediately after Tony left Monty alone in the window."

She smoked in silence for a moment and her dark eyes studied each of our faces in turn. When she spoke again there was a quality in her voice that made my skin creep, made murder a living, breathing thing, poised, and waiting there among us. Waiting in dread of discovery, but on guard and ready to strike again.

"Someone here in this room knows what happened in that interval," Sondo said. "Someone here among us now. I mean to know which one."

The look in her eyes wasn't quite sane. It was fanatic and revengeful.

"Will you tell me?" she went on with a sweetness in her voice that was terrible because of its mockery. "Or must I hunt you out?"

Owen Gardner's voice was harsh. "Stop your play-acting, Sondo, and get to the point."

His words released us from the unnatural tension. Bill offered Carla a cigarette and lit it for her, and the rest of us shifted our positions and tried to relax. I noticed that Carla and Owen seemed to be ignoring each other.

"Do you mind if I ask a question, Sondo?" Bill said, and went on without waiting for permission. "What did you do with the stone to that ring?"

I caught my breath and leaned forward. So that idea

156

had struck Bill too? Sondo drew lazily at her cigarette and gave him her curious, twisted smile.

"What stone to what ring?"

"You know well enough," Bill said, curtly. "But for the benefit of the others I'll do a little reconstructing myself. Either Monty, or the person who went to see him in the window had a ring in his possession. There must have been a disagreement about it, even a struggle. The stone must have been loose. It broke and the pieces flew out of the setting. But isn't it a little odd that the larger piece of the stone has never been found?"

Sondo shrugged and Bill went on.

"You don't suppose that stone could have dropped into the phonograph, do you? It wouldn't be possible that you suspected as much, and when Tony wanted to send the machine out to Universal, you allowed Keith to take the wrong one so that you could tinker with the other at your leisure? It wouldn't be possible that you have the stone to that ring?"

Sondo's expression was inscrutable. Her thick dark lashes shielded eyes that glanced lazily about the room. She was like some wild little jungle cat, moving gracefully, but filled with deadly power that could lash out and demolish when she chose to release it.

"Any other questions?" she asked.

No one spoke for a moment and then I burst out impulsively.

"Yes, I'd like to ask one." I opened the purse in my lap, took out the paper signed "E", and read them the note with its last sentence, 'There is still the ring.' "Does anyone know who wrote this?"

No one said anything, so I plunged again.

"All right then, does anyone know a woman named Lotta Montez?"

Again there was silence, but this time I could feel a certain tenseness. Not a movement, not a sound, nothing which had direction. I was sure that name had met with recognition, and possibly from several quarters. Certainly not from Helena alone.

But I could read nothing in the faces about me. Sondo's eyes were bright and watchful. Susan and Keith looked frightened. There was still more resentment than anything else in Owen Gardner's face, while Chris looked as if she were about to burst into tears. Helena was white and tired and Bill had an air that said, "What have you been into now?" and was addressed to me alone. As for Carla, except for her habitual melancholy, she was beautifully blank.

"What's this all about?" Bill asked.

I could be as mysterious as Sondo when I chose. I shook my head and put the letter back in my purse. Sondo's dramatic methods weren't getting us anywhere. Those who knew anything weren't telling and I resolved that the letter should go into McPhail's hands the next day.

Sondo, too, had evidently concluded that matters weren't moving ahead, and took charge again.

"We've wasted enough time," she said. "There was one other person in that window. I've suspected it all along. But now I know."

She walked over and stood threateningly above Chris Montgomery, and though she was small, and Chris much bigger, it was Sondo who dominated.

"You loved your husband very much, didn't you?" she demanded with venom in her tone. "But it might be that your love turned to hate when you married him and found he cared nothing for you at all. Isn't that true? Isn't it true that you hated him enough to kill him?"

Chris looked up at her wildly. "It's not true! I still love him! I always have!"

Her hands would have gone to her face, but Sondo reached out and caught her wrists with sinewy fingers,

158

held them down with a strength Chris was helpless to struggle against.

"Then what were you doing in that window when Monty was murdered?" Sondo asked in a low, cutting voice. "And don't try to lie. Bill heard the phone ring that time in the display department. He heard me answer it. It was you on that telephone, Chris. Remember?"

Chris tried feebly to pull her hands from Sondo's grasp, but the effort was useless.

"Shall I tell them what you wanted, Chris. Shall I tell them you asked where you could find Monty? And that when I told you, you said you'd go right down and look for him? Are you going to deny that you went to that window? Do you dare deny it?"

Chris went limp as Sondo released her. She turned her head helplessly from side to side, but the gesture was one of an animal trapped, not a motion of denial.

The thing had happened so quickly that not one of us had made a move. Now Susan Gardner flung a comforting arm about the girl's shoulders and faced Sondo defiantly.

"It's not true, any of it! You're a wicked person, Sondo Norgaard!"

Strangely, the life and animation seemed to die out of Sondo. There was a burning ember of purpose left at the core of her, but all the rest was cold ash.

"No," she said dully. "I'm not wicked. I want to see justice done. I want to find the person who killed Monty and make him pay, whoever it is. That's all I want and it's the thing I mean to do. None of you can stop me. Do you want to talk, Chris?"

I happened to glance at Owen Gardner and was shocked at what I saw. I've never seen such rage and hate in a human face. I almost cried out to Sondo to be careful, for his fingers moved convulsively as if he longed to close them about her thin neck. He was evidently too infuriated to speak, for no words came from his white lips.

"It's easy to reconstruct what happened," Sondo said, almost listlessly. "Chris went down to the window and found Monty there alone. She picked up that broken golf club Tony had left, and because Monty had hurt her so badly, she killed him with it."

This time Gardner came out of his chair, his face apoplectic.

"You're crazy!" he shouted at Sondo. "I've always known you were crazy! If you try to harm my girl I'll—"

Chris ran across and flung her arms about his neck.

"No, father! She's not crazy. She's telling the truth. I *was* in that window. I was there when Monty was killed!"

There was a long, hushed moment while we stared unbelievingly at Chris. And once more I was aware of little things—of the curling smoke from Sondo's cigarette, of the shine of Carla's hair, of Bill's right hand forming a soundless chord on the piano keys.

Then Owen Gardner put his hands on Chris's shoulders, patting them with awkward gentleness. "Of course you weren't in the window, Chris honey. You couldn't have been."

She pulled away from him and faced us. "Yes, I was. Sondo knows, so I might as well tell you what happened."

She went quietly back to her place beside Susan and it was as if she had gone through so much terror in the last two days that now it was a relief to tell the thing. Her voice was a monotone, expressionless, as if all emotion had been drained from her.

"After I talked to Sondo on the phone I went down to see if I could find Monty in the window. I heard his voice, so I just opened the door and went in. But the moment the door closed behind me I realized he was quarreling with someone and I was afraid to interrupt. I was afraid to be caught eavesdropping too, because he was so wildly angry. So I didn't go into the window proper at all, but just crept around behind a wing."

She stopped blankly and Sondo prodded her on.

"It all happened so much more quickly than I can tell it. I didn't see who was in the window with Monty. The other person didn't speak at all so I didn't even hear a second voice. Monty stamped around to the switch box and I squeezed back as far as I could into the corner so I wouldn't be found. I'd never heard him as angry as that and I was frightened. And then the other person went around after him and I heard the most awful sounds."

She broke off and put her hands over her ears, as if to shut out the memory of those blows.

"Then the—the person left the window and I—" her voice trailed off and suddenly she crumpled into a limp heap on the floor.

Bill picked her up and laid her on the couch. Sondo hung over her with a vulture look, until Helena and I pulled her away.

"You've done enough damage for one evening." I told her angrily. "Chris is hardly more than a child and she's been through all the horrors there are. Can't you let her alone?"

I doubt if Sondo heard me. She jerked herself free and dropped down on her knees beside Chris.

"What happened after that? Who was in the window with him, Chris? Who?"

The girl's eyelids fluttered and her lips moved in a whisper. "I don't know."

"You're lying! Monty must have said something that told you who the person was. You do know!"

Owen pulled Sondo away from the couch and pushed her roughly into a chair. I'm not sure but what we might have had another murder on our hands right then, if it hadn't been for Carla.

She had been sitting dreamily on the piano bench,

161

apparently undisturbed, looking at nothing. Suddenly she got up and crossed the room with incredible swiftness. Her slender hands rested lightly on Owen's arm, scarcely more than a touch. It was the first time she'd appeared to see him.

"This isn't the way," she said in her throaty whisper. "It doesn't matter now. He's dead. We all know Chris is innocent."

Her voice seemed to quiet him. His anger died out and to my surprise he went over to Susan and touched her arm.

"We must take her home," he said. "We must take her home right away."

Sondo made no effort to interfere. But she had one more little speech to make. It was apparently directed at no one of us, but it reached us all.

"There's just one thing," she said. "One thing that will make Chris's story all a lie. That's the stone of the ring. Bill was right. I have it. If it stands for what I think—but I shan't try to guess any longer. When McPhail comes to the store tomorrow I'll give him the stone and see what he can make of it."

If that meant anything to one of us, no sign was given. Chris, looking weak and shaken, was led out by Owen and Susan. She paused in the doorway and looked over her shoulder at me.

"I was in the window when you were there, Linell. I—I was afraid to leave right away. I didn't know what to do about Monty. And then in a little while you came and I had to wait till you left."

So there had been someone in the window watching me. Chris!

CHAPTER 15

When the door had closed, Sondo turned back to the rest of us.

"You mustn't go till you've had coffee," she said as pleasantly as though she'd been playing hostess at an ordinary party.

So we stayed and drank her bitter coffee. At least Bill did, and one or two of the others. I felt too sick over what had happened to swallow anything. To my surprise, Keith perked up a little and stopped looking as if he were afraid of his shadow. Not that he became the life of the party but, with the departure of the Gardners, one layer of fear left him.

When we were all served, Sondo settled into a winged-back chair and regarded us in cynical amusement.

"So you believed her? All that nonsense about hiding while someone else murdered Monty!"

"I think it's true," I said flatly.

Sondo didn't even glance at me. "Am I the only one who sees the discrepancies? Chris was supposed to be in love with Monty. If that was true, don't you think that no matter how frightened she was, she'd have rushed out of that window to give the alarm, to try to help him? Loving him, how could she possible stay there waiting her chance to escape unseen? How could she go off and leave him lying there?"

Her small hands were like talons gripping the edge of the chair as she waited for our denial. We made none.

"If I'd been in that window, do you think I'd have crouched there like a coward? Do you think I'd have left him?"

"Not you," Bill said, "You'd have been in the thick of things yourself. But your temperament is scarcely Chris's."

"One woman in love is very much like another." Sondo was defiant.

Keith, somewhat to my surprise, entered the discussion for the first time. "But what if she loved someone else besides Monty? What if raising the alarm meant she'd injure another person? If Monty was already beyond her help, maybe she'd behave just as she did behave."

Sondo threw him a speculative look and he flushed to the ears, already regretting his words.

Bill set his cup down and said, "There's one thing I want to know. Sondo, just how do you happen to know so much about what went on in the window?"

Her grin was impudent. "I wasn't there, if that's what you mean. But the fact that Chris was going to the window, coupled with the evidence of the ring, made me pretty sure. I'm more sure than ever now."

"Well," Bill said, "It's your party. But if I were you I'd get the stone from that ring off my hands as quickly as possible. Why don't you come along with me tonight to see McPhail?"

"Why don't you mind your own business?" Sondo told him. "I'll do things my way, or I won't do them at all."

Carla broke in unexpectedly. "Would you mind if I

stayed with you tonight, Sondo? I live so far away."

Sondo looked surprised, and then interested. "You can stay if you want to, Carla. If you're not—afraid?"

Carla shook her head gently. "Only those who have something to lose are afraid. I have nothing at all."

"Well, I like that!" Bill said. "And here I thought this was the beginning of a beautiful friendship."

Carla gave him a slow sad smile that might have meant anything. I couldn't figure her out at all. But I must admit that I was glad Bill wouldn't be driving her home. I was beginning to think he had a dizzy head on his shoulders.

In the end that was how it was arranged. Carla stayed with Sondo and Bill offered to drive Helena and me back to our apartment, and to drop Keith off at his bus stop on the way. Sondo stood in the doorway at the foot of the stairs, dramatic in her black, gold-embroidered pajamas, with Carla at her shoulder, tall and cool and lovely. Behind them lay dying firelight, flickering on the walls and shining on the red lacquer screen.

Somehow, little as I cared for Sondo, I was reluctant to leave her there alone with Carla. Not because there was any suspicion in my mind concerning Carla. It would have been the same no matter who had stayed with her. Two women alone, and one of them possessed of dangerous knowledge. Even though Sondo was often such a strange, disagreeable person, still there was something fearless about her I could not help admiring. And I knew only too well that the person who had killed Monty was ruthless and ready to stop at nothing.

I wanted to talk to Bill alone, but what with having Keith with us part way, and Helena all the way, I had no chance. I wanted to ask a few pointed questions about Carla, but I didn't want to ask them before Helena. However, when we'd dropped Keith, I told Bill a little of our adventure—that Chris and I had gone to Monty's apartment. I left Helena out of it, not only because she was right at my elbow, but because it didn't seem fair to bring her in until I'd a chance to talk to her.

I told him about the Lotta Montez letter without betraying what had happened to it, and he asked to have a look at the "E" note.

I opened my purse and fumbled about inside. Bill made a crack or two about filing systems for women's pocketbooks, and then I got a little frantic and dumped everything out in my lap right there in the car.

The note was gone.

"But, Bill!" I wailed. "It was right here. I had it at Sondo's. You saw me take it out and read it."

"Where did you leave your purse?" Helena asked.

"I didn't leave it," I told her. "It was right in my lap all the time. I know it was."

"Even when you jumped up to make room for Chris?" Bill asked.

I thought back in chagrin. No, I hadn't had my purse in my lap all the time. When all that excitement had started about Chris, I'd jumped up without regard for my belongings. I couldn't remember anything about my purse during that interval. I could recall vaguely that later I'd seen it lying on the couch or a chair—I wasn't even sure which—and had picked it up. But who had been near it during that time, I hadn't the faintest idea. Everyone in the room had seen me put the note away. Except possibly Chris. Though I couldn't even be sure about her.

"Nice going," Bill said dryly. "Between you and Sondo, McPhail is losing a lot of evidence. I think maybe you'd better have a little talk with him tomorrow and tell him all about what has happened.

I agreed meekly and Bill said that anyway it was a good thing I'd lost the letter. At least nobody would be murdering me to get it.

It was late when we got home and I felt so tired and upset that I didn't invite Bill up. He hadn't said anything about Carla Drake and it seemed to me that omission was very peculiar indeed.

He had a funny quirk to his smile when he said good night, and told me pointedly that I'd be hearing from him soon. I hoped my manner indicated to him how little I cared.

The moment Helena and I stepped into our living room, I could sense the uneasiness between us. She said nothing, and I said nothing and the silence grew into a chasm. We went about our usual preparations for bed as if nothing extraordinary had happened, but each was intensely aware of the other. I was waiting for her to speak, to explain, and she knew I was waiting. But she said nothing at all. She went off to the bathroom, came back with her face carefully creamed for the night and got calmly and silently into bed.

That was too much for me. I went over and sat on the edge of her bed, pulling my pajama-clad knees up to my chin. Helena had switched off the light and the room was dim except for moonlight at the window over by my bed. I didn't mind. Sometimes it's easier to talk in the dark.

"You'd better tell me," I said. "I have to know."

She lay with one arm thrown across her eyes and in the gloom I couldn't see her face at all.

"What if I don't tell you?" she asked.

"Then—then I'll have to go to McPhail," I said reluctantly. "How can the police work when all these under-the-surface things are kept out of their hands?"

"Such, for instance," Helena said quietly, "as the fact that you were the one who found Monty's body?"

Her words startled me. That was an attitude I'd never expected her to take. And she certainly had me. I knew that the part I'd played was perfectly innocent, and of no value to the police, but who else knew it?

167

As Hering had pointed out, I had a strong motive and McPhail was already treating me with suspicion. I'd be in for a siege if he found out.

"Helena," I said, "sooner or later I think everything is going to come out and that we'll both have to tell McPhail the truth. But in the meautime——"

Her voice was hard, unfriendly. "In the meantime let well enough alone."

But I couldn't do that. I couldn't go over to the other bed and go to sleep, wondering and guessing and suspecting. When it came right down to it, I didn't know an awful lot about Helena. I'd become acquainted with her when she'd first come to the store about a year before. I'd had to do a series of jewelry signs for the windows and Helena had helped me. She'd seemed very interested in what went on upstairs in the window display and advertising departments, and we'd struck up a friendship. When she'd suggested that we take a larger apartment together and split expenses, it had been a nice break for me. But in the months we'd lived there, I'd learned very little about her. Though, until now, that fact hadn't seemed important.

"Helena," I said, "did you know Michael Montgomery? I mean did you know him at all well?"

"I knew him well enough to dislike him," she said. "But I'm scarcely his type."

I followed up my thread of an idea. "Did you ever know him—in the past?"

"Of course I didn't know him." She said it a little too sharply and I had the same feeling that she was holding something back that I'd had when I'd asked her about Carla.

"All right then," I went on, "there's just one other thing, and I think you'd better tell me this. Who is Lotta Montez?"

She sat straight up in bed. "Linell, I'm very fond of you, and I know you mean well about all this. But you simply must let the questions go unanswered. If you don't, you may get some innocent people badly involved. One of them, at least, has suffered enough at Monty's hands. To turn that person over to McPhail now would do no good, and it might do irreparable harm."

She dropped back on her pillow and closed her eyes. Moonlight touched her face and her mouth looked bitter and twisted.

"Then you know who murdered Michael Montgomery?" I said in a low voice. "You do know, don't you?"

She turned her face toward the shadows. "I don't know anything. I don't know anything at all. Go to bed. Go to sleep."

I got helplessly off her bed, slid my feet into mules. It was no use. I had an idea that even if McPhail put her through the third degree, she still wouldn't tell what she knew.

The phone rang and I flew to answer it, with thoughts of disaster flooding my mind. Who on earth could be calling at this hour? Had something happened at Sondo's?

My hand was shaking when I lifted the receiver. It was Bill's voice and there was only impudence in it.

"Hello, baby," he said. "I knew you wouldn't be able to sleep until you hear how I fared with My Lady of the Silver Hair."

I wanted to slam the receiver down, but curiosity got the better of me.

"I suppose she confessed that she murdered Monty and threw herself on your mercy?" I inquired.

"Nothing of the kind," he said, and I didn't like his laugh. "We didn't talk about sordid things like murder. Too busy discovering common interests. Carla likes to rhumba and so do I. I think we're going to make quite a team."

"Look," I said, "I'm a working girl and it's way past

midnight. Didn't you even find out what time she went down to exchange that pin?"

"Well, no," he admitted. "It seems she doesn't remember either."

"But how did she look when you asked her?"

"Beautiful. That's the only way she ever looks."

"Oh, well," I said, "if you want to run around with old women it's no concern of mine."

"Jealous, baby?"

"I am not jealous," I said. And then I did hang up. Right in his ear.

When I went back to the bedroom Helena looked as if she'd gone to sleep, so I didn't bother her. I crawled into bed thinking murderous thoughts about the entire male sex and one member of the female in particular. But I suspect that I was rather enjoying myself. So long as it was Bill who pulled my pigtails, I'd just as soon have them pulled.

CHAPTER 16

Fortunately I didn't have to get to work early Friday. Tony's red windows were going in that night, and even with Tony in jail, the work had to go ahead. Lately Monty had had me stay to help him with the big State Street windows. On these occasions I came down late in the morning and worked late at night along with the rest of the department. That was my plan for the day, so it didn't matter if I overslept.

I awoke with a jolt and sat up in bed, feeling that it was going to be the worst possible sort of day. It wasn't raining, but clouds hung low, and the air was heavily oppressive. Not a breath of wind stirred at my window, but dampness cut through to the bone.

More than the weather disturbed me, however. My first waking thought was that something was about to happen. Something terrible that had to be stopped. It took me a minute or two to pull myself out of my deep sleep and figure out who I was and what I was concerned about.

Then I thought of Sondo. Had she and Carla come through the night all right? I had to know at once. I got up quickly.

Helena's bed was empty and her breakfast dishes stacked in the sink. She'd left without waking me, since she had to get to work on time as usual.

I looked up Sondo's number and called it. I waited for a dozen rings, but there wasn't any answer. That might, or might not be ominous. Sondo's hours depended on the work she had to do, and if she had to go down early and stay late, she often took some time off in the afternoon. On the other hand—but I didn't want to think about that.

I ate a sketchy breakfast and hurried for the bus, knowing there'd be no peace-of-mind for me, until I reached the store.

I'd told Keith he might help me in the windows, so he was working on the late shift, too, and hadn't come in when I reached the office.

I called window display, but the operator could get no answer. Which still didn't mean anything serious. I tried the fourth floor and got Carla easily.

"Where's Sondo?" I asked.

171

"Sondo?" She sounded surprised at the urgency in my voice. "Why, we left her place together this morning. Isn't she upstairs?"

Relief swept through me. "It's all right then," I assured Carla. "She's probably running around the store. Nothing—happened last night?"

"Of course not," Carla said in surprise. "Whatever would?"

Now that I could breathe again, I couldn't resist a dig. "Bill says you're a wonderful rhumba dancer, Carla."

She gave a queer little gasp. "Why, how silly! I've never danced the rhumba in my life." There was a blank pause and then she said, "Oh, there's someone calling me. Sorry," and rang off.

I put down the telephone. What on earth was the matter with her? Had Bill just been teasing me? But even then, there was nothing in the word "rhumba" to startle anyone. She'd acted as if I'd accused her of something awful.

I got up and moved about the office restlessly. So many things puzzled me. Chris hiding in the window at the very time when Monty was murdered. That was a terrible thought in itself. Helena stealing into Monty's apartment, burning that note. Later refusing to explain. And always Carla somewhere in the picture.

I felt as if I ought to do something. But I didn't know what. The vacant spot on my wall, where that picture had been, caught my eye tantalizingly and I made a face at it.

"Oh, you!" I said. "If I could just remember what you were!"

Keith chose that moment to walk in and was evidently not too reassured to find me talking to myself. He gave me a sidelong glance and slunk toward his desk.

"Well!" I said. "Good morning. How are you? I like people to speak to me when they come to work!"

He said, "You're feeling it again, too aren't you?"

I looked at him blankly.

"I mean it was like this the other day. Our nerves all tied up and waiting for something. And then Mr. Montgomery—"

"Oh, stop it," I told him. "Of course our nerves are wound up. That affair at Sondo's last night was enough to upset us all."

"It isn't just that," he said darkly. "Miss Wynn— maybe I talked too much last night."

"I can't remember your talking at all."

"But I did," he said. "And I shouldn't have. If you happen to remember, please don't mention it to anyone. Will you, Miss Wynn?"

"Of course not," I told him. I wasn't trying to remember what he'd said. My thoughts were concerned with Sondo and I was uneasy because no one answered the phone in the display department. Sondo had come to work early. So where was she? I ought to talk to McPhail and tell him everything I knew, but somehow I hesitated. There was that queer threat Helena had made and which I had an idea she might carry out. But most of all I didn't want to tie Chris up in a chain of circumstantial evidence.

Keith looked up suddenly. "It couldn't be, of course, but—that sounds like Tony Salvador."

It was Tony, all right, and he was furiously angry. As he approached my office I could hear Sylvester Hering attempting to calm him.

"Now take it easy, Tony?" Hering was saying. "She only told the police what was her duty to tell them. You can't blame—"

"I know what she did!" Tony broke in. "She built up a whole pack of lies just to get me arrested. Wait till I get my hands on her!"

They were coming down my corridor and I ran to the door.

"Hello, Tony. We all knew they'd have to let you go,

but we've been worried just the same. Thank goodness you're back to work on the windows tonight."

He gave me a black look and went right on raging. "Nobody can stop me from what I'm going to do to Sondo Norgaard. Not if they have to take me right back to jail for it."

Hering said, "Take it easy, take it easy," and trailed after Tony.

"I'll be right back," I told Keith and followed Tony and Hering toward the display department.

I wanted to see Sondo and assure myself that she was all right.

The department was deserted. None of the window decorators had come down yet and there was no Sondo anywhere. We gathered for a council of war in her workroom. The green plant still wore its Easter bonnet and on a table was one of Sondo's latest creations. A lamb made of rolled tubes of white paper. A fetching little creature with downcast, fringed paper eyelids. A screen to be used in the gray window was pulled out beside Sondo's work table, and I looked around it out of idle curiosity. What I saw made me gasp and reach weakly for Hering.

A woman's body, clad only in a pink satin underslip, lay twisted awkwardly face down behind the screen.

"She's here!" I cried. "Here on the floor!"

Hering pushed me aside and Tony crowded after him. They stood for an instant looking down in shocked silence. Then Hering turned back to me with a melancholy smile.

"It's okay, Miss Wynn. It ain't what you thought."

It wasn't Sondo. When I looked again I saw that the too-awkward position of the legs and arms wasn't due to death, but to the inanimate. Tony's Dolores lay there on the floor.

I started to laugh a little hysterically, but Tony knelt

174

beside the mannequin's figure and gave me a look that stopped me at once.

"If Sondo did this," he said, "there's just one more score to square with her."

I believe that in some strange way Dolores was a real person to Tony. He turned her over quite gently and I gave a cry of dismay. The whole side of the mannequin's head had been broken in. Not by a fall, but deliberately.

We knew it had been deliberately because as Tony turned her we saw the hammer under her body. Tony reached for it, but Hering put a quick foot on his wrist.

"Don't touch it," he said, "Fingerprints."

That was when I began to get the sinister aspect of the thing. The viciousness. It must have taken wild rage, or else a cold impulse toward destruction to have smashed the mannequin. And who would vent rage upon a thing of plaster and papier maché?

Yet there was no other sign of vandalism in the room. Nothing else had been touched. Hering found the mannequin's dress on a chair. A bright red dress she would have worn when they put her in the window that night.

The hammer was a small one Sondo kept on hand for tacks and the light carpentry work she sometimes attempted. I'd seen it often on her shelves. But there was no Sondo in the department, though Hering and I went through every room of it.

Tony stayed beside Dolores and I believe he was actually grieving. When we came back, he looked up at us.

"There's no use searching for her," he said. "This is just something else she's done to get even with me. But she'd have sense enough to get out of my sight after she did it. You needn't expect her here today."

Hering looked around the room. "It don't seem like the Norgaard girl would do a thing like this."

"A lot you know!" Tony told him. "It's exactly the

175

sort of thing she would do if the impulse struck her. Sondo's a devil."

"Just the same," Hering mused, "it don't seem like anybody who wanted to work for the store would go smashing one of those mannequins. They cost a lot of money, don't they?"

"Dolores came to a hundred and fifty dollars," Tony said.

"And there's another thing." Hering went over and picked up the red dress. "Of course I don't know much about the way you run things up here, but I've got a sort of picture in my head. I mean about these dresses you use in the windows. You don't just go throwing them around on chairs, do you?"

"Of course not," Tony said. "We get them fresh from the press room and then—"

"And then they go right on the dummy, don't they?"

"Mannequin." Tony corrected automatically.

"But you carry 'em around on hangers, don't you? And if you had to let a dress out of your hands, you'd hook the hanger over something. You wouldn't just go throwing the dress over the back of the chair."

Tony and I both looked at him. He had something there. Not a hanger in sight in the room.

"Of course I wouldn't know," Hering said, "but it looks like maybe that dum—mannequin was already dressed and somebody took the dress off her. Took it off in such a hurry that they didn't bother to look for a hanger to hang it up properly, just tossed it over a chair."

We found out very shortly that he was right about the mannequin having been dressed. The rest of the department started to straggle in and one of the boys admitted that he'd dressed Dolores before he went home the previous day. The mannequins had to be carried downstairs in sections, and were usually dressed in the windows, but in this case Sondo had wanted to try out

176

some effects and had asked that Dolores be dressed and left in her workroom.

This careful deduction got us nowhere. Tony finally dragged himself away from the "body" and Hering went to phone McPhail about the latest developments. It wasn't until much later in the day that Miss Babcock got into the affair and began to throw tantrums because the red belt that belonged with the dress was missing.

Meanwhile, I went back to my office to find Chris waiting for me. By the sudden silence that fell when I walked in and the guilty expressions on the faces of both Chris and Keith, I could surmise that I'd interrupted a little heart-to-heart talk.

"Oh, Linell!" Chris burst out when she had recovered from her momentary embarrassment. "I came to ask you not to say anything to the police about what came out at Sondo's party. You don't have to, do you? After all, it hasn't anything to do with Monty's death. I mean, since I don't really know anything—" A flush crept up her throat and into her cheeks and she stopped helplessly.

"Now listen to me," I said. "I'm beginning to feel practically like an encyclopedia of what the police department doesn't know. About every fifteen minutes someone new comes up and asks me please not to say anything to the police about such-and-such because, of course, it hasn't anything to do with the murder."

Tears began to well up in Chris's eyes. "Oh, Linell, how can you be so unkind? Of course father and Susan won't say anything. And I've already stopped by to speak to Helena and Carla and they won't tell either. Keith just promised me he wouldn't so there's only Sondo, Bill Thorne and you left. If you'd promise, then I could just go over to see Sondo and—"

"If you can find her," I said. "Just at the moment she's disappeared."

177

The flush drained out of Chris's cheeks.

"Oh, no!" she whispered. "Oh, no—it couldn't be!"

"Couldn't be what?" I snapped.

She looked around toward Keith, but he was watching me in wide-eyed horror and didn't see her.

"I didn't say she'd been murdered," I told them. "I only said she'd disappeared. Probably not even that. She came to the store this morning, so she may be around somewhere."

Chris was not reassured. She jumped up. "I'm going over to window display. I've got to find out! I've got to know!"

"Maybe you'd better stay away," Keith warned her. "After what Sondo did to you last night, they might go tying you in. Or they might tie—"

Chris whirled on him. "Don't you say it! Don't you dare say it!"

The glimmer of a most unpleasant suspicion began to stir in my mind. What was it Keith had been so uneasy about having said last night? It had been after Chris had gone. He'd accounted for her strange behavior in the window by suggesting that there might be someone else she'd loved as well as Monty.

For the first time that idea began to take hold in my mind. I'd thought from the beginning that she had never shown a natural hatred toward the murderer, even though he'd taken the life of the man she'd loved. And she'd been so frightened and hysterical from the beginning. There were two people Chris had loved besides Monty; two who loved her devotedly. Owen and Susan Gardner.

I leaned my elbows on the desk and put my face in my hands. My confusion of mind was so great that I couldn't seem to think in a straight line for two minutes consecutively. Sooner or later I'd have to go to McPhail with everything I knew. Everything. Which meant my own part in finding Monty's body, the part Bill had played, Helena's visit to Monty's apartment, the letters we'd found there, Sondo's suspicions of a possible explanation concerning the ring—anything and everything. But before I did that I wanted to have one last thorough talk with Bill.

"Chris," I said more gently than I'd spoken before, "I think you'd better go home and stay there. Don't talk to anyone else in the store. Probably Sondo is all right and will show up at any minute. But—but if she isn't all right—we'll all have to tell the truth. There's nothing else for it. Go home, Chris and rest. And I'll call you the moment I know anything."

She said, "All right, Linell," in a voice that was hardly more than a whisper and went out of the office as if she were walking in her sleep.

The moment she was gone, I sent Keith off on an errand and then phoned window display. One of Tony's helpers answered. No. Sondo hadn't shown up as yet. Hering was still there. Sure, he'd tell him I wanted to see him.

I sat back and waited. There were a number of things I couldn't tell Hering yet, but there was one thing I could. Until I made up my mind to confess the part I'd played, I simply couldn't go giving any of my friends away, but there was one person concerned who was no friend of mine.

"I want you to find out something for me," I said when Hering came in. "It's just possible there was another person near the window at the time Mr. Montgomery was murdered. I mean someone who hasn't figured very strongly yet."

He looked all ears and interest and I went on.

"Last week Carla Drake bought a pin down at the costume jewelry section. It didn't suit her and she went down Tuesday to exchange it. Helena Farnham waited on her on both occasions, but for some reason neither Miss Farnham nor Miss Drake can recall exactly what time of the day that exchange was made. Do you have access to the salesbooks?"

"I'll find out, Miss Wynn," Hering said.

"Of course there may not be anything to it," I told him. "I'm just curious, that's all. But there's one other thing. Yesterday a clipping came into my hands and it may have some significance. I wonder if you could look up the case referred to?"

"Well," he said, "I guess so. That Miss Drake sure is some baby, ain't she?"

"Et tu, Brute?" I said and smiled at his blank look. "I mean it would certainly be a shame if she turned out to be a murderess, wouldn't it?"

"Yeah," Hering said. "Tough to get a conviction. What's that clipping you were talking about?"

"I have it in my handbag," I said, and then wondered if I did. I'd read it over again on the way to work that morning, but what with the queer things that went on these days I couldn't be sure how long I'd keep anything.

I opened a drawer in my desk. I must have done it absently, because it wasn't the drawer in which I kept my bag and gloves. And then I sat quite motionless.

Hering must have noted the peculiar expression on my face because he came around the desk and looked at the contents of the drawer.

"Pull it out," he said. "Go ahead, pull it out."

I didn't want to. I didn't want to because suddenly and unreasonably I was afraid. I knew what was in that drawer and so did Hering. When I still hesitated, he reached in and pulled out the wrinkled green folds and shook them into shape.

The thing was Sondo's paint-smeared smock and out of it dropped the knotted yellow kerchief she so often wore about her head.

Hering regarded me darkly. "Where'd you get this?"

"I don't know," I said in bewilderment. "I mean I

didn't get it anywhere. Sondo must have put them there herself. But I can't imagine what for."

Hering looked increasingly mournful. "Maybe she did and maybe she didn't. You sure you don't know anything about this, Miss Wynn?"

I began to feel a little indignant. "I've told you I don't. What do you think—that I've murdered Sondo and—and—"

He shook his head at me reproachfully. "Don't get excited now. I didn't say nothing of the kind."

"But you thought it!" I cried. "I saw it there in your face. But why you should mind, I'm sure I don't know. I'd be a lot easier to get a conviction on than Carla Drake."

Hering said, "Aw, Miss Wynn!" and I began to feel a bit foolish. I hadn't meant to pull a Chris on him, but it just seemed as if so many things were piling up and that smock stuffed in the drawer of my desk was the last straw.

"It's all right," I said. "I'm sorry. I'm sure there's some simple explanation and as soon as Sondo shows up we'll hear about it."

"I'll have to take this over to show McPhail," he told me. "And now that clipping."

I found it and gave it to him. "It's about a fur coat theft at a style show run by the store where Monty used to work before he came here. Maybe there's a connection."

"I'll check on it," he assured me. "And don't you worry about this smock business."

Keith came back shortly after Hering had left and I told him what had happened. He looked sicker than ever and dropped limply into his chair.

"That means she's dead," he said in a hollow voice. "That's what it means!"

"It doesn't mean anything of the kind," I told him, but he shook his head at me.

"If she's dead I'm going to tell," he whispered. "I have to tell. I can't let it go on."

I was tempted to get up and shake Keith, the way Bill and I took turns at shaking Chris.

"Just what have you got on your mind?" I asked.

He only shook his head and I knew from experience that when Keith developed a mood there wasn't much chance of doing anything with him. He denied all knowledge of the smock and I believed him.

It wasn't until after lunch that we found out Bill had disappeared too, and that in all probability he'd been the last to talk to Sondo.

CHAPTER 17

But before that a few other things happened. McPhail arrived in a highly indignant state. He wanted to see Sondo about the wrong steer she'd given him in the Tony business, and he wasn't any too pleased over Dolores' broken head, or the smock stuffed in my drawer.

After a futile questioning session in which nothing new came out, he ordered a description of Sondo broadcast and set the whole police force watching for her. By that time he'd come to a satisfactory conclusion in his own mind. He'd been fooled by Sondo once and he didn't mean to be fooled again. Obviously she was our murderer and had done a neat getaway under the cover of Tony's arrest. Everything else—the smashed manne-quin, the smock in my drawer—were merely blinds by which he had no intention of being confused.

Tony was delighted with this idea and lost no time in revenging himself upon Sondo by telling McPhail everything he could think of against her.

Miss Babcock was called in and questioned about the red dress. She explained that it was a frock Mr. Gardner had particularly wanted shown in the window and that one of the display boys had taken it upstairs the day before. But where, demanded Miss Babcock indig-nantly, was the belt? In her eyes. I'm sure, the belt's disappearance was far more serious than Sondo's. In spite of the rumpus she raised, the belt wasn't found. Not then.

It was immediately after lunch that I had my odd encounter on the stairs.

All the stairways in the newer part of the store are enclosed and shut off from each floor. Since there are plenty of elevators and a wide escalator, they are sel-dom used. I'd been taking care of some matters per-taining to signs on the third floor and then I had to go down to the second to see the buyer of yard goods. As the stairs were handiest, I went through the door and out onto the third floor landing.

As I started down, I heard voices just below and one of them I recognized as Helena Farnham's. I paused and looked down over the rail. Carla Drake was with her and they were talking earnestly.

"I appreciate what you've done for me," Carla was saying. "I won't forget it. This way neither of us needs to be involved."

Carla's back was toward me so that I couldn't watch her expression. Of Helena I could see just the profile as she looked intently at Carla.

"He caused enough suffering while he was alive," Helena said. "There's no need for him to cause more, now that he's dead."

Carla held out her hand and Helena took it. It was like the signing of a pact. Then Helena started downstairs toward the main floor and Carla came up in my direction. I didn't linger to be discovered, but whirled and ran back onto the third floor, making my way to the escalator.

So there was something between Helena and Carla. Helena knew something about the model, something she was being quiet about. And I thought I knew what it was, in part.

My signal light went up before I'd finished what I had to do and I learned I was wanted in window display where McPhail was holding temporary court. Hering was with him and on Monty's desk lay the carbon of a sales slip.

"We've sent for Miss Drake and Miss Farnham about this pin business," McPhail said. "But first you can tell me what you know."

I explained that I'd had an uneasy feeling that the two women were being evasive about the time Carla had gone down to exchange the pin.

McPhail shoved the slip out of sight and nodded. "We've got the record here in carbons. The number stamped by the cash register shows that the pin exchange was made within an hour of closing time last Tuesday."

But he didn't get anywhere with them. Carla recalled vaguely that she must have made the exchange some time in the afternoon. Helena said she'd been too busy and there were too many exchanges for her to remember any particular one. When McPhail confronted them with the record, neither turned a hair. They'd expected something of the kind, of course, and both were schooled in self-control.

I didn't want to go too far until I was ready to go all the way, so I refrained from mentioning the meeting on the stairs. First I wanted to talk to Bill.

McPhail let Helena go, but he kept Carla for a while. Somebody had told him she'd spent the night at Sondo's and he was interested in getting an account of that. I was interested too and glad he didn't send me away.

Carla did a nice job of skimming the truth. Sondo had had a few friends over last night, she explained serenely, and when they'd gone home Sondo had invited her to stay. It was late and she'd been glad of the opportunity.

No, Sondo hadn't seemed any different than usual. They hadn't talked much. Sondo wanted to write a letter, so Carla had gone to bed on the studio couch in the living room. In the morning Bill Thorne had turned up bright and early on their doorstep and invited them to breakfast.

My interest quickened. Breakfast? Mm.

"But Sondo was in a hurry to get to the store," Carla explained. "She seemed to want to get down especially early. So Bill just took me to breakfast."

That made it still more interesting. I wanted to know all about that breakfast—where they'd gone and who'd said what. But McPhail didn't follow it up.

He said, "After Sondo left you to go to work, you didn't see her again?"

Carla shook her head. "I didn't. But maybe Bill did. He seemed curious about what she was up to and he said he thought he might as well run down to Cunningham's and have a talk with her before he went out to Universal. So he drove me to work."

Hering picked up the phone on Monty's desk. "Want me to call Universal?"

McPhail nodded and he put through the call. Bill hadn't been at Universal all day. But he'd phoned. He'd phoned from Cunningham's and said he had some things

185

to do and might take some time off. So nobody had been concerned.

Hering checked with a Cunningham operator who remembered a man's voice on the window display connection, asking for an outside wire early that morning. It looked very much as if Bill had had his interview with Sondo and then both of them had disappeared into thin air. Whether together or separately was anybody's guess.

I was beginning to get really scared. I didn't like the sound of any of it, and I didn't wait any longer to put in a few ideas of my own.

"I think something's happened to him," I told McPhail, while my stomach did back flip-flops at the very hint of anything happening to Bill. If he'd just show up quickly and all in one piece, I'd even forgive him for taking Carla to breakfast.

McPhail was unimpressed by my contribution. "I suppose you think maybe the Norgaard woman murdered him too? And I suppose a little half-pint squirt like her could just tuck the body under her arm and cart it out of the store?"

It was awful to hear Bill referred to as "the body."

"Maybe not," I said. "But she could have persuaded him to go out of the store with her and then—and then—" I couldn't go on.

Somebody had carried that pine spray of Tony's into Monty's office, and Hering had picked it up to test experimentally. He put it down now and turned to me.

"Look, Miss Wynn. What makes you think he didn't just go off alone on some hook of his own?"

I laid down my ace. "Because he wouldn't have come to Cunningham's and gone away again without stopping in to see me. Even if it was just to say 'hello,' he'd have stopped in my office."

McPhail looked me over in a way I didn't much like. "He had breakfast with the Drake woman, didn't

186

he?" he said, and the inference wasn't to be missed.

In McPhail's eyes I evidently wouldn't stand a chance against Carla, and probably Bill wouldn't have been interested in looking into my office.

I said, "If you're through with me, I'll get back to work," and went haughtily to the door.

Keith was waiting outside for me.

"I didn't know if I should interrupt or not," he said. "There's about twelve people waiting for you to call them up, and there's some trouble about the signs for the style show and—"

My heart wasn't in my work at the moment. All I wanted to know was whether Bill Thorne had called. Keith said he hadn't and, when my chin went down another notch, asked what was the matter.

"Bill's gone too," I said. "Sondo and Bill. They can't find either of them."

Keith looked so awful that I had to make an effort to take him in hand, instead of indulging in my own fears.

"Nothing's happened to Bill. He phoned Universal and told them he had some things to attend to. And McPhail thinks Sondo is the one who killed Monty and that she's tried to get away. He's sent out a description of her and they'll be sure to pick her up before long."

My words had a hollow sound because I didn't believe them myself, and Keith shook his head darkly all the way back to the office.

"I don't think so," he kept saying. "I don't think so."

Once during the afternoon I called Chris to see how she was and to ask if she'd heard from Bill. Susan answered the phone and said Chris was asleep, so I told her not to bother. But she was sure Bill hadn't been heard from there.

And then around four o'clock Owen Gardner sent for me.

There had been no news of either Sondo or Bill and

I was on edge with anxiety, and in no mood to look after the interests of Cunningham's. Though one good thing about a job is that it has to be done, and you can't give up even if you want to.

A look at Owen told me that his heart wasn't in his department either, though he made a pretense of having called me down about the window signs to advertise the style show.

"We're holding the dress rehearsal tonight, you know," he told me, "and the first show will go on tomorrow afternoon."

He might have been talking about the weather in South Africa for all the personal interest he appeared to be taking in the matter. He looked awful. There was no pinkness to his skin now. It was a gray, muddy color and his plump face seemed to have fallen into hollows and deep lines.

After a few more perfunctory remarks about the show, he stopped pretending.

"Anything new upstairs, Linell?" he asked. "Any word of Sondo?"

I shook my head. "Nothing. And did you know Bill Thorne is missing too?"

He didn't seem impressed. It was Sondo's disappearance that held his interest.

He said, "If she doesn't come back—I mean if—"

"You mean if something happened to her?" I asked directly.

There was horror in his blue eyes that were so much like Chris's. Then, with a quick rush of words, "If something's happened to Sondo, she can't go to McPhail with all that stuff about last night."

"You mean about Chris?" I asked.

"Yes. Linell, do you see what it means if they find out she was in the window? Do you see what they'll do to my poor little girl?"

188

"Perhaps they'll find the murderer before it needs to come out," I said without much hope.

If anything he turned a little grayer. "It's horrible—Chris being in the window when it happened. And keeping it all from us. I don't know what to do. I don't know how to save her."

He looked so broken and helpless that I leaned across his desk and patted his hand. "The police are sure to end it soon. There'll be a slip somewhere and they'll catch the person behind all this."

"And then what?" Owen said queerly and put his hands over his face.

He looked strange and rather terrible, sitting there with his plump hands over his face. As if he were dying a slow, torturing death inside, because of Chris, for whom he'd wanted so much, and with whom life had dealt so cruelly.

When I left his office I noticed the bustle of excitement in the department. Murderers might come and go in Cunningham's; people like Sondo Norgaard might disappear, but the models were concerned with their own lovely persons and ambitions. Tomorrow Cunningham's big semi-annual style show opened, and tonight was dress rehearsal!

When I got back to my office Keith was grinning broadly into the telephone and shouting, "Here she comes now! Wait a minute, Bill, wait a minute!"

I took the receiver from him and collapsed into my chair.

"Hello, baby," Bill's voice said. "Miss me any?"

Human nature's a funny thing. I'd missed him achingly until that very moment and then I'd have willingly killed him.

"Miss you?" I said coldly. "Why on earth should I?"

"Never mind, honey," he consoled me. "I'll take you to breakfast, too, one of these days. It's surprising the

189

things that come out over early morning coffee. Maybe you'd even discover how fond of me you are."

"Have you got Sondo with you?" I asked, ignoring that last.

"Sondo?" He sounded surprised. "Why would she be with me? What's happened to Sondo?"

"That's what we'd all like to know," I told him. "McPhail thinks she's the murderer and that she's skipped town."

I could hear Bill draw in his breath. "I saw her at the store this morning. Didn't you get the note I left on your desk?"

"Note? I didn't find any note!" I didn't want to pretend any more. The anxiety I'd felt broke through in words. "Oh, Bill, I've been so scared. I couldn't find where you'd gone, and what with Sondo's disappearing too, I thought maybe—maybe—"

Bill swore softly but distinctly. "I might have known better than to leave something like that on your desk. But you hadn't come to work yet and I thought I could be cryptic."

"What did it say, Bill?"

"Just to keep an eye on Sondo because something fishy was going on and that I was off to Mexico."

"Off to Mexico!" I gasped.

The operator came on just then and I heard the drop of coins. That was the first I realized that Bill wasn't talking to me from Chicago.

"Where are you?" I demanded.

"Listen, honey," he said, "the less you know the better. That crack about Mexico was figurative. I'm not very far away. I'll tell you just this much and you're not to repeat it to a soul. Understand?"

"I won't!" I promised fervently.

"Carla let something slip at breakfast. I don't think she meant to. She knows more about Monty than she's telling. It seems his unsavory qualities date pretty far

190

back. There was a girl he was tangled up with down in Mexico a long while ago, and there's a possibility that she's cropped up in his life again. If she has, we may have something. But the thread's a slim one, and right now I'm playing detective for all I'm worth. I'll be back in town in a day or so."

"What do you think's happened to Sondo?" I asked. "What did you mean about something fishy going on?"

"Well, she all but threw me out of the apartment this morning. She was rushing around in a feverish state and she told me to get out quick and stay out."

"You know that mannequin Tony calls 'Dolores'?" I asked. "Was that in the room?"

"Sure," Bill told me. "Dolores was there. She had on a red dress and Sondo was pulling it off in a great hurry."

"Did Sondo have on her green smock?"

Bill thought a minute. "I think she did. In fact I'm sure she did. Why?"

"Only that Hering and I found her smock stuffed in a drawer of my desk." I said. "And Dolores had her head smashed in. With a hammer."

Bill said, "Oh, God. And Sondo hasn't shown up?"

"No," I said. "Not a trace."

There was an urgency in Bill's voice that hadn't been there before. "Look, Linell, I'm coming back to town. But there isn't a train out of this dump till midnight. I'd like to phone you again before then. How late will you be home tonight?"

"I have to stay for the windows," I told him. "But I won't be any later than ten o'clock."

"Good. I'll call you at home. And, Linell—"

"Yes?"

"Honey, be careful. Don't take any chances. Promise!"

"I promise," I told him, with my heart doing a sort of highland fling in my breast because it mattered to Bill Thorne if I took chances.

191

After he'd hung up I sat there smiling idiotically at the telephone. Bill was safe. He'd had breakfast with Carla because he wanted information. He'd called me "honey," and I felt about sixteen and loved it.

I couldn't think of anything else. I couldn't think of the fact that I'd told him I'd be home by ten o'clock, which was one promise I'd not be able to keep. I wasn't even thinking about his warning me to be careful. Because how can you know when to be careful when you don't know around what corner danger lies?

CHAPTER 18

The red windows were going in.

Tony and his helpers were all at work. Sondo's backgrounds had been hung and the checkered floors were down. Tony was busy dressing the mannequin that was to take Dolores' place, though not in the dress originally intended for the window, because the belt was still missing.

It was my job to add finishing touches, to contribute any brilliant ideas I might have, and to keep in close touch with the window work in order to write better sign copy. Keith was anxious to learn something about the window decorating end and he was there too, mostly getting in the way.

Right at the moment I was wandering dreamily around the cosmetic counters selecting a few odds and ends I wanted for a window.

I don't think I was quite all there. Monty's death and Chris's grief and all the queer undercurrent things that I couldn't understand, had gone away from me for a little while. There was one spot in me that woke up every now and then and clamored, "What about Sondo?" But mostly I was moving around in a haze of happiness that was personally mine and that horror couldn't touch. I'd never felt like this about Monty. There'd always been a sure knowledge that I'd be hurt if I loved him too well. But I didn't think Bill was going to hurt me. Not for all his teasing. It was wonderful to have somebody who'd worry about me the way I'd worry about him. It was wonderful to have Bill.

So I moved around in my foolish, happy daze and I suppose it's just as well I had my little moment, because it wasn't going to come again for a while.

I picked out a small red tower of a box that held cologne, then a red and gold compact and a lipstick with a bright red container. After that I went over to costume jewelry and found a long strand of big red beads. I showed my selection to the watchman—the usual routine—and went back to Tony's window.

I hadn't been in a window since the day I'd found Monty, but I didn't think about that. I was feeling too happy about Bill for any queasiness. It didn't even matter that Tony looked like a thundercloud and snapped at everybody who spoke to him. I paid no attention, but carried my things to the right front corner of the window and knelt down to arrange them as a little eye-catching accent in red.

The heavy depression of the day had finally lifted. Rain pounded against the big plate glass window behind me. If I'd stopped to think, conditions were very much the same as they'd been on Tuesday. But my own golden haze kept me from thinking.

Under the circumstances, I don't know how it happened that what Tony was doing registered with me at all. I opened the box of cologne, tried various arrangements of compact, lipstick and coiled red beads. When I achieved a combination that satisfied me, I sat back on my heels to get the effect.

"How does it look, Tony?" I asked.

Tony's soul was still rankling under the indignities to which he'd been submitted, and he only glowered at me and went on trying to crush a hat that simply didn't belong there onto the head of a mannequin.

I said, "Heavens, Tony, stop it!"

The elaborate net and horsehair wigs they put on mannequins these days are stunning to look at, but they often drive the window decorators crazy because they lack the softness and pliability of more natural wigs.

"This hat's got to be used," Tony said grimly and made another attempt to arrange it on the stiff wig of the mannequin.

I came out of my haze enough to feel sorry for him. This series of red windows was Tony's own brain child. The whole idea was really a knockout and if it was done as Tony had planned, we all knew it would make a stir on the street. But Tony had had too much handed him and now that the opportunity to put the series across was actually in his hands, he was going to pieces with resentment over past wrongs, instead of trying to meet and fulfill his present chance.

I went over and took the hat out of his hands to have a try at it myself. But the hat and the mannequin were simply not to be mated.

"Look, Tony," I said, "this won't do at all. But what about that blond figure upstairs? You know—the one with her hair parted in the middle. I think you could use the hat on that one."

Tony said something intelligent and encouraging like "umph," and I knew he wouldn't do anything about it on his own. There was still a lot of work to be done in the windows and all his boys were occupied. Keith wouldn't know where to look if he went. I was the third hand that could be spared.

"I'll go get her," I offered. "Her coloring's good and she'll be much better all around."

"Dolores was the one," Tony said, but he didn't object to my going.

And I never thought about not going. I'd only have to carry a half figure downstairs and the figures we use now are very light. I never gave a thought to Bill's warning that I must be careful. It seems amazing that I could go blithely off on that errand, without a care in the world and all disaster forgotten. Just because the word "honey" had gone to my giddy head and I thought I carried a talisman against the powers of darkness.

The elevator man took me up and said he'd wait for me unless he got a signal. As we went past the fourth floor I caught a glimpse of bright lights from the dress section where the style show was being rehearsed.

I got out on eight and started toward window display. The passenger elevators were at the very opposite end of the floor and it was quite a hike. I didn't mind. It's a wonder I didn't skip as I went and maybe whistle a little tune. Never have I been so disgustingly carefree in my life—or with so little reason.

I went past my office, with my heels clattering gayly on the wooden floor. I hurried across the little draw-bridge effect leading into the department, without a thought for the gloomy depths of the freight elevator on one hand, or the old, open stairway on the other.

I didn't pause. I went straight on into the department. Only one or two lights were burning and I didn't bother to turn on any more. I knew my way around the manne-quin room, and I knew exactly where the half figures for the State Street windows were kept. There is something of a caste system among the mannequins. The older, cheaper figures are relegated to side windows, while State Street gets our prima donnas.

I went directly to the right cabinet and pulled open the door. Cabinets ranged as high as the partition in the mannequin room, but this was a low one, at floor level. Only a dim light came over the partition, but I knew what I was doing, and there was enough light to make out the figures in the cabinet.

I lifted out the first one, a luscious redhead, and set her to one side. Then I reached in for my blond. And knew immediately that something was wrong.

The next figure was wearing clothes, and the mannequins were never put away dressed. I put my hand on her hair and then froze where I stood. My throat was choked with horror. For one long, dreadful moment I couldn't even take my hand away.

Instead of the stiff net of a mannequin's wig, I'd touched hair that was soft and silky. Flyaway human hair that coiled about my fingers like something alive.

But not alive.

I stumbled backwards and closed the door quickly upon the thing that sat propped against the wall of the cabinet. I didn't want to look. I didn't need to look. I knew.

My surroundings began to crowd in upon me, awareness quickened within me and all my senses tensed to listening. The old trembling weakness ran through me and my knees refused to obey. But I could listen and watch.

I was aware of the lonely sound of rain whispering against the windows, and of all the dim, vast, echoing emptiness of the floor; the area of a huge city block. Far away the clang of an elevator gate told me the operator had not waited. I was the only living being on all that floor and within arm's length, separated from

196

me by only the thin wood of the cabinet door, lay something terrible and gruesome and dead.

Now, in my awareness, other shadowy figures about the room took on threatening guise and the whole place was horror-filled. But the culmination of all terror was still to come. Into that listening and waiting, came a sound that closed my throat and turned my flesh to ice. The eerie, ghostly sound of music, of a phonograph playing.

The needle had been set down in the middle of the record and the voice of the singer took up the words.

"Let the love that was once afire remain an ember;
Let it sleep like the dead desire I only remember,
When they begin the Beguine."

Sondo's favorite tune!

And then I heard the other sound. A queer slipping noise across the floor of Sondo's workroom and I knew there was something more terrifying than being alone on that floor.

I was trapped in the mannequin room. There was only one path of escape and that lay past Sondo's work-room, where that dreadful music played and something slipped and slid across the floor.

I took a step toward the door and some small object on the floor slid away from the touch of my foot with a tiny clatter. I stepped again and felt it small and hard beneath my shoe. Scarcely knowing what I did, I bent and picked the thing up, lest it clatter again, and slipped it into the pocket of my suit. And as I did so, I had the queer feeling that I was repeating a motion I had made long ago in the remote past, before I had ever reached a hand into a cabinet and touched silky hair that was no longer alive.

The weird singing went on and on and I knew I had

197

to escape before it stopped. I stole in stark terror into the corridor. The door to Sondo's room stood open, but from where I crouched I could see nothing in the dim light. I could only hear—the music, and that light, strange sound.

Was Sondo dead? Had it been Sondo in the cabinet? Or was it Sondo here in this room playing the music she loved? Was it perhaps—both?

I screamed then. I couldn't stop myself. There was no reason in me, but only a crazy tearing of sound from my throat.

"Sondo!" I cried. "Sondo! Sondo!"—as if by crying her name aloud I could make her be alive, and not a dead thing propped in a cabinet, not a ghostly dancer to that awful music.

But the music went on playing, though the other sound stopped abruptly. And nothing came out of that room. Nothing flew at my throat. No hands, living or dead, reached out for me, and I fled past the open door and ran wildly across the dark reaches of the floor toward the elevator.

There I stood shaking the gate crazily, screaming for help, until the elevator came rapidly upward, the operator round-eyed with amazement and a passenger in the car.

It was Sylvester Hering and never have I been so glad to see anyone in my life. I flung myself upon him, chattering hysterically and he simply put one big hand over my mouth and smothered me into silence.

He said, "Don't act like that! Pull yourself together. What's happened?"

I waved one hand wildly toward the display department. I could only gasp incoherently. Hering took me by the wrist and he and the elevator man started off on a run, with me trailing helplessly along. I didn't want to go back, but I was being dragged back. I couldn't even be allowed the privilege of hysteria.

The phonograph was still on in Sondo's workroom, the needle clicking round and round at the end of the record. But there was no one there, no one at all. Hering turned off the machine and turned sternly to me.

"Not here!" I told him frantically. "In the mannequin room!"

I had to go with them and show them which cabinet, but they didn't make me look. I shrank back against the door and covered my face with my hands. I couldn't shut out the things they were saying.

"It's the Norgaard woman, all right,"—that was Hering.

"Lookut what's around her neck!"—the elevator man.

I wouldn't look and I didn't know till later about the thin, braided suede belt that had cut off Sondo's life. A belt of bright scarlet—the color we were featuring for the year. The missing belt.

The next hour or so will always remain a little hazy in my mind. I've a memory of Hering trying to be in a dozen places at once. Trying to search all the enormous eighth floor, calling McPhail, giving orders that no one be allowed to leave the store.

We were all gathered in the department eventually— a more terrible repetition of the ordeal we'd gone through only a few days before. Tony and the boys from the windows, the models from the style show, Miss Babcock, Owen Gardner, and Carla Drake in her gold and white gown, looking like Juliet. Carla, protesting that she must be allowed to change her dress. Objecting and complaining till she was allowed to go and make the change. There were a few others too. Scrubwomen, anyone who had been in the store.

But out of us all there was simply nothing to be gleaned. Apparently everyone had been doing what he was supposed to do. I was the only one who admitted I'd been on the eighth floor.

After the police routine had been run through and the body examined, we found that Sondo had been dead since early morning. There was a bruise at her temple where she had been struck a blow, only enough to stun her, to make her helpless so that those cruel hands could draw the suede cord tightly about her throat. It was thought that the same hammer with which Dolores had been smashed had struck the blow.

This was more dreadful than Monty's death. That had been impersonal in the sense that it had little to do with us. Someone had hated him and killed him. But Sondo was dead, not because she was so bitterly hated, but because she had possessed knowledge that was dangerous. And that left each one of us wondering if he too knew more than it was safe to know. In a queer sort of way I suppose I'd liked Sondo. She was erratic and tempestuous and fiery, but she'd had a touch of genius and dauntless courage.

I told McPhail what I knew or surmised about the affair of the phonograph and the ring, and his men turned the place upside down searching for any trace of the stone, but if it was in the department, they didn't find it. Nor did they find anything enlightening when they later searched Sondo's apartment.

Bill had told me to keep still about everything until he saw me, so aside from what I knew about the phonograph, I said nothing. My mind was sick with speculation. If Sondo's suspicions had been correct, if she'd been following the right thread, then it was Chris she had prepared to trap. Every bit of evidence she'd uncovered had pointed to Chris. And she'd spoken as if she held back one final ace—the ring. Had that ring belonged to Chris? She'd been in the store that morning. Had she gone first to window display to try to recover her property? Had she—?

I could see the two of them with terrible clearness in my mind's eye. Chris, so big and strapping, and little wiry Sondo. A Chris capable of action when she was aroused—and not a limp crybaby.

I couldn't believe it.

Later I found myself in Hering's company at the lunch counter on the seventh floor, without quite knowing how I'd got there. Every night free coffee was served to the scrubwomen and anyone else who worked late. The free coffee business was flourishing that night.

I sat on a high stool beside Hering, while he handed me cream and sugar, and all but stirred my coffee for me. I'd gone so far along a road of horror since that moment in the mannequin room, that I couldn't feel much more about anything for the time being.

I do remember rousing myself once to inquire the time. It was after ten—which meant that I'd already missed my call from Bill. I hoped he wouldn't be too worried and that he'd come back to town tomorrow, but I couldn't even get very excited about that.

"What's the matter with your fingers?" Hering asked me, and I looked at my hand, not knowing what he meant.

Then I realized that I'd been rubbing my fingertips against my skirt, rubbing them again and again—and I knew why. It was as if I was trying to rub from them the silky feel of Sondo's dark hair.

"Why can't we do something?" I cried. "Why doesn't somebody do something?"

Others at the lunch counter glanced at me, then hastily away. For the first time I looked about to see who was there.

Carla Drake had changed to her blue suit and was wearing her usual beautiful, sad expression. I noticed with distaste that Owen Gardner had taken the stool beside her, but he was wasting no interest on her just then. He looked grayer than ever and the strong black coffee he drank seemed to be doing him little good.

201

Once Carla turned and said something to him in an undertone, but he only shook his head indifferently.

When I'd downed two cups of coffee, Hering pulled me off the stool and led me away from the counter. There was an exhibit of porch furniture not far from the lunch counters and he pushed me into a glider and sat down beside me. I was so numb and dazed that I had to be pushed and led.

"I found out about that fur coat business," he told me. "I had some time off this afternoon and I went over to the library and looked up some eastern papers around that date."

"Did you find anything that ties in?" I asked. I formed the words automatically because I couldn't really care. I didn't want to wake up and try to think. Every time I began to use my mind, I started through that experience in the mannequin room again. All I wanted now was to be numb.

"If it ties in," Hering said, "I don't know how. I took it to McPhail, but he was so bent on catching Sondo that he wasn't interested. I guess I don't look so smart from where he sits. Anyway, it seems Montgomery had a quite a finger in the style shows at that store in the east. They put 'em on like regular stage shows and he designed settings and arranged everything. Well, he had a dance team he was helping, and they went around appearing at all these shows between the dress displays. I guess he gave 'em a lot of good publicity."

I was barely listening. I'd begun to think of Bill again. Where had he gone? How long would it take him to get back to town?

"Well," Hering went on, "they had a fur coat show and some of the coats disappeared. I guess it even looked a little bad for Monty for a while. But they finally pinned it on these dancers he'd helped. They

202

arrested the man, but the woman got away. 'Luis and Lotta' they called themselves."

I came out of my apathy with a name ringing in my ears. "What did you say?"

Hering regarded me in despair, "Ain't you even been listening? I said they billed themselves as 'Luis and Lotta.'"

"Did the papers give their last name?" I asked.

"Yeah. Some sort of Spanish name. I got a picture of it in my head. Wait a minute."

"It wouldn't be Montez, would it?"

He fitted the name painstakingly to his mental photograph. "Yeah, sure. That's it. How'd you know?"

"I've probably heard it some place," I said.

Hering changed the subject. "Look, Miss Wynn, who do you think was up here playing that phonograph tonight?"

Everything came back with brutal clarity. I forgot about Lotta Montez.

"I don't think anybody ever played it, except Sondo and Carla Drake. And this time it wasn't Sondo. Carla was in the store all right, but why on earth she'd go sneaking upstairs to play that record, I don't know. And if it was Carla, why didn't she come out when I started screaming?"

"It could have been somebody who wanted you to think it was the Drake woman," Hering said.

"But why? It doesn't make any sense. And who would know I was there and take all the trouble to go up and scare me? Whoever it was had to walk up. The elevator man said he didn't take anyone but me to the eighth floor around that time."

Hering's melancholy deepened. "There's a lot that doesn't make sense till you get hold of a key. What did Sondo take the dress off that dummy for? And who smashed its head in?"

We were on the old treadmill of speculation again.

Tomorrow Bill would be back in town. Tomorrow I'd get to tell him everything I knew. And with whatever it was he had found out, perhaps something would make sense and we could go to McPhail with some concrete evidence that wouldn't hurt the wrong person.

One of McPhail's men came toward me "Hey! I been looking all over for you. You're wanted upstairs, Miss Wynn."

Hering took me up and I went into Monty's office, where McPhail was waiting for me. The department was bright now, with lights burning everywhere, and noisy enough to shut out the rain beating against the window panes. I knew the minute I sat down in the chair opposite McPhail, that something new had come up.

I found out almost at once. Although the fingerprints on the hammer had been badly smudged, they'd made out one clear thumb mark. It belonged to Bill Thorne.

CHAPTER 19

I forgot all other horror in this shock. I knew it was all right. It had to be. But it looked bad for Bill.

I told McPhail about the phone call I'd had from him late that afternoon and the detective pounced on the information eagerly.

"Where'd he call from? Where is he now?"

"I don't know," I said helplessly. "He didn't tell me."

McPhail didn't believe a word and I became a little frantic trying to convince him.

Across the room Hering was playing with the pine spray again, while he listened. He gave the plunger a little push and the office began to smell of Christmas trees. McPhail sneezed and barked at him.

"Get the damn' thing outta here!"

Hering took it away sheepishly and came back.

I explained to McPhail that Bill was on the track of something and that he'd thought it safer if I didn't know too much about it. I said he'd told me about seeing Sondo and that he'd sounded concerned when I'd told him Dolores had been smashed with a hammer.

"Sure," McPhail said, "he probably remembered his prints were on that hammer."

"He didn't say anything about the hammer," I told him. "He just sounded shocked and said he'd come back to town right away. There wasn't a train until midnight and he was going to call me again at ten o'clock. Only of course I wasn't home."

At the back of my mind I was thinking that all he'd need to know to settle us nicely was the part Bill and I had played in the discovery of Monty's body. Why on earth had Bill had to touch that hammer when he'd been in Sondo's workroom that morning?

The palms of my hands had broken into a cold sweat and I pulled a handkerchief from my pocket to dry them. Of all the times in the world to pull out a handkerchief, I had to pick the worst moment.

Something which had been caught in the folds flew across the room with a little clatter. Hering leaned down and picked it up. But he didn't hand it back to me. He studied it for a moment thoughtfully and then put it down on the desk in front of McPhail without a word.

His action was so odd that I leaned over to see what

it was. McPhail picked the object up in his fingers and turned it about. It was a large carnelian stone, deep red and highly polished, set in an oval of antique gold, evidently broken loose from the prongs of a ring. About a third of the stone had cracked off and the mounting was visible underneath.

McPhail spoke curtly over his shoulder and someone brought an envelope and laid it before him. He took out the ring that had been found clutched in Monty's hand and fitted the stone to it. The match was perfect. He looked at me, his eyes cold and deadly.

"Well?" he said.

I felt as if a net were being pulled in around me and I was suddenly too weary to fight the entangling mesh.

I don't know where it came from," I said. "I've never seen it before."

Someone was trying to incriminate me. That smock stuffed in my desk. And now the stone to the ring in my pocket. Who could hate me like that?

Hering's eyes were on me. "You try hard to think, Miss Wynn. You must have got that somewhere. Can't you remember anything about it?"

I put my fingers over my eyes and thought of everything I could remember handling that night in my work in the window. I went again through all the steps I'd taken on my way upstairs to the mannequin room, thought through the whole experience. And suddenly I had it.

No one had put that stone in my pocket. I'd put it there myself. I looked up at McPhail triumphantly.

"I remember now! When I was in the mannequin room. Right after—right after I found her. My foot kicked something on the floor and then I stepped on it. I picked it up and put it in my pocket so I couldn't kick it again. I didn't look at it or think about it, but it must have been the stone."

McPhail regarded me with open disbelief in those

cold eyes. "Pretty smooth with your stories, aren't you? First you find a piece in the window and then you lose it. Now you got the other piece. Come clean now— where did you get it? Why was it in your pocket? What were you going to do with it?"

He took me over the whole thing again and again, until I felt so weary that I wanted to give up. It was almost like the horrid fascination of looking down a well. I knew it was the end of me if I jumped, but I was tempted to go plunging down—to cry that of course I'd murdered Sondo, that the ring was mine, anything to get away from those coldly cruel eyes watching me. Somehow I clung to a shred of sanity because I knew I had to help Bill.

Hering finally broke the tension. He picked up the stone again.

"You know," he said, "I've seen this somewhere before."

McPhail turned. "Where?"

"I don't know exactly." Hering looked uncomfortable. "It's just that I got a picture of it in my head. And when I get a picture like that I know—"

"You and your pictures!" McPhail snapped. "If you've seen it before you'd better remember where."

Hering closed his eyes and went into one of his trances.

"It was on a hand," he produced at last.

"Well now," McPhail said heavily, "ain't that just too sweet! On a hand he says. You wouldn't by any chance know whose hand, I suppose?"

"Nope," Hering shook his head. "That ain't in the picture. But it was a woman's hand. With red nails."

McPhail turned his back in disgust and started over again on me. The little interlude had restored my balance to some extent, and I could go over the ground again without giving way.

Hering was still playing with the parts of the ring

and suddenly he exclaimed and stepped forward to show something to McPhail. There was a tiny hinge in the gold oval that held the stone and when he pressed above the hinge with his nail the stone tilted up to show a hollow beneath. It was a space in which a lock of hair, or a picture, or some such sentimental treasure might have been kept. There was nothing in it now.

McPhail glared at me. "I suppose you don't know what was kept in that ring?"

"Of course I don't," I said. "I've told you I've never seen the thing before."

He finally let me go, but only, I think, because he thought I might lead them to Bill. From that moment on I was followed every time I left the store.

There wasn't anyone to take me home this time and I have no clear memory of going out and catching a bus. I suppose I must have, because I turned up eventually at my own door.

Helena was sitting up in bed, reading a magazine. and she looked up anxiously as I came in.

"Linell! I've been so worried. You've never come home this late from the store."

I went over and sat limply down on her bed. "Sondo's dead. Murdered, just like Monty. I found her. I—I went up to the mannequin room for a figure. And when I put my hand into a cabinet I touched her hair and—"

Helena's magazine slid off on the floor with a ruffling of pages. She recovered herself as I talked, but there was a gray look about her mouth. "I knew it," she cried. "That party. I knew something awful would come of it. A thing like that gets out of hand."

I told her about that earlier attack upon me in the office and it was pleasant to have her soothe and cluck over me. But still I watched her a little uneasily. I hadn't seen her alone since the night before when she'd refused to tell me about Lotta Montez, and it seemed to me that Helena was looming up more and more as a mystery woman.

"I know about Lotta Montez," I said, when we'd exhausted the subject of Sondo's murder.

"About her?" The words were scarcely more than a whisper.

"Yes. That she was mixed up in that fur coat theft in the east. She and her dancing partner."

I watched her warily. Her expression was guarded and I couldn't tell how my news had hit her.

Lotta Montez. A stage name certainly. But who was the real woman behind the name? Why had Helena burned that note?

She leaned forward and put her hands on my shoulders, turned me so that I faced her.

"You're young. Linell," she said. "Only a few years older than Chris. Too young, perhaps, to have learned tolerance."

"Tolerance!" I cried. "How can you talk about tolerance when two people have been murdered?"

"Listen to me," she pleaded. "I'm not talking about murder. I'm talking about someone who is innocent and mustn't be brought into this."

I had to believe in her sincerity. I might not understand her motives, but I couldn't doubt that she was honest in what she was saying.

"There's nothing I can do anyway," I told her. "Hering looked up the fur theft and he put the whole thing in McPhail's hands. But right now McPhail is busy suspecting Bill Thorne."

"Bill!" Helena's tone was incredulous. Then she remembered. "He phoned you tonight. I told him you were working late and that everything was all right. He said he'd be seeing you and hung up."

That was a help. Not that I blamed Helena, since she hadn't known what was happening at the store. But if Bill took her at her word, he might not even come home tomorrow. And he had to come home. Quickly. In order to defend himself.

I gave Helena a further account of the evening while I was getting ready for bed, and the strangeness between us began to wear off. After all, Helena had as much right to shield someone if she chose, as Bill had to shield me, or I him. Probably none of us was obscuring the real issue. I couldn't help wondering who it was Helena was shielding. And why?

It took me a long time to get to sleep and then I had a queer dream. I was back in my office at Cunningham's and that missing picture was again in place on the wall. I *knew* it was there. But it was in place only so long as I had my back to it. The moment I started turning around, the spot on the wall was empty again. I kept trying and trying to sneak up on that picture and catch it in place—but always it just managed to elude me.

I woke up limp with fatigue, but came alive the moment I got out of bed. This was to be a day of action. If Bill wasn't to be arrested the moment he set foot back in town, somebody had to do something. And I knew one thing I was going to do—about that missing picture from the wall of my office.

I think I was a little shocked when I walked over from Michigan and found Cunningham's State Street windows alive with color and light. The curtains had been opened and the red windows were on display.

There were my signs, lettered in red on creamy paper. "Red is the Color of the Year!" with a crimson exclamation point. And Sondo's backgrounds bright and spectacular—when Sondo herself lay so tragically dead.

I had forgotten all about the windows from the time I'd found Sondo. But others had been more responsible than I. Sometime, between all the police procedure, Tony had managed to get his windows done. They were every bit as striking and effective as we'd hoped and I felt sick at heart to think Sondo couldn't see them. For all her scrapping with Tony, she'd loved her work and had taken a real pride in the things she did for the windows.

The store was in a state of confusion. The news of the second murder was out and I think every employee in Cunningham's had the jitters. The women, particularly, went to the locker rooms and upper floors in groups of two or three and during the day there were several resignations. Policemen were posted at every entrance and reporters lurked in every corner. Not even Mr. Cunningham could stem the tide now.

The day had a remorseless tempo. One thing led to another so swiftly that I seemed to be out of breath most of the time.

Keith started things off. He was already in the office when I arrived, and I knew by his face that he'd heard.

"I told you it would be like that," he said. "Something's loose now and it can't be stopped unless it's caught and bound. I told you it wasn't safe to know too much. Remember? So I'm going to be rid of what I know."

"What do you know, Keith?" I asked evenly.

His eyes were dark and haunted in his yellowish face. "It's all right to tell you now," he said, "because then I'm going over to tell McPhail. Remember Tuesday afternoon—before Mr. Montgomery was murdered—when you gave me those signs to take down to lingerie?"

I nodded.

"Well, I didn't leave the store right away afterward. I was going down to the basement to look at some shirts they had on sale. I took the basement stairs down from the main floor. The stairs at the front of the store. You know where they come in?"

I knew perfectly well. That stairway, with its head close to window five, cut down just below the front windows.

He saw my quickening of interest. "Just as I was starting down the stairs I heard somebody talking in the window. Somebody talking loud and angry. I'm pretty sure it was Mr. Montgomery, and I heard part of what he said."

I leaned forward. This was the thing Chris wouldn't tell.

"What did you hear?"

"He was swearing some. And then he said, 'You get out of here and get out fast. I'm sick of the whole tribe of Gardners and you're the worst of the lot.' "

My eyes were on Keith, but I didn't really see him. Certain little pieces of a puzzle were beginning to fall into place. But my mind shrank from accepting the pattern they presented. Monty might have addressed those words to Chris, though that seemed unlikely, if her story of hiding in the window during Monty's tirade was true. The other person to whom he might have been speaking was Owen Gardner.

Had Owen gone down earlier to see Monty? And then gone down again to discover the body? It was not only possible, but suddenly very likely. If it had been Owen in the window, then many things were explained. Chris's hysteria, her lack of hatred for the murderer.

That would be why she'd kept her presence in the window secret; why she refused to tell what she had heard. It explained Owen's behavior too. Torn between the necessity to save himself, the love for his daughter, and the need to keep her from being involved. Might it not even explain Sondo's death?

Owen, watching Sondo as she tortured Chris and threatened to involve her. It all dovetailed perfectly. The only trouble was that I had pieces left over. I had Lotta Montez, and Helena shielding someone, and a carnelian ring, and a mannequin with a smashed head.

Perhaps those things were really extra. Perhaps they

fitted no more than that stone in my pocket, or Bill's thumb print on the hammer.

Keith was watching the expressions that crossed my face.

"I've been afraid," he said. "But I'm not afraid any more. If I wait, maybe I'll be the next one after Sondo. So I'd better go talk to McPhail."

"Yes," I said, "you'd better go talk to McPhail."

He went off and I phoned Universal Arts to see if there'd been any word of Bill. But nobody had heard from him since the day before.

I took care of a few urgent matters on my desk and then put on my hat and coat. One last look at the vacant spot on my wall told me nothing, but I knew now what I might be able to do about it.

The public library was only a short walk and I went straight up to the periodical room and explained to the attendant what I wanted. I sat down at a table with an armful of magazines and started going through them methodically.

These were the magazines from which Keith and I had cut pictures to paste on the walls of my office. We'd chosen old ones to cut up, of course, so if I went back a few months before the time we'd papered the office, I ought to find a copy of the picture that had been torn from my wall.

I knew I was on familiar ground. Many of the pictures I had pasted on the office walls looked up at me from those pages. But though I went through the magazines carefully, with my hopes high at first, and then gradually dying, I found no picture which struck a responsive chord in my memory.

Just as I was about to give up, I was rewarded—not by finding the picture, but by discovering one I'd never seen before.

It was a beautiful photograph done in full color—rich golds and reds and black. A man with a young, narrow,

Spanish face smiling down at the woman in his arms. A woman in a dance frock of gold and red, and high-heeled gold sandals. Her head was tipped back to look up into his eyes and her glossy black hair swung to her shoulders.

My eyes dropped to the caption below the picture—"The dance team of Luis and Lotta, which has been making such a stir at style shows lately"—and then back to the profile of the woman.

I knew her in spite of the dark hair. Lotta. Shortened from *Car*lotta? Eventually Carla? There was no doubt about it. Lotta Montez was Carla Drake.

I sat back, wondering where the path led to now. Carla Drake, was Lotta Montez, and whose dancing partner had been sent to jail in connection with a fur theft at a store where Michael Montgomery had worked. Had she loved that much younger man in the photograph? Was he the "lost" husband Mrs. Babcock had mentioned? And what had become of him in the end? Hering had said that he'd been arrested. He'd said nothing of trial or conviction. But he'd said something else too—that the woman had got away.

I carried the magazines to the desk and headed for Cunningham's as fast As I could go. I left the elevator at the fourth floor.

Miss Babcock greeted me with a frantic wave of her hands. "The police are questioning Mr. Gardner again. And the style show's scheduled to go on at two this afternoon. What am I to do?"

So Keith had had his interview with McPhail.

"I want to see Miss Drake," I said. "Right away."

Miss Babcock went on for five minutes about Owen, the style show and the inconvenience of murders in general.

Then she said, "Oh, Miss Drake won't be down till later. She's not modeling this morning."

I was just as glad. There was something I wanted to see before I faced Carla.

"Do you mind if I have a look at that white dress she's wearing in the show?" I asked Miss Babcock.

The buyer motioned absently toward the racks where the style show dresses hung. I found Carla's lovely Juliet frock without any difficulty and lifted the soft material in my hands.

I could remember the tears in Carla's eyes when I'd told her how beautiful she looked. I could remember the graceful way she'd lifted the skirt. And the way she'd shied away from the slightest mention of dancing.

I ran the edge of the hem through my hands. There was a gray tracing of grime along the edge of the skirt. Grime never picked up from the soft, well-cleaned carpets of the dress section. I went back to speak to Babcock.

"Do you happen to remember where Miss Drake was during the rehearsal last evening?" I asked.

"Why—she was here, of course. Where else would she be?"

"But there were so many models. Are you sure? Would there have been any time when she could have slipped away for fifteen or twenty minutes?"

Miss Babcock considered. "Well, if it comes to that, I don't suppose there was one of us who was in plain sight all the time. Not even Mr. Gardner. Wait!" Something like a glitter came into her eyes and she put an excited hand on my arm. "There *was* a time. We had to wait for her once. In fact we ran some of the other girls through ahead. But she showed up right afterwards. She said she'd got bored and was looking around the department. It was strictly against rules for her to be out of the dressing rooms and I was very annoyed. You—you don't think Miss Drake has anything to do with—with all this?"

215

She looked disgustingly eager and I had no intention of satisfying her curiosity.

I said, "Oh, no. Certainly not," and left before she could stop me.

Now I was pretty sure about the mysterious hand that had played the phonograph last night. And where did it get me? If Sondo had been murdered around that time—but she hadn't. She'd been dead since early morning.

I went upstairs to my office and found Bill tilted back in my chair.

CHAPTER 20

"Bill!" I cried. "Oh, Bill, I'm so glad to see you!"

He nodded approvingly. "Now that's the sort of heartfelt greeting I like from my women. Maybe you'll appreciate me more when I'm around after this."

I didn't bother to take him down. I could do that later on.

"Bill, so many awful things have happened. Have you heard about Sondo?"

He dropped his joking manner and I saw how tired he looked, saw the anxiety in his eyes. He got up and pushed me gently down in my chair.

"Yes," he said, "I know. I've had a talk with Hering. I wish I'd been here. I wish you hadn't had to go through all that alone."

I remembered suddenly. "But, Bill, how did you get here without being arrested? I thought McPhail—"

"McPhail isn't interested in me just now. He's got his hands full. Keith told him what he'd heard in the window and he's having it out with Gardner and Chris."

I dropped wearily down in my chair. "I wonder if it's really over? Oh, I'd hate it to be Owen!"

"There's no telling," Bill said.

"What happened yesterday?" I asked him. "I mean when you went up to see Sondo. How did your fingerprints get on that hammer?"

He was airy about his explanation, but anxiety was still there.

"It's simple enough. The hammer was on a high shelf and she asked me to hand it to her. I don't know what she wanted it for—she wasn't hammering anything. I got the impression that she was setting the stage for something and that she wanted me out of the way in a hurry."

"She must have set it all right," I said. "When Mc-Phail gets through with Owen, you're going to have a lovely time explaining those fingerprints."

Bill shrugged.

"What about your trip?" I asked. "Did you find out anything?"

He shook his head. "I was on the trail of something, but it fizzled out. Carla knows more about Monty than she's telling. She almost gave something away and then caught herself up. She said it all went back to the time when Monty worked at a department store in a city in Missouri. There was some sort of scandal and he ran off to Mexico with the woman. So I followed the thread back to that store. But it must have been eighteen years ago, or more, and I wasn't able to pick up the last strands. Maybe if I'd taken more time—but I couldn't tell what you'd be getting into while I was gone, so—"

I broke in. "Maybe Carla's smarter than you think. I rather suspect she's had a little experience twisting men around her fingers. And you probably twist as well as the next one."

Bill's eyebrows went up in an amused quirk. "Meaning?"

"Meaning that she tossed you a few red herrings and you were gullible enough to bite. What better way to get you off the real track than by sending you down a side trail?"

"How can you love me and have such a poor opinion of my intelligence?"

I ignored that. "I've been following a few threads myself. I know a lot more about Carla than you do, and I didn't have to take her to breakfast to find out."

He grinned at me, but I went ahead and told him about my discovery at the library. About Carla being Lotta Montez. About her knowing Monty in the East and being mixed up in that theft of fur coats. That she was probably still wanted by the police. And about that tracing of grime on the hem of her white dress.

He let out a low whistle. "Next time, baby, I'll stay home and let you do the sleuthing."

There was more evidence against either Chris or Owen than there was against Carla. Or against Bill and me for that matter. There was, however, a possible motive in the light of what I'd found out. If Carla was wanted by the police and Monty knew it—? But then why would she come to the very store where he worked? If that had been accidental, why had she stayed? And what connection had she with the ring?

I began to feel more and more that the key to the puzzle of Carla lay in Helena Farnham's hands. If Helena could be made to talk! If she'd only tell us what really happened the day Carla exchanged the pin! Helena had seen something, knew something.

I picked up the phone and called the costume jewelry section. Helena was busy with a customer and I had to wait a moment. When she answered I wasted no time.

"You're having lunch with me," I told her. "What time do you go?"

"More questions?" she said. "It isn't any use, Linell."

"Oh, yes it is!" I told her. "It's got to be. Do you know what's happening up here? Do you know that McPhail is about ready to arrest Owen Gardner and that Chris is badly mixed in?"

There was silence at the other end of the wire and I knew I'd surprised her. I pushed my advantage hastily.

"None of us thinks Chris or Owen is guilty, but Bill and I come next on the list. So don't you think you'd better tell me what you know?"

Again silence. Then she said, "Linell, I honestly don't think it will help, but if you want the story, I'll give it to you."

I arranged to meet her and hung up, to face Bill triumphantly. "Now we're getting somewhere!"

"Maybe," he said.

I told him everything else I could think of, the things I'd had no opportunity to tell him before. About the queer way I'd found the stone to the ring, for one thing.

"Sondo must have had it in her possession," Bill said. "She could have dropped it on the floor of the mannequin room herself. Or it might have fallen out of her clothes when the murderer dragged her body in there and hid it in the cabinet."

I shivered. Every time the thought of those moments in the mannequin room came back to me I broke out in goose flesh.

Bill saw the look on my face and went on quickly in a matter-of-fact voice. "Or the murderer might have recovered the stone and dropped it himself."

"Or herself," I said.

Bill stood up just as Keith and Hering came into the room. Keith was yellower than ever, yet he looked relieved. As if he felt safer and more at ease with his conscience.

Hering said, "McPhail wants you, Thorne," and motioned with his thumb toward the display department.

Bill leaned over and gave my cheek a sharp pat. "If I don't come back, remember I love you."

"I'll write you letters in jail and come to the trial," I promised, but I didn't feel very funny.

Hering looked after him with his usual melancholy. "Nice kid. But he ought to lay off hammers."

"Don't be silly!" I snapped. "Sondo asked him to hand it to her. And he did. That's all there was to it."

Hering didn't say anything and I had a clairvoyant glimpse of what he might be thinking. A ridiculous picture of Bill getting the hammer down for Sondo, thumping her over the head with it and then calmly strangling her with the suede belt.

"Detectives are so stupid!" I told him. "It would take a crazy person to go smashing up that mannequin. To say nothing of taking off Sondo's smock and stuffing it in my desk. If you think Bill did any of that, you're crazy."

"Did I say anything, Miss Wynn?" Hering asked. "And you know, maybe we detectives wouldn't look stupid if we could get any co-operation out of people like you and Bill Thorne. Do you think it was nice not telling about that party at the Norgaard girl's apartment?"

"Oh, so you know about that?" I said.

"I told them," Keith broke in, looking at me defiantly. "I told them the whole thing."

"Now if I could just remember where I saw that ring," Hering complained.

He went off without remembering and left Keith and

me to work—or pretend to—in a long uncomfortable silence. I think we were alone for all of twenty minutes and then Carla Drake came gliding gently into my office to sit down in the chair opposite me.

"Miss Babcock said you were down looking for me," she announced, "so I thought I'd better come up and see what you wanted."

I promptly sent Keith on an errand, though I knew he didn't want to go. Then I faced Carla squarely, hoping that my manner was as cool as hers.

"Why did you go upstairs to play that phonograph last night?" I asked.

She smiled very sadly and sweetly. "It was wrong of me, wasn't it? But I was feeling so unhappy and I thought perhaps music—"

"You must have walked up four flights of stairs. Does music mean that much to you?"

She made an expressive gesture with her graceful, dancer's hands. "Music means everything to me. It is all I have left."

"But still the elevator is easier," I pointed out. "And more logical."

She was undisturbed and wearing her usual what-will-come-will-come manner. "Not when one is breaking the rules. I had no right to go about the store in that expensive frock."

"You *were* dancing, weren't you? You were up in that lonely place dancing. Why?"

For the first time she looked shaken. "It was the white frock. It was made for dancing. And that music was upstairs waiting—"

I had a sudden inspiration. *"Begin the Beguine—* Luis and Lotta used to dance to that, didn't they?"

She crossed her arms over her breast and drew her hands upward along them, with the gesture of one who is desperately cold. But she showed no surprise.

"Yes," she said. "We used to dance to that."

And the *Carioca* too, I thought. That explained her tears that night at Sondo's when Bill was playing.

"But you frightened me so," I protested. "I've never gone to pieces before the way I did when I heard that music. Carla, it was almost as if Sondo were in there playing it. Why didn't you come out when I screamed?"

She looked at me with lovely, haunted eyes. "I was afraid, too. I didn't know who it was, or what could have happened. And I—didn't want to be found there —dancing."

What was she hiding? Had she been frightened because she didn't know—or because she knew very well the thing that had caused my fright?

"Why didn't you want to be found dancing?" I persisted. "Was it because Lotta Montez is still wanted by the police?"

Her hands closed upon her own shoulders, her arms shielding her body as if from a blow. She made no effort to deny my words.

"Are you going to tell them?" she asked. "Are you going to turn me over to McPhail?"

She had that Lost Lady look in her eyes again, but this time I believed in it and I couldn't help being touched.

"I don't know," I said. "Perhaps I won't have to. I suppose it's enough that your husband is in jail, so—"

"My husband is not in jail," she said with quiet dignity. "My husband is dead."

Somehow I was completely taken aback and I don't know how I'd have answered her. As it happened I was saved by an interruption, because through the door of my office walked one the strangest figures I'd ever seen in my life.

We pass them sometimes on the street, characters so weirdly dressed, so queer in manner that we feel they belong only on a stage. And yet when we see them in a play we call them exaggerated and unreal.

This woman was real enough, for all her get-up. She

was short and broad, with an ancient, seamed face and black, wicked little eyes like coals set in yellow leather. She was dressed in a conglomeration that might have been the choice of a rag-picker's dream. Feathers and beads, bits of satin and silk, long faded in hue and set together in a crazy patchwork design.

"You're Miss Wynn, ain't you?" she said in a cracked voice. "I got a letter for you."

She came in, smelling to high heaven of an assortment of odors I made no attempt to analyze, and handed me a long envelope. My name was written across it plainly in black ink, the store's name, and the floor of my office.

I ripped the envelope open. There were two folded sheets of paper inside and as I pulled them out, something flew across the desk and dropped in front of Carla. It was a picture. A small snapshot cut in a tiny oval.

Carla picked it up to hand it to me, but something about it must have caught her eye for she looked at it a moment, then handed it across without a word. The expression on her face, though fleeting, was an odd one, and I took the picture quickly and looked at it.

Carla said, "I must hurry before it's time for the style show," and went out, circling my peculiar visitor by a wide margin. I scarcely noted her going, so puzzled was I by the snapshot in my hand.

It was only a tiny section of the original picture, showing the head and shoulders of a girl and a man wearing fancy dress—the man with a bullfighter's hat and an embroidered cape about his shoulders, the girl in a lace mantilla and Spanish shawl. They were both young, as nearly as I could tell, though the man's face was blurred a little. At that, it looked faintly familiar. I recognized the girl at once. It was Chris Montgomery.

I looked up at my visitor. "Who sent you?"

"My best friend," she said, preening a little. "My very best friend. Your friend too."

She paused and looked suspiciously about the office as if someone might be hiding there.

"Ain't no policemen in here, is there?"

"No," I said, "no policemen. Who sent you?"

She bent toward me and I held my breath against the aroma of gin, garlic and no baths.

"Sondo," she whispered. "Sondo Norgaard."

I'll confess that a cold finger went down my spine. My visitor managed to smile evilly and squeeze out a few tears at the same time.

"I'm Mrs. Dunlop," she confessed. "I got a room down in the basement near Sondo's rooms. And me and her was best friends. She never trusted nobody but me. And now she's gone."

I could get something of the picture. Sondo with her warped sense of humor, her derision for most of humanity. How like her to bestow a friendship of sorts on this bit of human wreckage.

"Well," she said, before I could recover from my surprise, "I got to be running along. Cynthia'll be waiting for me. Cynthia's my cat, you know. Sondo gave her to me. Poor Sondo. She was afraid all along something would happen to her. That's why she give me that letter to bring you, just in case."

She shook her assorted feathers and patches into place and departed with a coy wave of her hand for me. I went over and opened the window wide and then sat down to read the letter.

It was from Sondo, all right, and it gave me an eerie feeling to be sitting there reading words that she had written.

Dear Linell:

I'm writing this at my table before the fire just after you've all left. Carla is curled up on the studio couch watching me. I think she dislikes me as

224

much as the rest of you do. But there's no really telling with Carla.

You were all against me tonight for what I did to Chris. But in the long run you'll know I was right. And if by that time I'm not there to speak for myself, perhaps you'll forgive me. Not that I care whether you do or not. I only hope I'll be there to laugh.

Poor Chris! Poor sweet, helpless Chris! I could see it in your faces tonight—what you were thinking. But it's your sweet Chris who murdered Michael Montgomery.

Of course I loved him. Why wouldn't I? If I'd been a man I'd have wanted to be like him. Cold and ruthless and without mercy. That way you never get hurt yourself. But warm, too, with a fire that would draw women always. It drew even me, though I must scarcely seem a woman in your eyes. And I think in his way Monty was fonder of me than of all the rest. Because I understood him. I understood him and I loved him. The others only loved.

You know that queer Mexican desert thing I painted? I made a joke about that. I told him it was a picture of his soul. He got a kick out of what I said. But he didn't mind. He was flattered. I gave it to him and after he'd used it in a window at the store, he hung it in the place of honor in his apartment. He said he had a sentimental attachment for Mexico and this picture pleased him a lot.

But that isn't what I want to write about. Now that Monty's gone, I don't care what happens to me. I only want to avenge his death. I want to see Chris crawling on her knees to me for mercy—so that I can show her no more mercy than she showed him. Because it *is* Chris. I have the truth.

You and Bill were pretty smart about that pho-

225

nograph, but not smart enough. I found the stone from the ring, and there was a picture hidden beneath the stone. Chris's picture. That's why she was afraid to have it found. That's why she went out to Universal to try to recover it. Because it identified her so surely. I hoped she'd break down tonight and confess. But since she wouldn't I'm saving the stone for the ace I mean to play tomorrow.

Not the picture though. The picture goes in the envelope with this letter to you. I'm too wise for her. Even if she should succeed in what I think she'll try—still this picture will go to you and she will be caught.

But tomorrow I'll set a trap for her. A very dramatic little trap. And this is how it will go. I had one of the boys bring Tony's Dolores into my workroom this afternoon, because I thought I might need her tomorrow. Everyone will come down late in the morning, so I'll have the department to myself. And I'll dress Dolores in my smock, with my yellow handkerchief about her head. Then I'll sit her on the stool at my drawing table with her back to the door. I'll fix the lighting so it won't be too bright and she'll fool anyone intent on quick action into thinking it is Sondo Norgaard. Then I'll put the stone from the ring in plain sight on the drawing table, and I'll lay a hammer down handily near the door.

When my trap is baited, I'll hide behind a screen to wait for her to come. I'm not afraid. She's a coward at heart, really. And when she's struck at the mannequin, thinking it is me, she'll have so betrayed herself that she won't be able to do anything but collapse. I'll make her crawl then, before I turn her over to the police.

However, I know that human plans are fallible,

226

so I'm taking precautions. This picture and letter go into the hands of the delectable Mrs. Dunlop, and if anything goes wrong, they go into your hands.

Thanks, Linell.

Yours,

Sondo.

I sat there for a while with the letter before me and the cold lake breeze pouring in the window. I was too far away to feel it. I was seeing now exactly what must have happened. The trap being sprung—but not by Chris. By someone who was more of a match for Sondo than Chris would have been. A match in wits and will, not necessarily brawn.

Then the mannequin smashed and the ruse discovered. And Sondo stepping recklessly out from behind her screen, certain she could deal with the situation herself. Then what? The murderer standing there, hammer in hand, really caught—and this time attacking the flesh and blood Sondo. And when she'd dropped, unconscious from the blow, snatching up the first thing near at hand—that belt of braided suede?

But there was still the picture to leave me uncertain. Was this really such evidence as Sondo had supposed? I looked at it again, recognizing Chris's face, wondering about the identity of the man. If only his face were clearer! It looked familiar, yet not familiar.

I tried to recall the wording of that other note—the one signed "E," in which the ring had been mentioned. I tried to remember how Chris had looked when she read it. Had there been uneasiness, fear in her eyes? Could she have been the one, after all, to slip that note from my purse? I couldn't believe that Chris was guilty and I knew I couldn't take that picture and letter and lay her safety so surely in McPhail's hands. I got up to close the window and then hid the envelope containing both letter and picture between the pages of a magazine at the bottom of the pile on my window ledge.

Keith came back a few moments later and when I glanced at my watch I found it was almost time for my meeting with Helena. I'd have liked to see Bill again before I went, but he was evidently still busy with McPhail. My news would have to wait till later.

I found Helena in a more submissive mood than she'd been in for some time. The moment we'd ordered our lunch I opened my attack.

"I know just enough," I said, "so that you might as well tell me the rest. I know Lotta Montez is Carla Drake. I know about the fur theft and that she's wanted by the police. Now you can tell me what really happened down at the costume jewelry counter last Tuesday. Did you see her come out of the window?"

Helena didn't look at me. "No," she said in a low voice. "No, I didn't."

"But there's something," I said. "That evening right after Monty was killed, when we were all back at the apartment. I saw you looking at that scratch on your hand in an odd way. As if you'd just thought of something."

"I had," she admitted. "I hadn't remembered about Carla exchanging the pin until that moment. It struck me suddenly. But everything happened exactly as I've told you. I was around on the other side of the counter when she came down. One of the girls told me she was waiting for me and I went over to the end of the counter near the window, where she was. And while we were handling the pins my hand was scratched."

"But I still don't understand why you should have had that odd look on your face."

Helena shrugged. "It was because I knew she had a motive, I suppose. And at the time I couldn't help wondering."

"About that motive," I said. "Was it because Monty knew she was wanted by the police?"

"More than that. She was crazy about her husband. He was years younger than she, but they were very happy together. Monty sent him to jail. He was guilty all right. When Monty tried to connect Carla, Luis confessed and exonerated her."

"How did he die?"

"He hanged himself," Helena said. "While he was in jail. The police still thought Carla was in on the affair and they were looking for her. But she got away. You can understand her bitterness toward Monty. Luis was the emotional type who felt the disgrace was too much to bear. Particularly in Carla's eyes, because she hadn't known anything about what he was doing. But there was one thing, according to Carla, that never came out in the affair."

"What was that?"

Helena looked a little grim. "Carla claims it was Monty who should have been in jail. She says it was he who engineered the whole thing and that she had proof. Luis was weak and a tool in Monty's hands."

I didn't say anything for a few moments. I could understand many things now. Carla, mourning the death of her young husband, holding to her grief and pain. Some women get a perverse pleasure in the indulgence of pain. That accounted for the way music acted on her. It even made reasonable the temptation that had made her go upstairs the night before, to dance alone to the melancholy music of the *Beguine*.

And the motive it gave her!

"Then she must have come to Cunningham's deliberately," I said. "She must have followed Monty here."

Helena nodded. "She did. She wanted evidence that would trap him and put him behind bars where he belonged. When she found out how Owen Gardner disliked him, she told him the whole thing and the two of them set about the business of trapping Monty. That, you see, was why Monty married Chris."

I echoed her words stupidly. "Why Monty married Chris?"

"Yes. In an effort to save himself. I don't know all the details, but I believe Gardner threatened him with exposure. He was worried about Chris's infatuation."

I was beginning to see the whole thing. "So Monty, with his usual audacity, simply crossed Owen up by marrying his daughter and tying his hands?"

"Something of the sort," Helena said. "He knew her father would never expose him after the marriage."

"But how did he think he could keep Carla still?"

"By threatening that if he went to jail, he'd take her back with him. She's been desperately afraid of that."

"I wish you'd told me all this before," I said. "I didn't even know you were well acquainted with Carla."

"You can see what would happen if all this went to the police," Helena pointed out. "Carla's suffered enough at Monty's hands as it is."

I could see that. I could almost sympathize with her if she'd been driven to killing Monty. He'd been completely rotten. It nauseated me to think I'd ever imagined myself in love with him. And there might be others. Though if Carla had murdered Sondo, why hadn't she done it the night before when she'd slept in her apartment? She'd had the perfect opportunity then. Or would the evidence have pointed too surely to her in that case? The more I tried to analyze, the more confused I became.

We left the restaurant and returned to the store. Helena went on toward her department, and as I crossed the middle aisle on the main floor, I noticed two women walking ahead of me. One of them was Carla, the other Susan Gardner.

Now there was something to ponder!

CHAPTER 21

When I got back to the office Hering was waiting for me. I threw a hurried look at the stack of magazines on my window ledge as I went in, but they were evenly piled and hadn't been disturbed. Even though I wasn't going to do anything about the picture and Sondo's letter right away, I didn't want to lose them.

Keith went out to lunch and Hering sat down on the corner of the desk.

"What goes on?" I asked.

"Looks bad for Gardner," Hering told me. "But McPhail hasn't arrested anybody yet. He's moved down to Gardner's office on fourth so the style show can go ahead. Gardner needs to be on the spot and Cunningham's pulled strings to get him a break. But I think there'll be an arrest before night."

I believe Hering was feeling a bit lonely. My office was about the only spot in the store where he was listened to with respect. I gathered that the city detectives considered him on a lowly plane and felt his job was catching shoplifters, not dabbling in murders. In the end it was Hering who knew more about the case than any of the others.

231

Considering the gloomy mood which had held me so strongly in its grip the day Monty was murdered, I'm sure I don't know why I didn't feel something of the same thing that afternoon. My nerves were in a much more jittery state. I felt tense and jumpy and suspicious of everyone, and I did sense a mounting tempo. But I had no premonition that the climax was to come with such startling suddenness. In fact, I felt hopeless of a solution ever being reached.

"Where's Bill?" I asked Hering.

He was regarding my walls with his usual interest. "Oh, around. Universal's getting along without him these days. He said to tell you he'd be up to see you before he went home."

"Kind of him," I murmured and tried to turn my attention to the avalanche of work on my desk.

But Hering didn't take the hint. "Say, what'd you pull a picture off your wall for?" he inquired.

I looked up in surprise. "Don't tell me you didn't hear about that? I was a good little girl and told McPhail all about it. Whoever knocked me out with that book end must have pulled a picture off. Something else was pasted up in its place, but I took it down."

And then inspiration struck me so suddenly I almost choked.

"Mr. Hering," I said shakily, "you've looked at those pictures dozens of times. I suppose it would be too much to hope that you—might have taken one of your mental photographs of that wall?"

"Well now, I don't know," he said. "Maybe I did."

"Then tell me what the picture was that's missing" I demanded.

He closed his eyes obligingly and remained that way for a few minutes, while I held my breath. Then he opened them and regarded me in triumph.

"Sure," he said. "I got a picture of it. Just as clear as anything."

I bounced up and down in excitement. "Tell me! Tell me what it was!"

He was really enjoying himself. No one had ever taken his mental photography seriously before and he had to lengthen his big moment. He nearly drove me crazy with suspense.

He turned around with his back to the wall. "You check now and see if I'm right."

I could have shaken him. He proceeded to describe every picture in that row on the wall, from the door to the vacant space. When he came to that he paused maddeningly.

"Did I have 'em in order?"

"Every one," I told him. "But if you don't go on there'll be a murder right in this office."

He grinned at me and closed his eyes again. Closed his eyes and said one word.

"Seashells."

And I had the picture at once. But he went on in detail. "A woman's hands playing with seashells against something dark. Hands with bright red nails."

"You're wonderful!" I cried. "It was an ad for nail polish."

I remembered perfectly now. I hadn't found it when I'd looked at the library because I wasn't looking at ads. I'd forgotten we'd used any.

Hering positively beamed with pride. Now that I knew what the picture had been, I was hopelessly disappointed.

"It still doesn't mean anything," I pointed out. "It's just senseless. Why would anybody come in and pull a nail polish ad off my wall?"

He was holding back his trump and he leaned toward me with dramatic intensity.

"Because the woman whose hands posed for that picture was wearing a ring. A ring with a big, dark red stone in it." "You mean——?"

233

"Right," he said. "I knew I'd seen that ring before!"

I could remember it myself now.

"Then—then all we have to do—" I began, but he broke in on me.

"Miss Wynn, do you remember the name of the company that put out the ad?"

"It was the Nail Luster people, I think," I said. "Are you going to tell McPhail?"

He was halfway out the door, but he turned back and grinned at me. "And get laughed out of town? No thanks, Miss Wynn. I'm going to get busy and find out who posed for that ad. I'll be back when I know."

I settled down in my chair, limp with the aftermath of excitement. Hands. Graceful hands wearing a carnelian ring. I tried to remember the hands of all the women I knew, but I hadn't Hering's kind of memory.

The afternoon was endless. Keith came back and we both buckled down to a pretense of work. I could send him on errands around the store and run down to talk to various buyers myself. But I couldn't write copy to save my life.

Storm clouds were rolling in from the lake and it began to get dark in mid-afternoon. I felt restless with waiting. Would this evidence of the hands mean anything when we had it? I wanted to talk to Bill, but he didn't come around.

At three o'clock I went down to have a look at the style show. Owen had attracted a good crowd of our more exclusive customers for the first day and I got there in time to see Carla Drake (I couldn't think of her as Lotta Montez) go drifting effortlessly across the long platform. She was tremendously effective, but if the burst of applause she received meant anything to her, she gave no sign.

The door to Owen's office was closed and I had no wish to investigate. When I glimpsed Miss Babcock weaving toward me through the crowd, I left hastily, pretending not to see her.

The rest of that afternoon was all deadly routine until, around a quarter to five, Tony Salvador put his head in my office.

"Well, I've done it!" he announced.

I hadn't the faintest idea what he was talking about.

"Say, don't you work here any more?" he demanded. The windows! Everybody's nuts about 'em. Mr. Cunningham's secretary came down to congratulate me in person. Looks like I get the job."

"I'm glad, Tony," I told him. "You deserve it. But, Tony—no more phonographs. Please."

He looked a little sheepish. "Maybe you're right at that." Then the broad smile left his face. "You know something, Linell?"

"What?" I asked.

"I miss her like the dickens," he said. "Sondo, I mean. Place doesn't seem right without having her around to scrap with. And those are her windows as much as they are mine. I don't think I'll do so well without her."

"Of course you will," I assured him. "But I'm glad you said that. She'd have liked to get credit."

Tony grinned half-heartedly. "She liked credit all right, and she deserved it. Say—Carla's over in display now, packing up some of Sondo's records. We thought they might as well go to her. And she said she wished you'd come over for a minute. She wants to talk to you about something and you won't be interrupted over there. She wants you to bring a picture along. Says you'll know what she means. Well, the department's knocking off early tonight and I've got some shopping to do. So long."

What on earth did Carla want with that picture, I wondered. Keith shook his head at me.

"Don't you go, Miss Wynn. You stay away from display. Everything happens there."

Keith was forever playing Cassandra and it irritated me. "Don't be silly! It's daytime and I scarcely think Carla will murder me."

"You don't know," Keith warned. "You don't know for sure about anybody. And maybe it's daytime, but it's already dark."

It had been murky outside all day. Another storm was blowing up and the last traces of feeble daylight were dying out. But I wasn't afraid of Carla and I was curious as to what she might know of that snapshot of Chris.

I slipped the picture from its hiding place among the magazines and put it in my purse. Then I said, "Cheer up," and went off to window display, leaving Keith's mutterings behind me.

Tony had evidently closed the department for the night, because the lights were off, except for a single bulb in Sondo's workroom. What with the gloom outside, the place was dim and full of shadows. In spite of my brave words to Keith, I shrugged aside a twinge of uneasiness as I walked into the workroom.

Carla knelt on the floor, sorting a pile of records. She looked up at me soberly as I came in.

"Did you bring the picture?" she asked.

I tapped my purse. "Yes. What about it?"

"I want it," Carla said. "Give it to me please . . . it will be better for everyone if you give it to me."

There was something so strained in her manner that I was startled. It would be just as well, I thought, to keep Sondo's work table between Carla and me. If she made a single move, I could be out the door and away before she could reach me.

"Why do you want the picture?" I asked. "Why should a picture of Chris mean anything to you?"

For some strange reason the faintest flicker of relief

came into her eyes. Then she turned back to the records, reading the titles, placing one on one pile, one on another.

"The picture doesn't mean anything to me," she said. "It's just that—that it might get Chris into a lot of trouble. And why should you want to do that?"

"I don't want to get anyone into trouble she doesn't deserve," I told her. "But I'm not giving up that picture till I know what it's all about."

Carla laid the records aside and stood up. She pushed back a plume of hair from her eyes with a careless gesture—that silvery hair she had dyed black when she'd been part of the dance team of Luis and Lotta.

"It's for your own good," she said. "Sondo died because of that picture. If you keep it, something may happen to you."

I didn't like her tone, or the way she was looking at me and I inched backward toward the door.

"I'm not going to keep it," I told her. "I'm going to give it to McPhail."

"Don't be a fool," she said. "You mustn't do that."

I was almost at the door now. Another step and I'd make a bolt for it. My bravado was completely gone. This was a Carla I'd never seen before and I had no intention of letting her get near me.

And then to my relief, I heard footsteps coming down the corridor and into the department. But it was a relief shortlived.

Carla looked around, listening. "There she comes now. I had an idea you wouldn't want to give up the picture, so I asked her to come up and try to persuade you. You'd really better listen to us, Linell."

I felt trapped. Carla was there before me, and someone else was cutting off my retreat from the rear. I swung about quickly and my panic died. It was only Susan Gardner.

237

"You talk to her, Mrs. Gardner," Carla said and dropped to her knees to tie up a stack of records.

Susan came over to me, her hands aflutter with distress. "Miss Drake says you have a picture of Chris that may get her into difficulty. Won't you please let me have it?"

Carla gathered up her records and went past me to the door. "I've done what I could, Mrs. Gardner," she said. "It's up to you now. It's no use fighting destiny anyway."

"Listen," I said to Susan, when Carla had gone out, "I don't know what this is all about, or why a snapshot of Chris should mean much one way or another, but I'm not giving that picture to anyone but McPhail. I've held off because I didn't want to get anyone into unnecessary complications. But if this snapshot is as important as you and Carla seem to think, then I want to get it out of my possession right away and put it where it will help to clear everything up."

Susan stood there for a moment longer and she must have realized that my mind was made up. She looked distressed and unhappy, even a little puzzled, but she offered no further argument. Without another word, she turned and followed Carla.

So that was that, and there had been nothing to fear after all. I opened my bag to have another look at the picture that was causing all this controversy, but I could make no more of it than before. Who was the man? What part did he play in this? Was it, perhaps, his identity that held the answer to the riddle?

Another moment and I'd have returned the picture to my purse and left the department. I had no premonition whatsoever of what was about to happen. I heard no footfall, no sound of a hand creeping toward the light switch at the door behind me.

The light simply went out with a click and I stood there in darkness, filled with the knowledge that someone was in the doorway, cutting off escape. I fumbled at the catch of my purse and put the picture away.

"Susan?" I said. "Carla? Who is it?"

But there was no answer. The darkness was horrible and blank. I backed away, fumbling for a path of escape. If I could reach the wall, perhaps I could work my way around to the door. Escape I must. For I knew that Death stood in the doorway. The same death Monty had met, and Sondo. This time I might not be so lucky as I had been that day in my office.

Against the grayer darkness of the doorway I could just make out the blurred shadow that stood there. No outline, nothing to give height or form. Just a darker patch against more darkness.

Then a hoarse whisper came to me and I knew there was desperation here.

"The picture! Give me the picture!"

The voice was coarsened, unidentifiable. It might have been the voice of a man or a woman. Whatever it was, it sent terror streaming through the marrow of my bones. I wanted to scream, but I knew no scream could help me. One sound and I'd be done for, before anyone could hear and come to my help.

I moved again. Holding my breath, trying to control the trembling of my body. Back a step. Another step, and then a creak sounded that was like the crash of doom about my ears. I knew I was trapped.

I'd backed straight into Sondo's long work table and the sound had given my position away.

Hands reached for me in the darkness, brushed my face. I ducked beneath them, but I was cornered, caught. The hands were hunting for me. Cold hands with a deadly strength in the fingers.

I groped across the table behind me, searching for anything—anything at all that might serve as a weapon. My hand closed over a smooth tube of metal. I picked it up, not knowing what it was.

239

There was a hot breath on my face and hands touched my shoulders, moved upwards. I raised the thing in my hands, meaning to strike out with it. And then I recognized what it was. The pine spray Tony had used last Christmas to fill the store with the odor of Christmas trees.

I pulled back the plunger, thrust it forward, shooting the spray at short range straight into the face, the eyes of the shadowy figure before me.

There was a gasp of pain. I didn't wait for any more. I stumbled for the door, ran blindly out of the department, down the corridor. No purpose or direction. Wanting only to put distance between me and the horror that had reached for me in the dark.

The elevators were too far away and there'd be no safety in my office. I plunged down the stairway three steps at a time, falling twice, clinging to the rail, picking myself up to plunge downward again.

It was my abrupt collision with an indignant customer coming up the stairs that brought me to my senses. No pursuit sounded from above, and by running away I was giving the murderer every chance to cover her own escape.

The doors downstairs, I thought frantically. The exits must be stopped, the store searched. I left the protesting woman I'd nearly knocked over and rushed for an elevator, made the startled operator take me straight down to main. Then I tore down the middle aisle and ran straight into Keith, Bill and McPhail.

Keith gave a little scream as he saw me. "There she is! I told her not to go over to display!"

Bill put out his hands to stop my flight, caught my shoulders and swung me around. I clung to him for a moment, half hysterical with relief. Then I pushed him away and faced McPhail.

I couldn't have made very much sense, but he got enough of the idea to call one of his men from his post near a door and give sharp orders that every exit be watched.

"The pine spray!" I gasped. "I used it to get away. Shot it all over the person who came at me . . . over her shoulders and face and hair. She'll smell of it. If she tries to leave the store you can stop her."

"You keep saying 'she'," Bill said. "Have you any idea who it was?"

I hadn't. I was only using the 'she' because of Carla and Susan. I couldn't be absolutely positive it was one of them. It might just as easily have been a man.

"You take Miss Wynn upstairs to her office and keep her there," McPhail told Bill. "I'm going to round up everybody who's had any connection with this affair and we're going to have a showdown right now."

I didn't want to go back to the eighth floor again, but with Bill on one side, and Keith on the other, muttering I-told-you-so's, I was marched to an elevator and taken upstairs. Thank goodness, at least, that my two rescuers had no odor of pine needles about them.

Keith told me that shortly after I'd left the office, he had gone to get someone to stop me. He would never have been in time, but I was grateful just the same.

Sylvester Hering sat on my desk waiting for me. It was just closing time—I heard the jangle of the bell as we walked in.

"I'm on the trail!" Hering announced. "I got the Nail Luster people looking up the name of the gal who posed for that hand picture. They're gonna call me the minute they find out who she was. I told the operator I'd wait here." Then he paused and took in my distraught condition. "Say—what goes on?"

I could make a little more sense by that time and I blurted out the whole story. About the picture and Carla and Susan—everything. Hering had a look at the snapshot and shook his head in bewilderment. Then he passed it over to Bill, who sat down to study it.

"How is Owen getting along?" I asked, just to keep talking and stop my teeth from their nervous chattering.

Hering shrugged. "He still claims he wasn't the Gardner Montgomery was talking to in the window. They haven't been able to shake him from that. I guess McPhail is going to take him and Chris over to headquarters for a real going over."

Bill was still studying the picture, but didn't seem to come to any conclusions.

He said, without taking his eyes from it, "You know, I turned up something funny about Gardner on that trip I took."

"What?" I demanded.

Bill tilted the picture sideways and examined it from a fresh angle. "I told you about Monty working in a store down in a small Missouri city. And running off to Mexico with a woman who worked there. Well, Owen Gardner worked in that same store at the same time."

"Then—then Owen and Monty knew each other long ago, before they ever worked together here?" I asked.

"That's right," Bill said, as calmly as if he weren't throwing a bombshell into our midst. "You know something? I don't think the girl in this picture is Chris."

"Oh, don't be sil—" I began, but he looked so positive that I stopped and went to look over his shoulder. Then I said, "I think you're crazy. Of course it's Chris!"

He shook his head. "It can't be. Because of the man."

Even Hering craned his neck. "You mean you know who the man is?"

"I think so," Bill said. "And if I'm right, then this picture was taken years ago. So it couldn't be Chris."

The phone rang with startling shrillness and I could have tossed it impatiently out the window. But Hering picked up the receiver and it was his call. We all tensed to anxious listening.

"Yeah?" Hering said slowly. "You got her name? That's swell. . . . Sure, I'll write it down. Give."

242

Oddly enough, he didn't write. He stood there with his mouth open. Then he said, "Hey, come again! What was that name?" The name must have been repeated, for he listened blankly. "That's what I thought you said," he muttered and put the phone back on my desk.

When he looked around at us, it was with the stunned air of a man on whom a great light was beginning to break.

"I think Gardner's telling the truth," he said. "He wasn't in the window. It was a woman who killed Montgomery. The woman that ring belonged to. The same one who wrote that note signed 'E' and posed for the polish ad. And who killed Sondo because she wanted to get that picture back."

"But who is it?" I cried. "Tell us!"

Hering leaned over and tapped the picture Bill held. "The jane we're looking for is the one in that picture."

"You mean—you mean *Chris?*" I demanded.

"No," he said. "I don't mean Chris. Bill's right. That ain't no picture of Chris. It's a picture of the murderer. Her name's Eileen Gardner."

CHAPTER 22

      I repeated the name stupidly after him.
Bill whistled. "So! then I'm right about the man. It's
the only way it fits."

I shook him. "What do you mean? Who is the man?
What fits?"

"Calm down, toots. The man's Michael Montgomery,
of course. That picture was taken when he was young,
and it's pretty blurred. But that's who it is. The girl's
the one he ran away with to Mexico. Eileen Gardner.
Owen's wife. Chris's mother. Chris is fair-haired and
she told us her mother was dark. But the mantilla hides
the girl's hair in the picture."

I could remember something else. That night at our
place when Chris had mentioned an old picture she'd
found of her mother, mentioned how much it looked
like Chris the way she looked today. I was still confused.
I knew no one who looked like Chris Montgomery. I
was trying to understand, trying to get the fog out of
my brain, when McPhail put his head in the door.

"Come along," he said. "All of you. I've got the witnesses lined up over in the display department. Nobody's
been acting funny. Nobody's tried to leave the store
except Mrs. Gardner and Tony Salvador and we stopped

them. But if there's a whiff of pine on one of the lot, you better locate it, Miss Wynn. We can't."

I had only to use my nose. McPhail stationed me at the door to the display department and I stood there with my eyes closed while, one after another, the people he'd gathered there went past me. I sniffed each time and then opened my eyes, but it was no use.

There was nobody missing. Tony, Owen, Chris, Helena, Susan, Carla. They even sent Bill and Keith past me. But on not one of them was there the faintest odor of pine. And there were no signs of clothes having been changed either. The women were all wearing the same dresses they'd worn earlier, and as far as I could tell, the men had on the same suits.

McPhail collected us in Monty's office and then turned to me in disgust.

"Why does everything have to happen to you? And why does it always happen without you seeing anything? Couldn't you just once get a useful idea that would give us a hint about who could have attacked you?"

I looked about the room helplessly, as much at sea as ever. I had a feeling that it ought to be either Susan or Carla, but I hadn't a clue in the world to go on.

McPhail was just about to dismiss the lot of us when the idea hit me like a thunderclap in a clear sky.

"Wait! I think I know what might have happened. Look—" I was so excited my words were tumbling out, "—what if the person who tried to kill me was wearing a smock, or a wrap, or something? What if her hair was covered? The spray would have gone on the outer garments, so that if she took them off and washed her face with soap, maybe the smell wouldn't cling."

"Maybe you got something there," McPhail admitted.

"And here's another idea!" I cried. "If that's what happened, then she'd have to get rid of that smock, or whatever it was, quickly. She wouldn't dare go out in the store that way. And if it was the person who killed

Sondo, wouldn't the first place she'd think of to hide anything be the mannequin room? Wouldn't she—"

Hering was already off on a run to the mannequin room. We could hear cabinet doors banging for a moment while we waited in silence. A deathly silence in which not one of us dared look at his neighbor.

Hering came back with a rolled bundle in his hands. He shook out a long black coat and held up a black turban.

The reek of pine needles filled the room.

Something seemed to twist inside me and I turned and leaned my forehead against Bill's sleeve. I was too sick with shock to look at the woman to whom that coat belonged.

I'd recognized it at once. It was Helena Farnham's.

It is hard to write of those moments immediately following. Even though she tried twice to kill me, I cannot hate Helena. Strangely enough, I think she was always rather fond of me. She was a woman with an obsession, a single purpose, and when I stood in her way, threatened the object of her love, I ceased to exist as Linell Wynn, her friend.

She made a statement to McPhail then and there, in the presence of all of us, and she made it in a manner so cool and withdrawn that it was difficult to believe she was a woman with blood on her hands. I sat listening in disbelief and horror, trying to understand that this woman was Chris's mother. She resembled the girl now only in her big-boned frame. All facial likeness had been lost with the years and the fading of Helena's beauty.

She told McPhail simply that she had known Michael Montgomery long ago and that she had gone away with him to Mexico. He had treated her cruelly, deserted her. Then, recently, she had met him again here at Cunningham's, and all her grievances against him had eaten at her, until, when the opportunity had offered last Tuesday, she had killed him. And she had killed Sondo too, because Sondo had found her out.

That was all. Nothing of Owen or Chris, or all that miserable tangle. Bill and Hering and I exchanged puzzled glances, but McPhail was happy. He had his confession and there would be no more murders at Cunningham's. He asked her only one question—about the ring.

"I'll show you," Helena said and went quietly over to a shelf of books behind Monty's desk.

What followed is something that will never be erased from my memory as long as I live. The book shelf was next to the closed window. Helena picked up a heavy volume, crashed it through the glass and hurled herself after it. She was through the window and gone—gone before even McPhail was aware of how she had caught him off guard.

Carla screamed and I put my hands over my ears. There were shouts from below and McPhail leaned out the window. He looked a bit white when he stalked past us out of the office.

The police stenographer and detectives hurried after him. Keith rushed off to be sick, and the rest of us sat there in the office, too stunned and horrified to move.

Carla put her head down on Monty's desk and began to cry softly. Owen Gardner put an arm about his daughter's shoulders, patting her awkwardly, with a hand that trembled.

"Come along, my dear," he said. "Come along."

Susan followed them, whimpering and fluttering. But it is Chris's words I will never forget.

"The poor thing," she said. "Another woman Monty hurt. I'm glad she won't have to face a trial."

They went off and there were just four of us left in the office. Hering and Bill and Carla and I.

"Chris doesn't know," I said. "She doesn't know that it was her own mother who killed Monty."

247

Carla raised her head, wiped tear-stained cheeks. "That's the way Helena wanted it to be. So Chris would never know."

It was Carla then who drew together the missing threads and gave us the story. Because Carla, through no desire of her own, had been nearest to the whole thing from the beginning. Not even Owen had known for sure who Monty's murderer had been.

"He thought it was either Helena or I," Carla said. "He tried to get it out of me one day at lunch. But I knew how awful it would be for him to know that Chris's mother was a murderer. The blow to Chris in her hysterical state, the effect it might have on her mind would have been too much for him to face. So I held off telling him and he was afraid to have the wrong one arrested."

"Why did you try to protect her?" Bill asked.

Carla flung her head back. "Because Michael Montgomery caused the death of the one person I loved. I was glad when he died. I—I didn't care if his murderer was caught or not."

There was a stormy pause and then Carla's unusual spurt of defiance died.

"I saw Helena when she came out of the window after she'd killed Monty. I was waiting to exchange that pin and no one else saw her come back to the counter. She was so nervous that she scratched herself. But I didn't think about it till later. Then I knew. Helena and I had been thrown together to some extent because of our mutual hatred of Monty and I'd heard most of her story. So I let her know I wouldn't talk."

The pieces began to fit into place. Eileen Gardner had lost track of her daughter for years. Then she had read about her in the newspapers when Chris had won a dress-designing contest. She had dropped her work as a model for hand ads, taken the name of Helena Farnham, and come to Cunningham's to be near Chris.

Owen no longer felt bitter against the wife he had divorced so long ago. When he saw how she had changed and aged, so that all her youthful resemblance to Chris had faded, he told her that he would not object to her remaining in the store where she could see Chris occasionally. But he warned her that she would have to keep her identity a secret.

Helena promised. What emotion there was left in her was bound wholly in Chris. She struck up an acquaintance with me merely because Chris was something of a protegé of mine and she could see her more often by cultivating me.

And then life played one of its scurvy tricks. Monty, anxious to leave the East, which was getting a little hot for him because of the fur coat affair, came to Cunningham's as window display manager. The stage was set for tragedy.

Helena and Owen were both frantic when they saw that Chris was becoming infatuated with Monty. Owen was just about to help Carla bring her evidence against Monty, when Monty played a bold counter hand and married Chris. That morning I'd seen Monty and Carla together, she had been threatening to give evidence against him anyway, but he'd caught her by the shoulders and shaken her roughly, warned her that he'd take her to jail with him if he went.

Monty's marriage to Chris had set Helena off. All she cared about in the world was Chris's happiness and Monty was wrecking it. So she went into the window that day to threaten him with exposure. She had an old locket-ring he had given her with a picture of the two of them in it and she meant to show it to Chris in an attempt to get the girl to leave Monty. So that Owen could act against Chris's husband. Helena herself had been that member of the "tribe of Gardners" Monty had shouted at in the window.

There had been a struggle over the ring. The stone

had been broken once before and it chipped into two pieces and flew out, the part containing the picture falling into the phonograph attachment. All Helena's hatred of Monty must have spilled over. When she saw her chance, she picked up the heavy end of the golf club and killed him.

Helena had been desperate about the loss of the stone from the ring. She'd gone to my office to get the smaller piece, fearing the picture might have adhered to it. And then she'd seen on my wall that old ad for which she'd posed. A picture that showed the very ring Monty had given her. She'd worked quickly to get it down and replace it with another picture. But she hadn't been quick enough and I had nearly trapped her.

If only Sondo hadn't begun to suspect Chris! Sondo was already curious about Chris's possible visit to the window, and when she got the stone with its picture out of the phonograph, she thought she had certain evidence against Chris. Helena, of course, had fallen into Sondo's trap and gone to Universal to break into the wrong phonograph. Then she'd given us the slip and hurried home, to try to get Bill on the phone in an effort to stop any suspicion on our part.

Helena had not known about the Lotta Montez note, though she knew Carla's story. She had gone to Monty's apartment to try to recover the note signed "E," which had mentioned the old set-up existing again—meaning Owen, Helena and Monty in the same store—and had mentioned the ring. When she saw the Montez note, she had chosen to destroy it in an effort to throw me off the real clue. Later, at Sondo's in the confusion over Chris, she had taken the other note from my purse.

And then Helena had walked again into a trap of Sondo's. She had been frantic because Sondo was torturing Chris, trying to pin the murder on her. And she was afraid that if the old picture got into the hands of the police the truth would come out. Her fear now was not so much of discovery—she was past caring much about herself—as of desperation lest Chris learn that her mother was a murderer.

So when she had walked into the little scene Sondo had arranged, she had done just what Sondo had anticipated. She had picked up the hammer and attacked the mannequin. But Sondo had been caught in her own trap. Instead of meeting Chris, whom she thought she could handle, she had met a woman obsessed by a single idea, and she had been no match for her. Helena had evidently worn gloves in handling the hammer and had left no prints, merely smudging over most of Bill's.

Helena's disappointment at finding the picture gone from the part of the ring Sondo had so carefully laid out with her trap, must have been bitter. How she had dropped the stone later for me to find, we'd never know.

Her next move had been to hide Sondo's body in the mannequin room. Then she had returned to the workroom to pull the smock and handkerchief from the broken figure of Dolores. To have left them there would have been to make Sondo's ruse too evident to the police. Perhaps she thought that if the smock were missing altogether, it would be taken for granted that Sondo had gone out of the department wearing it. And the hue and cry would not be immediately raised.

The logical thing would have been to hide the smock with the body, but perhaps by that time Helena was too anxious to get out of the department. So she took it with her, saw my office empty and thrust it into a drawer. That was after the conversation I'd had with her when she'd vaguely threatened me. It was just possible that the gesture of hiding the smock in my office was one more scrap of evidence against me, and as such, might serve to keep me quiet. Bill's note lay face up on my desk and she had taken that, since it suggested that Sondo was up to something.

When Carla had happened in my office at the time I

251

got Sondo's letter, she had seen the picture and had recognized it at once as the one Helena had told her about.

Until Sondo's death, Carla's actions had been apathetic. She had a strong tendency toward fatalism in her nature and she felt that Luis' death had now been avenged. As far as the future went, what would be would be.

And so she'd gone her dreamy way, listening to Sondo's sentimental records, living in the past, not caring very much about what happened in the present. Though she did bestir herself sufficiently to stay with Sondo that one night, in an effort to keep Helena away from her.

But she had not really roused from her apathy until Sondo was murdered.

As Carla sat there in Monty's office, trying to explain her actions, I began to get a picture of her confusion and fear, her futility. The dreamer thrown abruptly against ugly reality and unable to cope with it decisively. Unable even to decide upon a course of action.

She was appalled by Sondo's murder, but could not even then bring herself to go to the police. She was half afraid she would not be believed and that her own motives might come to light. Owen was already suspecting her of Sondo's murder because of her foolish dancing that night in the display department. On the other hand, she was beginning to fear Helena, to wonder when the other woman might strike out to silence her. So, torn many ways, she must have moved endlessly on her treadmill of indecision, unable to settle on any course of action.

Then, when she saw the picture Sondo had left for me, she was seized with the conviction that if she could get that picture for Helena, the tragedies would stop. She counted on me to make the same mistake Sondo had made and take the picture for one of Chris. So she did her best to get it from me, even to the extent of enlisting the aid of poor, bewildered Susan, who knew nothing of the truth at all. But when I refused to give up the picture, Carla dropped helplessly back into her fatalistic attitude.

Helena, however, had not been content to leave matters in Carla's hands. She had got off work early and had come upstairs wearing her turban and coat. Not even Carla had known she was hiding there in the department, listening to everything. When Carla and Susan had failed with me, Helena had made her final, desperate attempt to get the picture.

That was all.

"You see the pattern?" Carla said. "The way Helena tried to the very last to stick to her purpose of protecting Chris? That's why she made that statement to the police just now that left out so much of the truth. She knew she had to give them something that would serve as a confession, and then die quickly before the answers came out. To protect Chris, she even took her own life. There's been a—a sort of fate acting through this whole thing. So now, must the pattern be changed? Must Chris know the truth?

She stopped and there was a long silence. We were all looking at Hering, and he was looking at none of us. Hering was the police. It was up to him to go to McPhail with the true story.

The wailing of an ambulance siren came up to us. I shivered, knowing what the sound meant. Hering listened for a moment and then came over and picked up the tiny oval snapshot I'd laid on the desk. The picture of a girl who looked like Chris.

And while we all watched him, scarcely daring to breathe, he took a packet of matches from his pocket, lit one and held it to the picture. It flared briefly and then floated in black ash from his fingers. He dusted his hands and walked out of the room without a backward look for any of us.

We had our answer.

Carla wandered off by herself, looking more lost than ever, and Bill and I went downstairs. I'm afraid I was clinging to him as if he were a lifeline which I never meant to let go.

"Bill," I said, my voice going up into unexpected quavers, "I don't want to go back to the apartment. I couldn't face it. All Helena's things. Her empty bed. Knowing that I've been so close to her all the while and—"

"Of course you're not going back," Bill said. "You're coming home to meet my mother. I've been telling her all about what a lucky girl you are and I think it's high time she had a look at you."

But I couldn't even rise to that bait.

"I don't want to be teased any more!" I wailed. "I don't want—"

Bill put an arm around me. "Look, baby, one of these days when you've had time to get over all this, you're going to have a proper proposal. With all the trimmings. But this isn't the time, the place, or the atmosphere."

Together we went past the watchman and out the revolving door.

PHYLLIS WHITNEY

SEVEN TEARS FOR APOLLO

She awakened with a start and saw that the balcony doors were now gaping open. And then she saw the shadow . . . moving across the room to where she lay . . .

Ever since the tragic death of her husband, pretty Dorcas Brandt lived in constant fear. Too many frightening and seemingly inexplicable things had begun to happen – the fatal accident to a close friend, the mysterious warnings scrawled on her mirror, the ransacking of her room . . .

In desperation, she fled to Greece – only to find the shadow of fear that had stalked her for so long grew even more oppressive, until it threatened to unhinge her mind and take away her reason.

Post·A·Book

A Royal Mail service in association with the Book Marketing Council & The Booksellers Association.

Post-A-Book is a Post Office trademark.

ALSO AVAILABLE IN CORONET BOOKS

PHYLLIS A. WHITNEY

All these books are available at your local bookshop or newsagent, or can be ordered direct from the publisher. Just tick the titles you want and fill in the form below.

Prices and availability subject to change without notice.

CORONET BOOKS, P.O. Box 11, Falmouth, Cornwall.

Please send cheque or postal order, and allow the following for postage and packing:

U.K. – 50p for one book, plus 20p for the second book, and 14p for each additional book ordered up to a £1.63 maximum.

B.F.P.O. and EIRE – 50p for the first book, plus 20p for the second book, and 14p per copy for the next 7 books, 8p per book thereafter.

OTHER OVERSEAS CUSTOMERS – 75p for the first book, plus 21p per copy for each additional book.

Name ....

Address ....

....